Wade-Giles, a Romanization system for Mandarin Chinese, was devised to simplify Chinese language characters for the Western world. It was widely used by foreigners from the late 19th century to the 1950s. In 1958 the People's Republic of China instituted Pinyin, a new system of romanization for Mandarin Chinese.

Given the time period of this novel, Wade-Giles is used in the text rather than Pinyin.

Vicky and Ed,
Fellow author and
good friends,
Best wishes always,
Love,
[illegible]

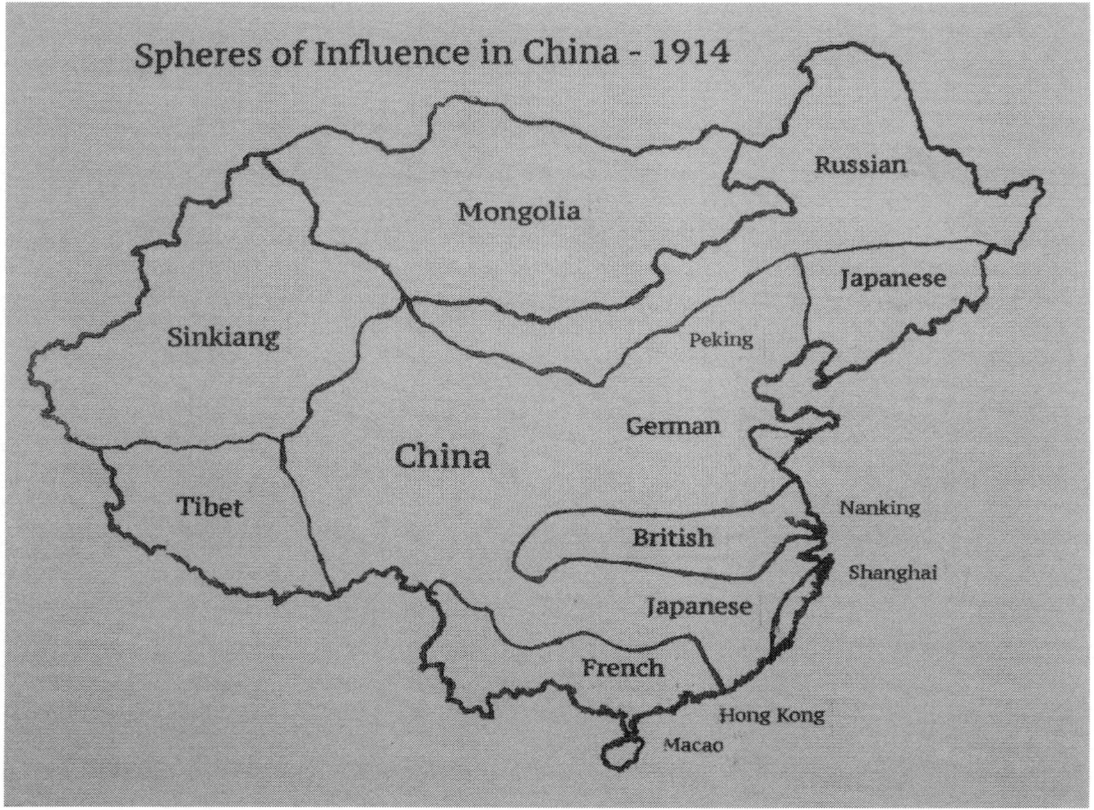
Spheres of Influence in China - 1914
Russian
Mongolia
Japanese
Sinkiang
Peking
German
China
Tibet
Nanking
British
Shanghai
Japanese
French
Hong Kong
Macao

REFUGEE OF THE HEART

REFUGEE OF THE HEART

JANE IWAN

ISBN-13: 9781546603085
ISBN-10: 1546603085
Library of Congress Control Number: 2017907699
CreateSpace Independent Publishing Platform
North Charleston, South Carolina

for Larry

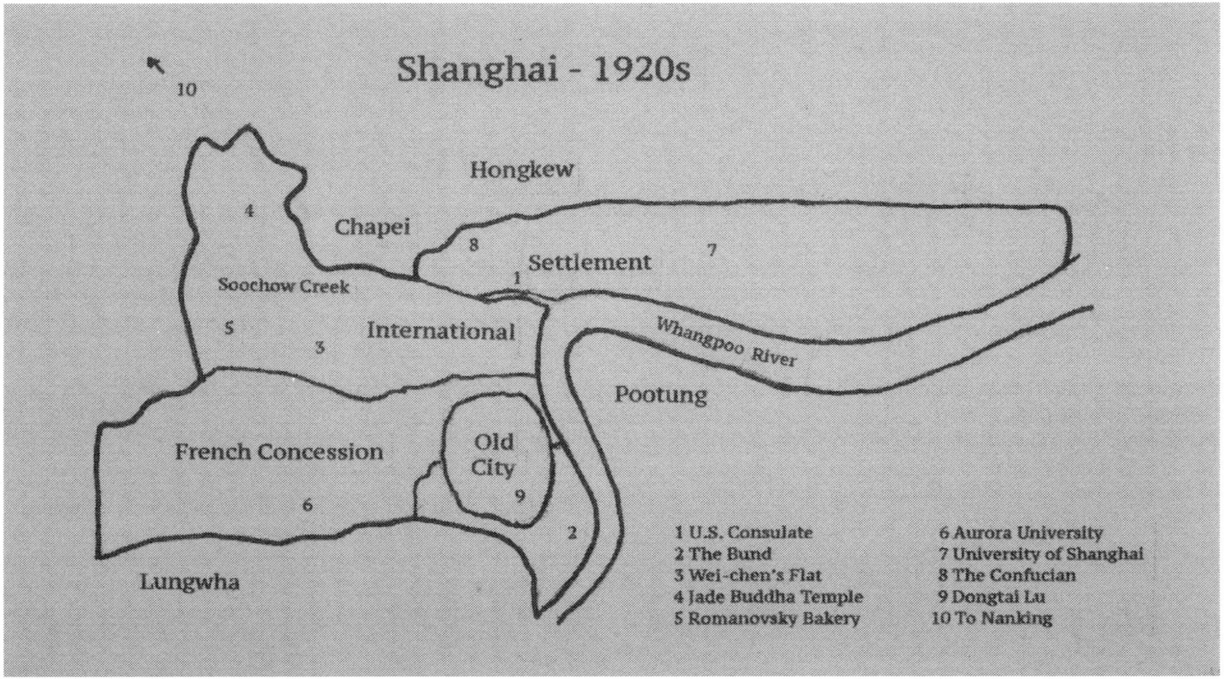
Shanghai - 1920s
10
Hongkew
4
Chapei
8
Settlement
7
1
Soochow Creek
5
3
International
Whangpoo River
Pootung
French Concession
Old
City
9
6
2
Lungwha
1 U.S. Consulate
2 The Bund
3 Wei-chen's Flat
4 Jade Buddha Temple
5 Romanovsky Bakery
6 Aurora University
7 University of Shanghai
8 The Confucian
9 Dongtai Lu
10 To Nanking

CHINA

One

1919

Wei-chen watched family friends snake down the cemetery's terraced hillside, just outside the town of Chia-hsing. Now alone at his uncle's grave, he committed his first betrayal of the day. Bending down on one knee, he pressed his palm into the turned earth. Forgive me, Uncle. I am leaving tonight. Without you, there is no reason to stay here any longer.

At dusk Wei-chen returned to Lin Porcelain Ware, his uncle's shophouse. Closing the shutters, he jammed cash from the safe into his pockets, then stuffed his savings in a leather pouch. He grasped the Kuan-Yin statue from the kitchen shrine and wedged it in the suitcase. Each morning Uncle had burned incense before the Goddess of Mercy. Wei-chen wanted and needed her continued protection.

Sneaking out the back door, he headed down the alley to Mr. Wong's puppet shop. This was the hardest betrayal of all. Fleeing without letting friends know was one thing. But leaving without saying good-bye to Uncle's best friend - and his too - was cowardly and disrespectful. He slid an envelope under Mr. Wong's back door.

A silver moon guided him through backstreets to the train station. The first-class ticket was indulgent but he could not risk close contact with anyone. The moment the train for Shanghai pulled in, he boarded it and released a deep breath. No one he recognized was on board.

Wei-chen took a window seat and focused on the night sky, avoiding contact with other travelers. He thought about the note he left behind for Mr. Wong. To write it, he had needed to keep his emotions in check. Now his heart questioned his mind. How could he have done this to an old friend?

> If I do not leave tonight, I might never have the chance to get away from Chia-hsing. A matchmaker has been stopping by the shop for months. Several times I overheard her talking to Uncle. She was trying to arrange a marriage between her friend's daughter and me. I am sure the girl's parents knew Uncle was failing. It was an attempt to acquire his shop and secure a marriage for their daughter.
>
> Having just turned eighteen, I am not ready to commit the rest of my life to someone. My dream is to attend university. Assuming I marry someday, I want a modern marriage. In Shanghai some couples are marrying for love, not because their families arrange it. But right now, that is the last thing from my mind.
>
> Uncle's heart spells were getting worse, but I never thought he would pass this soon. Looking back, I realize he knew how serious it was. Two weeks ago Uncle and I went over his legal papers. Every document is in this envelope. I am transferring ownership of the shop to you. I apologize for my disrespectful exit. I will write as soon as I have an address in Shanghai. Please forgive me for not stopping by before I left.

The train lurched around a curve waking Wei-chen. He didn't remember drifting off and made sure his bag was secure. A dream, or maybe a distant memory, floated at the edge of his consciousness. He was a small child again, standing on a train station platform, terrified. A stranger, who turned out to be his maternal uncle, picked him up and spoke gently to him. Then the vision disappeared.

The first few years after his mother's death, Wei-chen sometimes sensed her presence. But that was a long time ago. His ties to the paternal family line were severed when Uncle adopted him. He no longer carried any memories of his father or brother.

When the train entered Shanghai's outskirts, he caught himself thinking about his favorite teacher at the Methodist Mission Academy, another person he chose not to say good-bye to. It was rude of him to leave without expressing his gratitude. This man was the reason Wei-chen was heading to Shanghai today. The teacher, one of Uncle's regular customers, arranged a scholarship for Wei-chen when he was seven years old. His education at the mission school changed the trajectory of Wei-chen's life.

When he started school, foreign powers still controlled large areas of China and China's fledgling republic was struggling to survive. Uncle recognized a western education would prepare his nephew for the changing world, but he also understood the mission school could lure Wei-chen away from him, make him hunger for a bigger world.

By the time he started secondary school, Wei-chen was determined to attend university in Shanghai. When he wasn't working in Uncle's shop, he worked extra hours at Mr. Wong's puppet shop to save money. His plan was working until Uncle's sudden death. That crushed Wei-chen's expectation for a smooth transition out of Chia-hsing.

When he stepped off the train, the frenetic scene at the station threw him off guard. He stopped beside a newsstand to calm down, pressing two fingers on the underside of his wrist. Uncle had taught him to slow his pulse like this when he was little and got upset. It usually worked.

Wei-chen had dreamed about this moment the past four years, but it was not happening the way he had imagined. He forced himself to settle down. This was no time to give into anxiety. He needed to open a bank account and find lodging by nightfall.

Unfolding his map, tattered from years of reference, he located the tram line to Nantao, the Old Chinese City. He stepped off the tram at Dongtai Lu, the district renowned for its porcelain ware and the likeliest place for him to find a job. Shops and stalls jammed the streets with arrays of celadon, blue-and-white porcelain and multi-colored patterns. Close to feeling overwhelmed, he walked into a teahouse to make a plan.

He must have looked upset because the shop owner came over. After taking Wei-chen's order, he asked Wei-chen if he was all right.

"I just arrived in Shanghai. I want to live in this area and need to find a room to rent."

The shop owner eyed Wei-chen's suitcase. "There is a small hotel near here that rents rooms by the week. It is secure. You look young to be on your own."

The man seemed kind, almost solicitous. Wei-chen decided to trust him. "Perhaps you could also recommend a bank."

After depositing his savings, he found the hotel. It was located on a hutong, one of the little alleyways that spill off larger streets. It would do for now. When he entered the room, he collapsed on the bed and allowed Uncle's passing to land full force on his heart.

The next morning he sat in a noodle shop and rehearsed the reasons someone should hire him. Fortified by dumplings and broth, he explored the neighborhood, evaluating the shops in terms of clientele and the range of porcelain ware. The trees, their leaves a beautiful spring green, provided shade when he needed to sit down and rest for a while.

By evening he felt exhausted. No shopkeepers he approached were willing to hire him. Fear gnawed at his self-confidence and kept him awake. The next day produced the same results. On the third afternoon he discovered a new side street to explore. He entered a teahouse and ordered jasmine tea. It reminded him of Uncle brewing jasmine tea at the end of each workday, a soothing ritual Wei-chen attempted to recreate today.

A porcelain shop across the street caught his eye. It had an understated look but he would wager the back of the shop held some valuable old pieces. A foreigner stood in the doorway with a package tucked under his arm. He waved good-bye to the owner.

Wei-chen watched the man walk away. He stood at least six feet tall, with hair as black as any Chinese but wavy. He carried himself just like the

American teachers at his mission school, with a bigger sense of personal space than most foreigners. Wei-chen wondered what he was carrying. He finished his tea, screwed up his courage and crossed the street.

The owner glanced at Wei-chen when he entered the stop and then seemed to dismiss him. He nosed around the front of the shop, checking the porcelain patterns. The inventory was much larger than Uncle's. He worked his way towards the back of the shop where the owner sat at a large desk.

"Nei-hou," the owner said, wishing good day. "Could I help you with something?"

"Nei hou. You have quite a selection of patterns. The antique pieces behind the counter are exceptional."

"Thank you. You don't speak Shanghainese. Where are you from?"

"I just moved here from Chia-hsing, but I will learn the dialect quickly."

"You seem to know porcelain."

"I worked in my Uncle's porcelain shop. He taught me many things and gave me an appreciation for fine work."

"Does he no longer have the shop?"

"No, he passed on recently."

"And you decided to move here."

The shop owner's tone implied a question so Wei-chen seized the moment. "Yes. He was my only family. I think Shanghai will offer me more opportunities than Chia-hsing. I just graduated from the Methodist Mission Academy there and am looking for work. I have worked in a shop since I was quite young."

"So, are you asking to work in my shop?"

"Yes, it is different from the other ones I have observed. The selection and quality remind of my Uncle's shop."

"Well, I do not need any extra help just now."

"If you would please let me work tomorrow, I would show you what I could do. You would not have to pay me. I noticed a bit of dust on some of the stacks, which makes it seem those patterns have not sold recently. Customers like to think the ware in your shop is desirable to others too.

"Also, I observed the foreigner who just left here. I expect you have regular customers who are interested in your antique pieces. I could help with other customers when you are working with your patrons. And I speak English, which might increase your business with foreigners. I have noticed quite a few of them in the shops."

"The man who just left speaks excellent Mandarin."

"But I think most tourists do not. I am sure I could attract some business by standing outside the shop and enticing people to come inside. Also, I could change your window displays frequently." Wei-chen didn't know what else to say.

"All right, I will let you work tomorrow afternoon and we will see how you manage. My name is Mr. Liu." The initial frown on his face shifted to a slight smile.

"I am Chan Wei-chen. Thank you for the opportunity." He bowed slightly and left the shop.

When Wei-chen arrived for work the next afternoon, Mr. Liu instructed him about what he wanted done. Late in the afternoon a foreign woman came into the shop. Mr. Liu was involved with a customer so Wei-chen approached her.

"May I assist you?" he asked in English.

"Yes. I am looking for a gift, perhaps a small vase." He couldn't identify her accent. Perhaps it was French. Definitely not British or American.

"We have many small items that are beautiful. It is just a matter of deciding which one you would like."

She smiled at him, and he directed her around the shop. She found a vase she liked and also a blue-and- white porcelain teapot. After Mr. Liu handled the sale, Wei-chen walked her to the front door and wished her a pleasant evening.

Mr. Liu called him to the back of the shop. "That was a nice sale for your first day. Would you like some dumplings? My wife just brought some."

"Yes, thank you." The scent reminded him of the dumpling shop where he and Uncle usually ate. His eyes were liquid.

"Let us talk about how your first day went. I watched you closely. You accomplished everything I requested and even a few things I did not ask you to do. It is almost summer, one of my busiest times. I could use your help for the next few months but in the fall you will need to find other work. Because weekends are busy, your day off will be Wednesdays."

"Thank you, Mr. Liu. I will not disappoint you." That night Wei-chen wrote a letter to Mr. Wong, giving him his address and telling him he had a temporary job.

On his first day off from work, Wei-chen took a tram to the International Settlement, which comprised the original British and American Settlements. A substantial Chinese population resided there as well as large numbers of trading companies, embassies and universities. With his fluency in English, he hoped to find a job with a trading company by fall.

He sauntered along Soochow Creek, watching somnolent boat traffic. Suddenly he remembered something. Last year a traveling monk spent a month in Wei-chen's neighborhood temple. At the end of his stay, the monk mentioned he was leaving to study at Jade Buddha Temple in Shanghai. Wei-chen looked at his map. The temple was about a mile away. Hoping something might develop from this connection, he set off at a fast pace.

The temple's imposing saffron walls ascended directly from the sidewalk. When he passed through the gate, shafts of reflected light captured him. He felt safe. An old ginkgo tree on his school campus filtered the same golden light each fall. He had always felt protected by it and sensed the same protection now.

In front of the main building, people were lighting joss sticks at a large incense burner. Wei-chen joined them and burned an offering for Uncle's soul. Wreathed in smoke and wrapped in sadness, he lost track of time.

Somewhat later he stopped a novice walking past. "Is there a Monk Wei here?"

"Earlier this year a monk who travels in the cloud stayed here. His family name was Wei. He left several months ago to continue his journey of purification." The novice bowed and walked away.

Wei-chen knew Monk Wei wanted to study with other masters, to move through life like a floating cloud, without attachment, but he couldn't help feeling disappointed. The monk was always kind to him, and he could use some emotional support right now. He spotted a quiet courtyard and went to sit on a bench. Leaning back against the wall, he closed his eyes.

"Good afternoon," someone said, breaking Wei-chen's reverie. Standing in front of him was a gentleman he had noticed at the incense burner. He stood up and returned the greeting.

"I observed you earlier. It appears as though this is your first time in the temple," the man said.

"Yes, that is right." Wei-chen judged the man to be in his mid-thirties. There was something peaceful about his bearing. Perhaps he was some kind of monk even though he wasn't dressed like one.

"My name is Mr. Cheng. I am a Buddhist scholar and work with the novices here. Perhaps I could show you around the temple. Its construction was finished two years ago. I think you might appreciate seeing the Jade Buddhas."

"Thank you. My name is Chan Wei-chen. I would like to see the temple."

When Mr. Cheng led him to the main altar, Wei-chen stepped into another world. Incense blanketed the room from offerings of devotees' hearts desires. They removed their shoes and the scholar showed him the small, reclining Jade Buddha. Then they climbed steep stairs to the larger Jade Buddha. Bustling Shanghai seemed far away.

"Well, young man, it is obvious you like the temple. I often come here to meditate." Mr. Cheng guided Wei-chen to a quiet courtyard. "We can sit on this bench. What a lovely day to watch incense carrying prayers to the heavens." He hesitated for a moment, then said, "I sense you are missing your family."

"That is true. How do you know that?"

"I think someone very close to you passed on recently. Is that right?"

"Yes, my Uncle, my only family. The rising smoke reminds me of him. Every morning and evening he burned incense at our kitchen shrine." His dry eyes couldn't hide the sadness in his heart.

"Are you from Shanghai?"

"I lived with my Uncle in Chia-hsing. I have been here for two weeks."

"Just as I thought. You do not have the air of a big city boy," Mr. Cheng said.

"How do you know about Uncle and me?"

"Since I was a boy, I have been able to read many things inside people's minds and hearts. It is not always wise for me to reveal what I see, but I can tell you are searching for truth. I want to reassure you that you are on the right path.

"In time you will learn family can shift and change, like a plant that continues to grow after it has been damaged. If you cut off a branch, it forces new growth elsewhere. I do not diminish the deep bond between you and your uncle. But someday, after your grief subsides, you will find people who will become like family to you. Coming to Shanghai was the right decision for you."

While Mr. Cheng talked, tranquility draped a cloak over Wei-chen's shoulders. The tension inside him dissipated somewhat. He studied the man. Although slightly shorter than Wei-chen, he appeared taller because of his erect bearing. The black mandarin jacket and trousers emphasized his lean build. He decided Mr. Cheng led an austere life.

Light filtered through the trees, spreading lace patterns across the courtyard. "It is time for me to leave. It was no accident that we met. We will meet again." Mr. Cheng stood up.

"I would like that." Wei-chen watched the scholar walk away, then glanced up at the second story of the temple. Shadows of novices shape shifted against the windows, adding to the mystery of his day.

Taking a different route back to the Old City, Wei-chen wandered down a side street off Haiphong Road. The aroma of fresh-baked bread drew him to a small bakery. Round breads spilled out of baskets in the front window. His mouth watered. It was the first time he felt truly hungry since Uncle's passing.

"Nei hou, young man." A foreign woman standing in the doorway smiled at him. "Would you like to try something?"

Her Shanghainese was difficult for him to understand. He couldn't place her accent but it definitely was not English. Curly red hair framed her face, but it was the maternal look in her eyes that arrested him. He thought she was beautiful.

"Yes, I will try something. What are the little round breads?" Wei-chen responded in English.

"They are bagels. Come in. I will give you a sample." Her eyes crinkled when she smiled. She appeared relieved to speak English.

"This reminds me of mantou, our steamed bread." With the first taste, an image of Uncle's kitchen flew through his mind.

"Do you live nearby?"

"I live in the Old City, but I was just at Jade Buddha Temple."

"My husband and I also go to temple. We go to the Jewish temple in the French Concession."

"I have not seen that temple. The bagel was delicious. Thank you."

"My name is Mrs. Romanovsky. I hope you will stop by again." She extended her hand.

"I will do that. My name is Chan Wei-chen." He concluded her firm handshake resulted from years of kneading bread.

When he fell into bed that night, a glimmer of hope for his future tucked him in.

Before he closed the shop Saturday evening, Mr. Liu said, "On Sunday I usually go to the Ghost Market. If you would like to join me, meet me here at five o'clock tomorrow morning. We will need to be back to open the shop at ten."

"That would be a dream come true. Uncle told me about that market. I will be waiting outside your shop early tomorrow."

The concept of the ghost market fascinated Wei-chen. Vendors arrived near daybreak to set up their wares in stalls or on cloths spread along walkways. In the afternoon they dispersed like mist spirits that hover above a lake and disappear when the air warms.

Before sunrise he and Mr. Liu took a tram to the outskirts of the Old City. From there they walked to Fuyou Lu Market, the Ghost Market. Having staked out their spaces, the vendors were already conducting business. The collection of goods - ceramics, jade pieces, rattan ware, textiles, antiques of all kinds - astonished Wei-chen.

"This market always amazes me," Mr. Liu said. "I never know what I will find here. The inventory changes each week. It all depends upon what the sellers have managed to glean from the countryside."

Mr. Liu guided Wei-chen through the market, introducing him to his preferred vendors. Watching the bargaining, conducted in a relaxed manner, reminded Wei-chen of his home town. He noted which stalls had old porcelain. Once he secured a stable job, he planned to return to them. There were some treasures to collect at a good price.

"Exactly when did your Uncle pass?" Mr. Liu asked on their return trip.

"It has been almost three weeks."

Mr. Liu sighed. "I wish I could do more for you. You are a bright young man and a good worker."

"You have already helped me by hiring me. I will find another job by fall. Somehow it will all work out." Wei-chen spoke in a firm tone but that belied what he felt inside. At night fear of not finding work kept him awake for hours.

When they got off the tram, university students and workers were blocking the streets - another protest against the terms of the Paris Peace Conference. The demonstrations started in Peking on May 4 when the treaty terms were telegraphed to China. Thousands of university students instantly protested the handover of Germany's leased territories to Japan rather than their being returned to China. Demonstrations continued to fan across the country. Wei-chen identified with the protesters.

"I grew up hearing Uncle and his friend talk about China's future. They resented foreign powers for staking claim to Chinese territories. When The Great War ended, Uncle paid close attention to the treaty negotiations. He never trusted Europe's intentions for China. How Europe carved up its countries did not concern him. He just wanted their spheres of influence returned to China."

"He was right not to trust them," Mr. Liu said. "I also follow the political situation closely. Early this year it seemed the European Allies would return

Germany's leased concessions to China. They led the Chinese negotiators to believe the unequal treaties would be abolished. It turned out to be a complicated betrayal."

"What do you mean? Because of Uncle's passing I am not aware of the latest developments."

Mr. Liu nodded. "Here is what happened. While those treaty discussions were going on, Japan signed secret agreements with several European countries and also with our warlord government. Instead of the German concessions being returned to China, the warlord government ceded them to Japan. The warlords signed the agreement behind our own negotiators' backs because the Japanese promised to make investments in Shantung Province. In effect, it was a bribe. The warlords are the ones who will benefit from those investments.

"The dreams of our republic have melted like spring snow. Dr. Sun struck a bargain with the devil when he brought warlords into his government. I understand it was the only way for him to gain military strength, but it compromised his position. It compromised all of us."

"Do you think the protests will make the Western powers change the treaty?" Wei-chen asked.

"No, it is too late for that. To keep Japan in the war, the Allies agreed to Japan's claims to Germany's Shantung concessions. Besides, it raises a much larger question. If the German territories had been returned to China, how could the other Western powers justify holding onto theirs?"

Wei-chen looked back at the demonstrators and stumbled.

"I can tell your heart is with them."

"Yes. When I was little, I often fell asleep listening to Uncle and his friend Mr. Wong talk about Dr. Sun's Republic. Their voices were filled with hope. But as the years passed, concern and despair drowned out hope. When will China control her own destiny? I am tired of foreigners staking claim to our country." Wei-chen's tone carried frustration.

"One day China will have a strong government. One day we will be free from foreign control. I firmly believe this. From now on, when you leave work

I will give you my copy of *Shen Pao*. You will have a better idea of what is taking place."

Each night Wei-chen devoured *Shen Pao*, Shanghai's Chinese newspaper. He also read the *North China Daily News* to learn the Western slant on issues and look at job listings. Every Wednesday he spent the entire day in the foreign concessions searching for work.

After six weeks his efforts had produced nothing. The trading companies he approached weren't willing to hire him. It rattled him that his command of English wasn't enough to land him a position. Attending university would have to wait, but he had already determined his school of choice - the University of Shanghai.

Each week on his day off, besides searching for work, he stopped by Jade Buddha Temple to make an offering for Uncle. He always looked for Mr. Cheng but hadn't seen him since their first meeting. The same with Mrs. Romanovsky. Whenever he walked past the shop, a gentlemen was behind the counter so he kept going. He was deeply disappointed on both counts.

In late July Wei-chen was about to enter the temple when he noticed Mr. Cheng and a foreigner sitting at a teashop across the street. Something about the man looked familiar. He was sure the foreigner was the same person he had seen leaving Mr. Liu's shop two months earlier. Wei-chen found it all very odd and couldn't help staring. Mr. Cheng saw him and nodded. Wei-chen returned the nod and entered the temple, wanting Mr. Cheng to find him later.

When he was burning incense Wei-chen sensed someone at his side. "Mr. Cheng, it is a pleasure to see you."

"The pleasure is also mine. You look better than the last time I saw you." The scholar guided Wei-chen to a small courtyard. "This is a good place to talk." A jasmine tree dappled shadows across the stonework. "Have you had any luck with your search for a new job?"

"No. I keep submitting applications, mostly to trading companies. Nothing has worked out, but I am sure of one thing. I want to attend the University of Shanghai when I have saved enough money." The desire for education constantly refocused him when he panicked at the thought of remaining destitute.

"I believe your diligence will be rewarded soon. The position you find will be quite a surprise for you." Mr. Cheng looked at Wei-chen and smiled. "No, I have no idea how it will happen."

"This might seem intrusive but I was wondering about the foreigner you were drinking tea with."

"He is one of my students. You look surprised. Perhaps I did not tell you that, besides my work with the novices, I teach Chinese literature."

"He looks a bit old to be a student."

The scholar laughed. "One is never too old to be a student. There are always new things to master. Besides being fluent in Mandarin, this gentleman has a great appreciation of Chinese culture and history and is obsessed with learning more."

"The way he carries himself reminds me of the teachers at my mission school. Is he American?"

"Yes, that is a good observation on your part."

Wei-chen wanted to know more about the American but Mr. Cheng changed the subject. After about an hour Wei-chen said, "I am sorry but I have to leave. I have identified several companies I want to approach. Is it possible you will be here next week?"

"Not next week but the week after that. We could meet here, early in the afternoon. I wish you good fortune on your search."

Wei-chen approached three businesses that afternoon. Only one asked him to submit a job application. Anxiety gnawed at him, chewing away his self-confidence. He decided to stop by the bakery before heading back to his room.

"Chan Wei-chen. How nice to see you." Mrs. Romanovsky walked from behind the counter.

"Good afternoon, Mrs. Romanovsky. It is good to see you too." She looked happy to see him.

"You must stay and have some tea. I need to get off my feet for a few minutes." She motioned Wei-chen to a small table near the front window. Within minutes she served tea and cookies.

Wei-chen's mouth watered when she set down the plate. "What does that say?" Wei-chen pointed to a small sign on the counter.

"It is in Russian. Our business keeps growing so we need to hire someone. We came here in 1918, along with many other Russians, and more keep arriving. Most of our customers are American and European."

"Why did you come to Shanghai?"

"After the revolution, society came apart. Not that life was perfect before the tsar was overthrown. Jewish communities have always struggled in Russia, but it is quite unsafe now. We came to Shanghai because it is a free port. We could enter without travel documents."

"Do you have family here?" Wei-chen asked.

"No. Our sons decided otherwise. They fled to the West and are now in France, on their way to Palestine. We arrived here with family photographs, our memories and enough savings to open the bakery."

She looked sad. Wei-chen understood what it meant for a son to be separated from his mother.

"What about your family? Where do they live?"

"It is a bit complicated but, by the time I was three years old, both my parents had died. A maternal uncle adopted me, and a paternal uncle adopted my brother. I have not seen him since. I regard Uncle Lin as my father. I moved to Shanghai in May after he passed away."

Mrs. Romanovsky's tea cup clinked on the saucer. "Oh my, you have had to grow up so quickly. Sometimes life tests us." She patted his hand.

Wei-chen blinked quickly, hiding tears. Her maternal touch scratched the surface of distant childhood memories. The empty teapot signaled him it was time to leave.

"Thank you for the tea. It was good to see you. Just one more thing. Would you please tell me what the sign says."

"It explains our requirements for an employee. We need someone to start work at five o'clock in the morning to help my husband make deliveries and then work in the shop until mid-afternoon."

"Does this person have to be Russian?"

"No, we have no nationality requirement." Mrs. Romanovsky smiled and walked him to the door.

Two days later Wei-chen asked Mr. Liu if he could leave work early, then took a tram to the bakery. Looking through the window, he checked to make sure the job notice was still there. When he walked into the shop, a man appeared from the back room. He looked strong, with bulges pushing against the sleeves of his shirt.

"Good afternoon. Is Mrs. Romanovsky here?"

"Good afternoon. You must be Chan Wei-chen. I am Jakov Romanovsky. I will get my wife."

Mr. Romanovsky walked with a slight limp. Wei-chen wondered what caused it.

"What a nice surprise." Mrs. Romanovsky burst into the front of the shop, smudges of flour across her apron. Tendrils of auburn curls escaped from her headscarf.

Mr. Romanovsky stood beside her and looked at her tenderly. Not used to seeing this kind of affection, Wei-chen glanced out the window.

"I would like to apply for this position." Wei-chen pointed to the sign. Before the Romanovskys could respond, he continued, "I used to work in my Uncle's shop selling porcelain. I also kept the shop in order. I am not a baker but I could learn and also help with many other things. For example, I could teach you some Chinese and help you bargain for supplies. I am sure my current employer would give me a good reference. I am a hard worker." Wei-chen stopped and held his breath.

"So you think my husband and I should learn more Chinese?" Mrs. Romanovsky asked.

Her smile encouraged Wei-chen. "Your Chinese is quite good, but I could teach you even more. Our four-character idioms contain a lot of wisdom."

"Well, then you would have to learn some Yiddish in return," Mr. Romanovsky said.

"What is that?" Wei-chen liked the sound of the word.

"It is a language Jews created in Eastern Europe and is based on thousands of years of experience. I think we could learn much from each other." Mrs. Romanovsky's tone made clear the job was his.

Wei-chen remembered Mr. Cheng's prediction that his new job would be something unexpected. Life had just matched two interlocking puzzle pieces. He heaved a sigh. He was beginning to trust in the future.

That evening he wrote Mr. Wong.

> Mr. Wong, I have been waiting to write until there was something positive to tell you. From the first day I started working at the porcelain shop, I knew the job would only last until September.
>
> Yesterday I found a new position. A Russian couple hired me to work in their European bakery. The bakery is located in the International Settlement so I plan to move there in the fall.
>
> I will write again when I have a new address. Each day I think about you and remember the many ways you touched my life. Please give the shop dog a pat on the head. I hope you are well.
>
> Your friend,
> Wei-chen

Two weeks later, when Wei-chen got home from work, there was a letter from Mr. Wong.

Wei-chen, reading your letter brought me happiness and relief. Your efforts at creating a new life are beginning to bear fruit. You will shine like the evening star in an indigo sky.

This past week I negotiated the sale of your uncle's business. Please send the details of your bank account so I can transfer the proceeds to you.

I miss you greatly, as does the shop dog. He crosses the street each day, hoping you will come out of the porcelain shop. I hope you will return next May for the first anniversary of your uncle's passing.

In friendship,
Mr. Wong

Wei-chen read the letter twice to make sure he understood it. He was tired but he left and walked to a neighborhood teashop. A doorway to his future was opening. His mind raced with the implications. He ordered jasmine tea and tried to settle down.

After Uncle's passing, Wei-chen's immediate concern was to get to Shanghai and transfer Uncle's property to Mr. Wong. He didn't expect Mr. Wong to sell the shop. He felt a weight lifting. His dream to attend university was within reach.

Mr. Wong's comment about the shop dog made him smile. When he helped Mr. Wong make puppets, the dog always nestled against his leg. With its square snout, bristly hair and sturdy build, it looked like all the other village dogs - except for its eyes. With one blue eye and one brown eye, its peculiar look frightened most children. But not Wei-chen. He felt an affinity with the dog, somehow identifying with its oddness. When Wei-chen scratched its back, the creature smelled like the dust it rolled in. He remembered the dog's earthy scent and looked down at his tea, restraining tears.

He wanted the puppet maker to keep half the proceeds from the shop. Mr. Wong's wife passed away years before Wei-chen came to live with Uncle. Their children died young, victims of a typhoid epidemic. With no one to care for him in his old age, it was the absolute least Wei-chen could do.

Two

1920

Wei-chen stared at the passing landscape. The train hurtled past rapeseed fields covered in their yellow springtime blanket. A journey much longer than the distance between Shanghai and his hometown was taking place within him.

No mule-drawn cart was available at the station so he walked to his old neighborhood, the commercial area where shophouses lined the streets. He slowed his city pace, ambling like a horse returning to its stable. Dust clinging to his clothes dulled the metropolitan veneer. The town seemed smaller to him, too small to live in ever again. Shanghai had altered the scope of his personal universe.

When Wei-chen knocked at Mr. Wong's shop door, the shop dog whined. He listened to the puppet maker shuffling to the door.

"Come in. You are taller, and you have gained weight. What a handsome young man you have become." Mr. Wong stared at Wei-chen. "Sit down. I will make some tea. I bought your favorite dumplings for dinner."

The warm welcome surged through Wei-chen's heart. His shoulders relaxed a bit. Establishing a new life in Shanghai this past year took great effort but he had achieved it. He was back in Chia-hsing by choice, not because he had failed.

"I brought some materials you could use for puppet outfits. When I roam the antique markets, I keep you in mind. Here are some new brushes for you." Wei-chen spread the gifts on the kitchen table.

Mr. Wong wiped something from his eye and poured tea. The shop dog draped a firm paw over Wei-chen's foot and nestled against his leg.

"Tomorrow we will visit your uncle's grave. I bought paper money to burn for our offering. I give thanks we are together to observe the first anniversary of his passing." Mr. Wong pretended to study something in his tea cup.

"Yes, it is hard to believe how quickly this year has passed. I go to Jade Buddha Temple each week to burn incense for Uncle's soul. I think of him everyday." Wei-chen regarded the puppet maker. When his face creased in a smile, wrinkles radiated like veins in a leaf. A lifetime told its story in those intersecting seams.

"You and your Uncle were very close. One day your deep sadness will be replaced by loving memories of him."

"That is hard to imagine." Wei-chen ruffed the hair behind the dog's ears.

Before burning their offerings the next morning, they cleaned Uncle's grave. Wei-chen followed Mr. Wong's every move. They were sitting beside the grave when a cloud of cranes floated down from the sky. The birds posted sentries, then stalked among the tomb stones.

"I have never seen this many cranes at one time. There are at least one hundred." Mr. Wong spoke in a hushed voice.

They watched the birds, mesmerized. When they stood up to walk home, whooshing wings filled the air. Flying in close formation, the cranes banked simultaneously. Sunlight sparkled on their wings for an instant.

"It is a sign from the gods. Your uncle's soul is at peace," the puppet maker whispered.

Wei-chen draped an arm across his friend's shoulders.

Mr. Wong steeped a pot of jasmine tea after dinner. "These leaves are some of the best from last year."

"Thank you. This reminds me of Uncle making tea each night. I stopped by the mission school today to make sure my transcripts are in order. I plan to attend the University of Shanghai this fall. While I was at the school, I talked to a friend who will graduate this year. He also plans to attend the university, so I will have a friend in Shanghai."

"Has it been been difficult for you to make friends? Is it because you work long hours?" Concern traced furrows across Mr. Wong's forehead.

"It is mostly because of work, but I will make new friends at the university. Also, the Romanovskys are quite good to me. Mrs. Romanovsky hovers over me like a mother, always making sure I have enough food. She misses her sons very much. After working at the bakery nine months, perhaps I have become a bit of a substitute for them.

"Also, have I mentioned Mr. Cheng, the Buddhist scholar? I meet with him at Jade Buddha Temple about once a month. We have interesting talks. I consider him a guide, someone to help me avoid life's pitfalls, like you and Uncle did."

"You are fortunate to have met this scholar." Relief flashed across Mr. Wong's face. "What kinds of things do you talk about?"

"Sometimes he gives me books to read, and we discuss them the next time we meet. Also, he teaches me about Chinese writings and the ways of Buddha." Wei-chen left unsaid how much Mr. Cheng had guided him through the grief of Uncle's passing.

"There is something I want to say before you leave, something I would have said to you last year if you had not left so abruptly." Mr. Wong's porcelain teacup clinked on the saucer. "In a city like Shanghai, there are many people who would take advantage of a small town boy. Remember, your eyes must see six roads. Your ears must listen in eight directions. Always look all around you. The same with your ears. Listen carefully from all directions. Sharpen all your senses before you open your mouth. Remember, a word spoken is past recalling."

"I promise to be careful. I will do as you say." Chagrined at the memory of his hasty departure, Wei-chen stared at tea leaves drifting in his cup. Mr. Wong was only saying what Uncle would say if he were still alive.

"Your uncle guided you on the Eightfold Path of Buddha. Try to live the things he taught you. Act with right intention and right mindfulness. Remember to see the world without hatred or greed. Please write to me each month. I have always believed you will succeed in whatever you choose to do. I want to know how you develop your talents." Tenderness and concern underlay everything Mr. Wong said.

"I will not forget your advice and promise to write each month."

"There is one more thing. Before selling your Uncle's shop, I found this small bamboo chest hidden behind some boxes. I think he set it aside for safekeeping years ago and then forgot about it. I am quite sure it belongs to you."

Wei-chen opened the chest and carefully lifted out a silk child's vest.

"I think your mother made it for you. Look closely at the embroidery in the butterfly wings. You will see the characters of your name."

Wei-chen studied the embroidery, then pressed the vest to his face, searching for the memory of his mother's caress. "Her face is a blur to me. I wish I could remember her." He folded the vest and kept it on his lap, placing a hand over it.

"Even if you cannot see her image, there are memories buried inside you. I have always known you were well loved in those first years before your uncle adopted you."

Roosters screeched at sunrise, waking Wei-chen. He finished packing, the scent of congee drifting up the stairway.

After breakfast they stepped outside to wait for the cart. The shop dog sat next to Wei-chen and leaned against him. Wei-chen bent down to scratch his ears. "If it is all right, I would like to come back next year for Lunar New Year."

Mr. Wong smiled. "That would please me. Do you know you look like your uncle? You have the same slightly arched nose and the same shock of hair that falls across your forehead."

"Long ago Auntie told me a nephew should look like his maternal uncle. When I am old, maybe I will have a beard too."

"I think you would look good with a beard and perhaps a mustache." The puppet maker smiled, then looked away. He brushed his eyes with his shirt sleeve. "I will remember you and send blessings from afar. Smooth travels, Wei-chen."

Wei-chen climbed into the cart. At the end of the street when he looked back, Mr. Wong extended his hands in a blessing.

The next morning Mrs. Romanovsky embraced him as soon as he entered the bakery. "After the breads are in the oven, we would like to talk to you."

He wondered what the Romanovskys wanted to talk about. He had made every effort to fulfill whatever responsibilities they gave him. He needed the security of this job in order to attend university.

With the bakery still closed for business, they sat at a table near the front window. Shop owners across the street were beginning to open their shutters.

"Did your visit to Chia-hsing go well?" Mrs. Romanovsky asked.

"Yes. I stayed with Mr. Wong, Uncle's best friend. When I was growing up, I spent a lot of time in his shop. I helped him make puppets, and he spent most evenings with us. It comforted me to see him again. Also, something beautiful happened at Uncle's grave."

When he described the appearance of the cranes, Mrs. Romanovsky's eyes rimmed with tears. "That was a sign. Your uncle's soul is at peace. We have a saying that all things grow with time except grief. I hope this is true for you."

"It is beginning to happen. I will never forget the appearance of the cranes. It consoled me." The words spilled from him without his usual filter. He felt safe with the Romanovskys.

"Before we get back to work, there is something we want to ask you," Mr. Romanovsky said. "We would like to increase your responsibilities and have you be our shabbos goy, a type of assistant. For one thing, you would be in charge of closing the shop on the Sabbath."

"I would like that. I am honored you asked me."

"I will go over your new position after work today. Here is your paycheck for last week."

When he looked at the check, Wei-chen blinked and read the amount twice. "Mr. Romanovksy, you forgot to deduct my time away from work."

"Observing your uncle's passing was an honorable act. We support what you did." Mrs. Romanovksy embraced Wei-chen, leaving a smudge of flour on his shoulder.

Her words shadowed Wei-chen all day. He wore the smudge of flour like a badge, making sure it remained on his shirt.

In mid-June Wei-chen arranged to meet Mr. Cheng. Before walking through the entrance to Jade Buddha Temple, he glanced across the street to see if the scholar was at the teashop. Instead he saw the American who studied Chinese literature with Mr. Cheng. Over the past year, Wei-chen had seen the American in various parts of the city but mostly in the International Settlement.

A striking woman was sitting at a table with him, their hands clasped. He wondered if she was Russian or perhaps Middle Eastern. After working at the bakery for nearly a year, he was better at identifying the various nationalities in Shanghai. Because of the Russian Revolution and the splintering of the Ottoman Empire, the city was filled with foreigners escaping turmoil in their homelands. Even from across the street, Wei-chen could sense the heat between them. One day he wanted to find a woman who would make him feel that way.

Wei-chen found Mr. Cheng in a side courtyard. "Nei hou."

"A Mi Tuo Fo." Mr. Cheng offered a blessing, palms pressed together across his chest. "You look the happiest I have ever seen you." He motioned for Wei-chen to sit on a bench. "There is a sense of peace about you. Tell me what you have been doing."

"My trip to Chia-hsing was good in many ways. Observing the first year of Uncle's passing with Mr. Wong was comforting. He had a strong friendship with my Uncle, and I now have a closer relationship with him. I promised Mr. Wong to return for Lunar New Year."

"Yes, you will see him one more time."

The statement rattled Wei-chen but he decided not to pursue it. Mr. Cheng's prophetic pronouncements always turned out to be right, at least so far.

"The Romanovskys promoted me. I am now their shabbos goy. One of my responsibilities will be closing the shop on the Sabbath. Under Jewish law, they are not allowed to work that night. They are good people. Mr. Romanovsky is a member of a council that helps émigrés. Mrs. Romanovsky constantly gives bread to people who cannot afford it. She says it is stale and she needs to get rid of it, but the truth is she cannot bear to see a hungry person."

Mr. Cheng nodded as if all this were happening according to some larger plan.

"Just before I entered the temple I saw your Chinese literature student across the street."

"Ah, yes, I noticed him too. He has been a bit distracted lately." The scholar sighed.

"Well, it could be worse. Not many distractions are that beautiful."

Mr. Cheng laughed. "One day you will meet Gabriel Knight, but this is not the right time."

———

Early summer swathed Shanghai in heat and humidity. Wei-chen's clothes were soaked by mid-morning. In July he realized the heat from the ovens was forging much more than bread. Whether it was the absence of their sons or simply because they liked him, Mrs. Romanovsky hovered about him and Mr. Romanovsky exerted a gentle guidance.

One afternoon, when he was about to leave work, the Romanovskys insisted he have tea with them. This was unusual. He wondered why they were interrupting their schedule.

"There are several things we want to discuss with you. First of all, since last September you have proven your worth. Besides being a trustworthy employee, you have become a friend. Because of this, we would like you to refer to us on a first-name basis." Mr. Romanovsky looked into Wei-chen's eyes.

"I am honored to have gained your trust and friendship. I would appreciate calling you Mrs. Mera and Mr. Jakov. It is a sign of our closeness. Thank you."

"The title of Mr. or Mrs. is not necessary," Mrs. Mera said.

"But it is necessary for me. I must show my respect."

"There is something else. With you starting university in the fall, we would like to help in some way. If you would like to live with us, we think the small room at the back of the shop would be perfect for you. It would save you rent money," Mr. Jakov said.

"That is a most generous offer but it is too much." Wei-chen looked away from Mrs. Mera's penetrating eyes. He didn't want to be pitied or have them feel obliged to shelter him. But, in his heart, he couldn't think of a better place to stay.

"It is no trouble for us. Since we live above the shop, you would not be in our way. Of course, we understand if you prefer to live somewhere else." Mrs. Mera's eyes looked a bit sad, the light gone from them.

"There is nowhere else I would rather be. I just do not want to trouble you."

"Then it is agreed. We will make the room suitable for you over the next few weeks. We only wish we could do more." Mrs. Mera beamed a smile into his heart.

"Many thanks to you both." They were treating him like family, an intimacy almost unimaginable for an orphan.

Wei-chen moved into the room in August. Across from his bed, a window opened onto a hutong that ran through the neighborhood. Children were playing games outside. Wei-chen smiled, remembering his childhood in Chia-hsing.

"We have something for you." Mrs. Mera stood in the doorway.

Mr. Jakov walked in with a bamboo chest and set it under the window. "This scholar's chest is for you. We found it near Dongtai Lu market. When the shopkeeper told us the meaning of the calligraphy, we knew it was a perfect find."

"The characters are from an old poem. It is a beautiful chest. Thank you." Deeply touched, Wei-chen's wall of self-sufficiency crumbled. Finally in safe moorage, that night he fell into a deep, peaceful sleep.

Before he could register at the University of Shanghai, Wei-chen was required to present his transcripts. He couldn't remember where he had stored them. Finally he looked in the rattan suitcase Mr. Wong gave him on his recent visit. It contained all the paperwork from Uncle's shop. Mr. Wong said it was the very suitcase sent with Wei-chen when Uncle adopted him.

He emptied it on his bed and found the transcripts shoved between some other papers. Before repacking everything, Wei-chen noticed an edge of paper wedged into a corner. The suitcase appeared to have a false bottom. Running his fingers along the side, he found small toggles holding a rattan layer in place. He removed the layer and found three photographs. One of them showed a young couple, perhaps a bride and groom on their wedding day. In the second one the same woman was standing with two boys, one on either side of her. The third one showed two little boys sitting on a bench. The vest on the smaller boy looked like Wei-chen's baby vest.

The Romanovskys were preparing Monday's baking schedule when Wei-chen exploded into the front room of the bakery.

"For heaven's sake, what is wrong?" Mrs. Mera asked.

"'Nothing. Look at these photographs. I think this is my family. I found the photos in my old suitcase."

Mr. Jakov looked at the photos spread on the counter. "So your uncle never showed you these photos?"

"He could not have known about them. They were hidden under a false bottom in my suitcase. I discovered them when I was looking for my transcripts. The vest on the little boy looks exactly like my baby vest. I think I am the one on the left." Wei-chen spoke rapidly, trying to keep pace with his thoughts. "Look at the young couple. I think they are my parents. The same woman is in this one with the boys."

"Of course, that is you. I see a resemblance between you and the younger one. And also between you and the woman. She has to be your mother. What a handsome boy you were. Even then you looked inquisitive. And look at your parents, such a lovely couple." Mrs. Mera kneaded his hand.

Like a bird in a rain puddle, Wei-chen drank in the comments.

Mr. Jakov left the room and returned with a box. "I want to show you some photographs of our family. Here we are on our wedding day." He looked at Mrs. Mera and smiled.

"My parents are posed the same way. Maybe it was their wedding day too." Wei-chen couldn't help imagining his family history.

"Here are our sons. It was the last photo taken before we left Russia." Sadness settled on the baker's features. Mrs. Mera stood up and walked behind him, placing her hands on his shoulders.

"You miss them very much."

"Everyday we miss them, but they are making a new life for themselves." Mrs. Mera made a feeble attempt at a smile.

While the Romanovskys talked, images of their past bled through the veneer of their life in Shanghai, like the pentimento on an oil painting. Wei-chen now had a better understanding of their compassion for refugees and how deeply they missed their sons.

It made him want to search for his family. "One day I am going to find my brother," Wei-chen declared.

Three

1924

Now beginning his fourth year at university, Wei-chen was amazed how quickly the first three years had raced past, like leaves that run before the wind. Given his economics major, he fully expected to land a job in Shanghai's bustling trade sector. When he was returning home from an evening class, he stopped short outside the bakery. The Romanovskys were sitting at a table in the back of the shop. Mrs. Mera looked upset.

Mr. Jakov looked up and waved Wei-chen inside. "Come join us for tea."

Wei-chen looked at them and assessed the situation. Mr. Jakov seemed to be fine but Mrs. Mera's eyes were red. "You are up late tonight. Is everything all right?"

"Two Russian cadets stopped at the shop just as we were closing. Mera asked them to come in and sit down while she packed some food for them. She has been upset since they left."

"They are so young and sad. The desperation in their eyes haunts me." Mrs. Mera wiped away tears.

Wei-chen understood completely. A month ago, in early September, three-hundred-fifty young cadets, sons of Russian officers killed in the revolution, had landed in Shanghai. Since then cadets stopped everyday at the bakery asking for bread. An orphan himself, Wei-chen identified closely with the boys. Each time it happened he felt deeply unsettled.

"Shanghai has become the mother of the dispossessed, and foreigners are not the only ones seeking refuge. Chinese are fleeing the countryside because of the warlords. Their unending battles are destabilizing China," Mr. Jakov said.

Mrs. Mera flinched at the tension in her husband's words. Wei-chen felt sure Mr. Jakov was recalling their flight from Russia.

"What you say is true. Sun Yat-sen's Republic cannot control the warlords nor protect its citizens. I was naive to be so hopeful. My country is paying a massive price for this failure." Wei-chen stared into his teacup.

"What do you think that price is?" Mr. Jakov asked.

"The price is double standards, the price is accepting foreign restrictions. One night last spring my friend Dong-hsing and I peeked in the windows of a Western club. We wanted to see what those places are like, the clubs that forbid Chinese to enter."

"What did you see?" Mrs. Mera looked concerned.

"The atmosphere was hazy but there were beautiful women, maybe Russians, talking and dancing with foreigners. The band members were the only Chinese there. Some guards chased us away so we were only there a short time. Not only are Chinese denied entry to these clubs, we cannot even look in the windows."

"You need to be careful. The settlement police might not treat you kindly." Mr. Jakov's tone was firm.

"Mr. Cheng has also warned me. I find the security situation ironic. The Chinese fleeing here want to end up in the foreign zones. It is well known the foreign police provide better protection. The rest of Shanghai is just not as safe. That is the reason I wanted to live here too, but I still resent being treated as a second-class citizen in my homeland."

The dichotomy rankled Wei-chen. It was true that all residents, Chinese and foreign, were safer in the foreign-occupied zones. But in return China was forced to accept foreign occupation in key areas across her land. England, France, Germany, the United States, Russia and Japan all claimed various parts of China.

"Before the Tsar was overthrown, the Russian nobility had much greater privileges than what you see in Shanghai," Mr. Jakov said. "I remember walking down the streets of our town sensing the old order was coming to an end. When the revolution occurred, we fled as quickly as possible. It was our chance to finally be free. We have lived here seven years, and I see change coming just as it did in Russia. It will not happen quickly, but China's simmering political situation will boil over one day."

Mr. Jakov's prediction concerned Wei-chen. He wanted an end to foreign domination but was concerned about a messy, painful transition. He did not want a repeat of what had occurred in Russia where one form of oppression replaced another.

In early December Wei-chen sipped tea at The Singing Bird, waiting for Mr. Cheng. Only a few bird cages were hanging in the teashop. A frigid chill prevented most owners from bringing their feathered pets out for fresh air. He was shocked when Mr. Cheng walked through the door with the American.

After Mr. Cheng made introductions, Gabriel Knight said, "I have been looking forward to meeting you. Mr. Cheng tells me you've done very well at the University of Shanghai. What are you studying?"

"My concentration is economics but I have minors in mathematics and English. The mission school I attended in Chia-hsing gave me a good foundation in the language." Wei-chen clamped onto his teacup with both hands, willing his nerves to settle down. Finally meeting this man was a wish come true. Mr. Cheng looked at him and smiled.

After some small talk, Wei-chen said, "One of my university instructors is from New Hampshire. Are you from the American Northeast?" He seized the chance to learn a few things about Knight. Mr. Cheng was always cagey when it came to discussing him.

"That is a good guess. I'm from Massachusetts, not too far from Boston. Your English is excellent, by the way."

"Thank you. Mr. Cheng says your command of Mandarin is exceptional. Have you lived here very long?"

"I came here in 1915 to work for the United States Consulate. It is normal to have only one or two tours of duty on an assignment but, after I had completed two tours, I wasn't ready to leave. I have been fascinated with China most of my life and was fortunate to land a job with Jardine Matheson and Company. Perhaps you are familiar with them." Knight smiled and seemed to relax a bit.

"Yes, I am. It is one of the largest hongs, founded in Canton nearly a century ago." Wei-chen was quite familiar with it. This foreign trading conglomerate had made its fortune trading smuggled opium, tea, and cotton before expanding to railways, shipping and insurance. He hoped he would never have to work for a European company.

"Do you return to America very often?" Wei-chen asked.

"Not really. After the Great War I returned to see my parents. Then, this past year, my father passed away so I was gone for a couple of months. I couldn't wait to return to Shanghai. This is my home now. I intend to remain here as long as possible."

"What would make it impossible to stay here?"

"There is a perceptible increase in the resentment against foreigners. When I returned from my home visit, I was looking for a coolie to haul my luggage to the taxi queue. Just when one came to pick up my bags, I heard someone cursing a foreigner. I turned to see what was going on and realized I was the one being sworn at. I understand the antagonism against Westerners, but that was more blatant than anything I have ever experienced."

"Did they spit on you? That has also been happening."

"No. I guess it could have been worse. On the same note, yesterday I met with several missionaries who fled here recently because it is too dangerous to remain in the countryside. They hope to return to their missions, but I'm not confident that will happen."

"Do you think it was a mistake for you to return?"

"No. I don't want to leave China. The tension between the haves and have-nots has been building for years, and it is justified. If Westerners and the Japanese want to continue doing business here, they will have to make some accommodations."

"Yesterday after class, a student handed me a pamphlet. Students are boycotting Japanese businesses to protest Japan's occupation of Port Arthur and

Dalian. I support the boycott. Those ports belong to China and should be returned. When I was young my Uncle and his best friend were concerned about Japanese expansion, and it still continues."

"Did the student ask you to take part in any protests?" Mr. Cheng snapped back into the discussion.

"Yes, he did."

"Promise me you will not get involved in any protests. You are kind-hearted. People will take advantage of you. I cannot predict the date, but the blood of students will be spilled."

The scholar's insistent tone jarred Wei-chen. Mr. Cheng stared at him, waiting for a response. "I will do as you wish." Wei-chen acceded but with some resentment. If he needed to avoid demonstrations, he would find other ways to support the students' efforts.

"I understand why you sympathize with this cause. I also think those ports should be returned to China, but you must be careful how you get involved. The protesters will be under surveillance. Photographs will be taken. Names will be recorded." Mr. Cheng looked hard at Wei-chen, making sure his comments registered.

The comments registered but Wei-chen didn't like feeling boxed in. He wanted to get involved with the protests. Wei-chen glanced at Knight. The American seemed to be assessing him. But then, he was also assessing Knight.

"The Japanese aren't the only ones interested in those Manchurian ports," Knight said.

"What do you mean?" Wei-chen wondered if Knight was trying to change the subject.

"Since 1889 Dalian and Port Arthur have gone back and forth between Japan and Russia. With their link to the Trans Siberian Railway, they're strategic to the Soviets."

"So you think the Soviet Union wants to regain control of that area?"

"Yes. I think that's part of the reason the Soviets offered to help Dr. Sun's party form a new government."

"I find it interesting the Soviet Union, which has many needs of its own, would so generously assist China." Mr. Cheng's tone reeked with sarcasm.

"It is more than interesting. My friend Dan McGuire, a reporter for the *North China Daily News,* believes it's because the most direct route from Moscow to Vladivostok runs across Manchuria. Perhaps the Soviets think an indebted Chinese government would drive the Japanese from Manchuria and welcome their assistance in doing this," Knight said.

"And who would fill the vacuum if the Japanese left? The Chinese or the Russians?" Mr. Cheng left the question hanging in the air.

"I have heard this conversation since I was a child. China is still struggling to form a republic more than ten years after the revolution. Will China never control her land?" Frustration roiled Wei-chen.

"It took hundreds of years for the Han Chinese to bring an end to the Manchu Ching Dynasty, but it will not take that long for China to retake the territories now occupied by foreigners. One day China will control all her land." Mr. Cheng spoke as if it were a foregone conclusion.

"In my lifetime?"

"It will happen long before you are an old man, and the toll exacted on our people will be massive."

The edge in Mr. Cheng's tone sent a chill down Wei-chen's back. It was the first time he had heard the scholar speak with such undeniable conviction.

Wei-chen wrote to Mr. Wong each month, and the puppet maker always responded, except for the past two months. In the last letter, the old man's handwriting was nearly illegible. Knowing he couldn't delay a visit any longer, Wei-chen traveled to Chia-hsing for the Lunar New Year in January.

Before he entered the shop, Wei-chen studied the exterior. The shop looked uninhabited. The display hadn't been changed in years, and the shop sign dangled at an angle. He knocked at the door and waited, then knocked again. Finally, shuffling footsteps approached the door.

Wei-chen had tried to prepare himself but Mr. Wong's appearance alarmed him. He was bent over a cane, his back arched in a painful angle. Cloudy eyes gazed at Wei-chen as if from a faraway place.

"Welcome, Wei-chen. Do I smell dumplings?"

"Yes, I stopped at the noodle shop down the street. We will celebrate the New Year properly. I will steep some tea."

At midnight a string of explosions filled the air and continued intermittently throughout the night. Wei-chen slept fitfully. On New Year's Day he and Mr. Wong sat outside to watch the Lion Dance. Dancers crouched and leaped their way past shops and homes. Musicians brought up the rear, scaring away evil spirits with loud percussions. Wei-chen took comfort in this ancient routine, all done to attract good luck in the coming year.

After people returned to their homes, the clacking of mah-jongg tiles filled the air. When they were back inside the shop, Mr. Wong said, "There are some things I want to talk about." Wei-chen poured tea, and the puppet maker continued. "I have a condition similar to your uncle's. When I pass, it will happen quickly. My affairs are in order. There is no need for you to come back again. It is much more important that you came now. You have been like the son I never had. I treasure this time with you."

Wei-chen stared at his friend, not sure how to respond.

"You must not worry. I am not afraid. When it is your time, you will not be afraid either."

"I should be the one consoling you, but it is you who consoles me. I will never forget this day. We are family." Wei-chen went to bed thinking he and Mr. Wong were like bookends, one looking back on life, the other looking forward to his future. A quiet trance settled over the city but it took him a long time to drift off.

Early the next morning he placed a hand on Mr. Wong's shoulder in farewell, then hoisted his bag into the cart. When the cart was about to turn the corner, Wei-chen looked back. The morning breeze molded Mr. Wong's jacket against his thin body. He waved, an old bamboo stalk, roots atrophied, about to succumb to the next strong wind. His face radiated peace.

In the early months of 1925, the Communist Party organized over twenty strikes against Japanese textile mills. They also enlisted university students to solicit contributions for striking workers. Wei-chen managed to support the boycott against Japanese businesses and still keep his word to Mr. Cheng. He avoided demonstrations and signed his name to no documents, but he solicited for and contributed to the workers fund.

Knight cautioned him the Communists were using students as unwitting foot soldiers to further their political aims. Initially Wei-chen shrugged off the warning, but over the past couple of months he had witnessed the manipulation of students. They were like tinder, easily inflamed. In late May the settlement police arrested students for their fundraising in support of striking workers. The trial was set for May 30.

On May 31 Mrs. Mera asked Wei-chen to run out and buy a copy of *Shen Pao*, the Chinese newspaper. When he returned she said, "Come and sit at the back table. Tell me what it says about yesterday's demonstration."

Not only did Wei-chen know one of the students who was arrested, his donation to the strikers' fund ran through that student. He gripped the newspaper with sweaty hands. "The first part of the article explains about the student arrests last week. It goes on to say the Communist Party organized a major demonstration for the day of the trial to protest the arrests. The Chinese General Chamber of Commerce and the Shanghai Student Federation also supported the demonstration." Wei-chen glanced at Mrs. Mera. She looked tense, hanging on each word.

"Now the article gets to the demonstration. Yesterday students and workers marched down Nanking Road in an anti-Japanese protest. An alert was sent to all police stations, warning them things might spiral out of control. When the protestors approached the Louza Police Station, Chinese and Sikh policemen blocked Nanking Road. The station chief arrested twenty-three students but hundreds more appeared, demanding the release of the students.

"The crowd continued to swell, and the station chief threatened to shoot if they did not calm down. A short time later he gave the order to fire. Four people were killed immediately. Five people were critically wounded and many others were injured. In response to the killings, a general strike against the foreign community has been set for June 3." Wei-chen stopped short when Mr. Jakov came into the shop.

"I was just at the emigré meeting. We discussed the strike. We will have to close the shop."

"For how long?" Mrs. Mera asked.

"No one knows. We hope things will return to normal soon." Mr. Jakov stood near the front window, hands clasped behind him.

"But what is normal? When we fled from Russia, I thought we could build a future here. Now I am not so sure. Our sons made a good decision not to move here." Mrs. Mera's face locked tight with concern.

"Please, Mera, you must not worry. The foreign banks and businesses will be forced to make some concessions. Then things will improve." Mr. Jakov walked over and patted her shoulder.

Two weeks after the strike began, Wei-chen and Knight met at a noodle shop in the Old City. After their first meeting in December, they continued to meet once a month, sometimes with Mr. Cheng and sometimes not. Wei-chen regarded the developing friendship with Knight as a tremendous gift.

Knight was different from other foreigners Wei-chen knew. He wasn't caught up in an extravagant lifestyle and didn't have an inflated ego. When Wei-chen questioned Knight about his work, he never responded in any detail, almost brushing it aside. He kept his personal life private. Knight never mentioned the beautiful woman who looked somewhat Eurasian. The last time Wei-chen saw them together, she was crying. He assumed she was no longer a part of Knight's life.

Wei-chen looked down the streets. "All the shops and stalls are open for business. It's eerie how quiet the streets are in the Settlement. With the foreign businesses shut down, there's no traffic. It's a stark contrast to the activity here in the Old City."

"Last night I saw Dan McGuire, my friend who works for the *North China Daily News*. He talked about the anti-foreign protests spreading across China. Unarmed protesters were shot in Nanking and Chungking, but the most brutal crackdown occurred in Canton. British and French military killed fifty-two protesters. With the killings on May 30 and now this, the foreign powers have detonated a powder keg of resentment. The old order is broken, like a vase that's been dropped and shattered. No matter how they try to put it back together, it will never be the same.

"Beyond that, the warlord generals in Peking are losing their stranglehold on the country. It's unfortunate Dr. Sun didn't live to see it. Above all other individuals, he was the most dedicated to creating a republic. Now we'll see what the Nationalists and Communists put in place." Knight tapped the table with his fingertips.

"Mr. Jakov thinks the strike will be over in a couple of weeks. The municipal government has shut off power to Chinese factories, forcing them to close. With their revenue cut off, they cannot continue to finance the strike fund. Workers will soon be forced back to work."

"Even so, I maintain the balance has shifted. History is being made as we speak, and it's going to be messy." Knight spoke with conviction.

Shortly after the fall semester started, Wei-chen's English professor asked him to stop by. When he knocked at the office door, the professor told him to come in.

"Good afternoon, Professor Smith." He stared at his teacher, who peered back at him over piles of papers. Wei-chen wondered if something was wrong. He hoped the knot in his gut didn't register on his face.

"Please sit down. I imagine you are wondering why I wanted to see you."

"I assume it concerns your literature class."

"Ah, young man, it's much more important than that. I want to talk to you about your future. You are modest about it, but you far surpass the other students in your English fluency. As for your Chinese, I am told you speak it like an old scholar."

Wei-chen, relieved nothing was wrong, wondered where the conversation was heading.

"I have also noticed you get on well with your fellow students. They respect you. You would make an excellent teacher. I know you still have another year to complete your degree, but it isn't too soon to start thinking ahead. If you decide to teach and need a recommendation for a position, just let me know. I would be glad to write one for you."

"Thank you, Professor. I appreciate your support." Relief coursed through Wei-chen. Their conversation continued until dusk descended.

As a young boy, Wei-chen loved studying the stars with Uncle. Perhaps part of the attraction was that his name meant brilliant star. Tonight, when he left the office, the night sky was unusually clear. Fang, his favorite constellation, twinkled in the Green Dragon quadrant of the eastern sky. Knight said it corresponded to the western constellation Libra. Just as Fang had its place in the heavens, Wei-chen was determined to find his proper place in the world. He walked home, hopes floating above his head, the path to his future stretching in front of him.

He fell asleep when the moon dropped behind the rooftops. In the middle of the night, a vivid dream captured him, sweeping him into Yu Yuan Garden in the Old City. The five-sided teahouse stood just ahead of him. He went upstairs to the second floor and took a table overlooking the pond. Sensing someone staring at him, he looked across the room. An old man with a long beard and piercing eyes nodded to him. Wei-chen was about to join the man but at just that moment Uncle sat down beside him. A waiter appeared with a pot of tea.

"There is something I must tell you," Uncle said. "In one of her letters, your mother wrote a little story about you. When you were two years old, you climbed into a persimmon tree. A branch broke and cut your arm when you tumbled down. It caused that scar on your left arm."

Wei-chen looked at the scar. Suddenly he was a little boy again, crying, frightened by the blood on his arm. A slightly older boy, perhaps his brother, tried to comfort him.

"In her letter she said your father's family was in some financial difficulty. You were all living with them." Uncle stood up. "I must go now."

"Do not leave. I want to know more."

Uncle's image vanished.

Instantly the old sage was standing beside him. "Your teacup is empty. I have come to read the leaves." He sat down, took the cup in his hands and studied the dregs. "You will undertake a quest that you will fulfill in your lifetime. Your journey will not always be easy, but deep friendships will offset the difficulties you encounter. I see a phoenix. It symbolizes your life. Like the mythical bird that rises from its ashes, you have the ability for self-renewal. We will meet again." The seer stood up, crossed the room to an open window, shape-shifted into a large crane and flew away.

In the state between dream and reality, Wei-chen turned on the bedside lamp. Holding his left arm under the light, he traced a faint scar. His heart pumped fast. As if looking through a mist, he recaptured the memory of his bloodied arm and his brother standing beside him. Taking pen and paper, he wrote down every detail he could remember about the dream and his memory.

The next afternoon he went to the temple. Mr. Cheng, who was burning incense at the main altar, nodded to him. "Wait for me in the courtyard. I will be there shortly, and we will discuss your dream."

Even after years of witnessing it, Wei-chen never took Mr. Cheng's prescience for granted. He never knew when it would occur and always found it comforting, as if the universe were synchronized somehow. He sat in the shade of a jasmine tree and waited.

Mr. Cheng strode across the courtyard and sat beside Wei-chen. "Now, tell me about your dream, my friend."

After relating everything, Wei-chen said, "The story about my fall could be true. Look at this scar. I feel sure the boy in the dream was my older brother. I can visualize him."

"There is something basic about your dream. You want it to be true but, if it is true, you wonder why your uncle did not tell you about this event when you lived with him."

"Yes, I want so much to believe the dream."

"You must not doubt the knowledge you received. I believe it to be true. Maybe it is better you learned this now rather than when you were too young to do something about it. The dream occurred because you want to find your brother. You have talked about this ever since I met you. Perhaps now is the time to search for him, and perhaps that is the quest the sage mentioned in your dream."

"Where should I start?"

"We shall begin at the ending. The last you knew, your Uncle Chan's family lived outside Soochow. Each village temple keeps administrative records. I will work through Jade Buddha Temple and find individuals to search the records in that region."

In October Mr. Cheng gave Wei-chen a letter. It said the Chan family left their village some years ago and moved south towards Canton, leaving no trail. Someone with great wealth now owned the Chan family land.

Disappointed, Wei-chen walked through the maze of side streets in the Old City. Wandering aimlessly, he suddenly felt compelled to turn into a hutong. Halfway down the narrow street, Wei-chen noticed a sign above a shop door - Teller of Fortunes. Intrigued, he peered through the front window. Dried herbs hung from the rafters. A bird cage dangled on one side of the window. On the other side, an old man sat in a shaft of light reading a tattered book. Wei-chen's shadow fell across the floor, catching the man's attention. The seer looked up and walked to the door.

"Good morning, lao ban." Wei-chen used the honorific to show respect for an elder. The old man looked exactly like the sage in his dream. Wei-chen didn't understand how this could be possible.

"Good morning. I am Mr. Lee. Young man, you look shocked."

"I am shocked. You look exactly like the wise man I saw in a dream. He read my tea leaves. Now, to see you here, I am puzzled."

"Is this the first time you have seen into the future? It can be a bit disconcerting the first time it happens. Please come in."

Wei-chen sat on a bench near the seer's chair. The scent of lavender and sage drifted down from the rafters, calming him. When Mr. Lee nodded, Wei-chen asked, "Did you know you were in my dream?"

"No, but I frequently glimpse things that come to pass. When I was a little boy, my mother noticed I often responded to questions before she asked them. Because her paternal grandfather was a seer, she was familiar with this form of knowledge. She encouraged me to develop this sixth sense but cautioned me to be wise in what I revealed to others."

"You mean sometimes you do not reveal what you see?"

"Yes. For example, several years ago a friend came to see me because he was concerned about his eldest grandson. The young man, a university student in Nanking, was active in political causes."

Wei-chen shook his head.

"You know what I am going to say. I told my friend his grandson must stay away from demonstrations, that the police were going to respond with great force. I sensed the young man would likely die within the year, but I could not prevent it. He was killed in the student protests this past spring."

Wei-chen was quiet, thinking about a friend who had died during the April demonstration. "What about interpreting dreams? Can you do that?"

"Dreams fascinate me. They open doorways to the past and the future. Much can be learned from them. Perhaps it is time for you to tell me about your dream. After all, that is why you wandered past the shop today."

Wei-chen related the dream, then continued, "Since that night I cannot stop thinking about my brother. I have tried to find him. A friend arranged for a search of temple records in the Soochow area. He learned that my uncle moved south with his family. I suspect he lost the family land."

"It was the right place to start searching, but I think you will not find your uncle's family any time soon. I see many home moves for them. Everything happens in its own time. There is a saying that fate will bring two people together even though they are separated by one thousand miles, and that fate will prevent two people from meeting although they are standing face to face. You must be persistent. I believe eventually you will find your brother."

He wanted to find his brother now. He stared out the window, trying to collect himself. "What do you think the future holds for China?"

"Within the next ten years, living conditions will become extremely difficult. Fighting between the Nationalists and Communists will begin, and there will likely be a war with Japan."

Wei-chen now wished he had not asked about China's future. He didn't want to hear about war with Japan. But Mr. Lee was only confirming what Wei-chen already feared inside, which was why he had posed the question in the first place. There was one more question he wanted to ask but decided against it. He was not sure he could handle another negative response.

Mr. Lee nodded. "You have another question but you are reluctant to ask it. I know the question you want to ask."

Wei-chen's heart longed for a perfect mate. He hadn't discussed it with anyone, not even Mrs. Mera. He was not in a rush to find someone. His concern lay elsewhere. "Because of my family situation, meaning that I do not actually have one, most parents will not consider me a suitable match for their daughter. A woman's family would have to compromise to accept me as their son-in-law. And there's another thing. I do not want to compromise on the qualities I desire in a mate. Given all of that, the question I hesitate to ask is, do you think I will have a wife and family of my own someday?"

The old man's eyelids closed halfway, seeing a world that lay far beyond the room. "An old proverb says you cannot catch a tiger cub unless you go to the tiger's lair. Because you have been focused on your education, you have been somewhat reluctant to pursue young women. This will change within the next few years. I see a woman coming into your life. She will bring you great happiness, and you will do the same for her."

Hope fluttered in his heart. Wei-chen wondered when they would meet and how he would recognize her.

Four

1926

On the second day of the Lunar New Year, Wei-chen met Knight and Mr. Cheng at The Confucian restaurant. Wei-chen looked forward to their periodic meetings, which were always stimulating and provided an interesting break from the company of his university friends.

"Are you still planning to finish university this year?" Knight asked.

"Yes, but after fall semester rather than spring semester. It has taken some extra time, but I will finish debt free."

"Have you determined what kind of career you would like to pursue?"

Wei-chen felt as if Knight were pressuring him. It made him defensive. With graduation less than a year out, he knew it was time to investigate potential employers. Keeping his emotions in check, he took a deep breath. "I have not approached any companies yet, but I want to work in trade development. If that does not work out, one of my professor thinks I should teach English. I hope it will not come to that, but it is an option."

"If you don't find a position with a trading company, you might also consider working for the American Consulate General. With your command of the English language and background in economics, you could work in their commercial attaché section. I think you would make an attractive candidate. I have some contacts if you ever want to explore that route."

"Thank you. I might take you up on that. I will start looking this semester." Once he realized Knight was only trying to be helpful, Wei-chen felt foolish. He glanced at Mr. Cheng. An unfathomable expression masked his face. Having witnessed this before, Wei-chen knew the scholar glimpsed something and was not ready to reveal it.

—

For the first time since starting university, Wei-chen didn't attend summer session. He continued to work at the bakery, while researching possible employers and spending evenings with friends. But he also did something else. After an unwavering focus on school and work for the past six years, he took a painting class for the sheer pleasure of creating.

This past spring he met a Chinese artist who had studied in Paris and was now teaching in his flat. Wei-chen liked his work and decided to study with him. When the Romanovskys learned this, they insisted on paying for the class, telling him it was an early graduation gift.

Like a butterfly in a cocoon, Wei-chen felt a metamorphosis taking place. His being was filled with a new sense of energy. Holding a brush in his hand again felt like second nature. It reminded him of making puppets for Mr. Wong, losing himself in the act of creating and entering a space where the world dropped away. By summer's end he was capturing vignettes of Shanghai street scenes.

—

In November Wei-chen found a small flat to let. He struggled with how to break the news to the Romanovskys that he had decided to move out. He knew Mr. Jakov would understand his need to be independent but Mrs. Mera would take it personally.

It didn't make it any easier for Wei-chen when Knight said, "I don't think the Romanovskys are in any rush for you to move, especially Mera. She misses her sons. It's been good for her to have you with them."

"I am ready to live on my own. I also think the timing is right for this to happen. Yesterday Mrs. Mera was the happiest I have ever seen her. Their older son wrote to say they arrived in Palestine and are working on a kibbutz. She is relieved their sons are safe and starting a new life."

"Then maybe it will be a good time for you to move. How are things progressing with finding a job? Have you heard from the Consulate?"

"Yes. I have a second interview tomorrow. I think I might get an offer."

"I do too. In fact, I would bet on it."

Knight looked as if he were stifling a smile. Wei-chen wondered just how close a relationship Knight had with his contact at the Consulate.

After his chat with Knight, Wei-chen went to the bakery. Mrs. Mera was standing behind the counter. "Is Mr. Jakov here?"

"He will be here in an hour or so." Her eyes locked onto Wei-chen's face. "You look different. I think you have something to tell me."

Concern flew across her face. Heaven only knew what she was thinking. He couldn't delay his news until Mr. Jakov got home. "Nothing bad has happened. I am thinking of moving to a small flat in December. You and Mr. Jakov will have your privacy again."

Looking down Mrs. Mera patted her hands on her apron, creating a cloud of flour dust. When she looked up, her lips trembled and tears spilled down her cheeks. "I understand your desire to live independently. I was just hoping it would not happen so soon. It is nature's design, having young birds fly away from the nest. I have been through this before, and it is not any easier this time. You are the son of my heart."

Not exactly sure how to comfort her, Wei-chen walked over and embraced Mrs. Mera. She leaned her head on his chest. Tears dampened his shirt. "And you are the mother of my heart." His heart pounded with loyalty to his adoptive mother.

On his final night at the bakery, Wei-chen cleaned the shop while Mrs. Mera prepared a hearty meal, a continuing endeavor to put more meat on his lean frame. When it was dark, she served dinner at a candlelit table.

Wei-chen looked across at them. Moonlight pouring through the window gilded his Russian icons. After dinner he went to his room and returned with a package wrapped in indigo fabric.

Mrs. Mera carefully unwrapped the gift. A smile played on her face as she studied it, then handed it to Mr. Jakov. "This is our shop. What a charming painting. Did you paint this in your class?"

"Yes. I stood across the street, made some sketches when the shop was closed and finished it in class. I wanted to surprise you."

"These characters at the bottom must be your name. We need to have a chop made for you. Your paintings will look more professional with your name stamped on them. We are proud to have this. Thank you," Mr. Jakov said.

"It will always remind us of the years you lived with us." Mrs. Mera served tea and they sat in silence, marking a rite of passage.

In January he moved to a flat not far from the Romanovskys. While he was packing he promised Mrs. Mera to stop by each week, the only way she would give Wei-chen her blessing to leave.

Thanks to Knight's connection, Wei-chen was now employed at the United States Consulate General, working as support staff for the commercial attaché. In mid-February Knight rang him and asked to meet him after work. Hunching his shoulders against the frigid wind, Wei-chen caught a tram to the French Concession and headed to Le Papillon, Knight's favorite bistro. The smoky haze permeating the cafe cloaked each table in seclusion. Wei-chen finally saw Knight and Dan McGuire in the back. He knew McGuire and liked him.

"Dan just returned from Nanking." Knight pulled out a chair for Wei-chen.

Wei-chen was grateful for the chance to speak directly to McGuire. He wanted to sort out the truth from rumors flying around the Consulate. "What was the situation in Nanking when you left?"

"It was stable. The warlords are gone, and the Nationalist Army is in firm control."

"Foreign women and children are boarding outbound ships because they are concerned Nationalist troops are advancing on Shanghai. Is that true?" Wei-chen asked.

"Yes, it is. They're heading here. Under Chiang's command, the Nationalist contingent and Communist army are working effectively together. I'm amazed to see what their joint Nationalist Revolutionary Army has accomplished in the past two years."

"How are they treating foreigners?" Knight asked.

"Missionaries are fleeing the countryside. Most foreigners are leaving cities before the Nationalists have a chance to capture them. Their strategy is quite effective. The Communists advance first, attacking warlords and organizing workers strikes. Then, when the Nationalist troops arrive, their combined forces occupy schools, hospitals and churches and set up local governments based on the Soviet model," McGuire said.

"Do you think the same thing will happen when they reach Shanghai?" Wei-chen wanted political change but not the Soviet model. The upheaval occurring in Russia was too destabilizing.

"Shanghai is quite a different situation. Before the Nationalist forces reached Nanking, Britain had already abandoned Hankow and Nanking. But here the foreign powers will make a stand. Forty thousand troops are being deployed to protect the International Settlement and French Concession. You've seen the barbed wire barricades and trenches ringing the concessions. The foreign governments are preparing for an attack." McGuire delivered his assessment in rapid-fire bursts.

"Do you think some kind of accommodation can be reached?" Knight asked.

"If I had to bet on it, I would say yes. For the time being, I think the Nationalist Revolutionary Army will settle for controlling Shanghai except for the foreign concessions. The concessions are stable because they have their own police and military forces.

"It's the rest of the city that's out of control with armed robberies and kidnappings occurring daily. On top of that, the Communist-dominated labor unions have paralyzed Shanghai with their general strike. I think the Chinese business community will offer no resistance to the Nationalist forces and will actually welcome them to stabilize the city.

"Chiang-Kai-shek is the person to watch. In 1923 he went to Moscow to study the Soviet army's organization. Since then he has advanced quickly through the ranks. He is ambitious, and perhaps ruthless, but wise enough to calculate the situation very carefully before taking on the Western forces."

"So you think Chiang will leave the concessions alone?" Wei-chen said.

"I am sure he would like them under Chinese control, but I think he has a more immediate purpose for his troops. The Nationalists and Communists seem to be cooperating, but that alliance has always been a strained one. I think Chiang wants complete control of the military."

"Are you suggesting he would turn the Nationalist army on the Communists?" Knight looked surprised.

"Yes, I am. We'll see how it plays out."

When Wei-chen returned to his flat, he brewed tea and sat at his kitchen table. McGuire's comments about Chiang unsettled him. Several of his former classmates were organizing support for the labor strike. He was concerned the Nationalists might round them up for their involvement in the strike.

He flashed back to childhood memories. More than once he had crawled out of bed and crouched at the top of the stairs, spying on Uncle and Mr. Wong. When the two old friends discussed their daily routines, they hummed like bees hovering over flowers. The droning usually comforted Wei-chen, but there was one evening in particular he could never forget.

He was nodding off on the landing when the intensity in Uncle's tone jolted him. He and Mr. Wong, with unusual passion, were discussing the political and social changes taking place in China's new republic. The banning of bound feet was good. The end of Mongol rule was necessary but the new government, long on idealism, was short on military might. Building a republic from the ashes of a corrupt dynasty was a massive task. Sun Yat-sen, the father of the Republic, was in a difficult position. He was compelled to rely on warlords to provide security, but it would come back to haunt him.

When Uncle compared Japan to a bird of prey, swooping down to pick China clean, Wei-chen crawled back into bed. He felt unsettled, frightened. During the night he dreamed about a blood-red dragon descending from the sky. He fled from the monster, taking refuge in an ancient temple. The temple's thick incense and burning candles provided a strong shield. The creature was powerless against it. But, hearing its raspy breathing, Wei-chen knew the beast stalked outside.

Breathing hard, Wei-chen had shot up in bed. Fighting to emerge from the dream, he looked over at Uncle. Finally Uncle's deep, relaxed breaths lulled Wei-chen into a sound sleep.

Tonight, fear hovered over his table. What if the blood-red dragon was the Nationalist Army? What if they were to go after his friends? What if they decided to come after him because he had supported the strike?

In late April Wei-chen arranged to meet Knight at Le Papillon. He usually loved this time of year when warm breezes coaxed blossoms to burst open. But tonight anxiety overshadowed any sense of beauty. He drummed his fingers waiting for Knight.

When Knight sat down, he stared at Wei-chen. "What's wrong? I have never seen you like this."

Wei-chen waited until the waiter left. "A university friend was killed in the April 12 attack. He was involved with trade union demonstrations. Somehow the Nationalists got his name. The killings still continue. People are being seized. There are no trials - just executions."

Knight poured more tea for Wei-chen. "These are dangerous days. I am very sorry about your friend. Thank God you're all right. I met with Dan McGuire last night. He has managed to piece some things together. He was right about Chiang turning the Nationalist army against the Communists. Two weeks before the April attack, some Communist members of the Nationalist Party told McGuire they suspected Chiang Kai-shek was about to betray them. One of them had seen Chiang meeting with leaders of the Chekiang-Kiangsu group, the capitalists who dominate Shanghai's business sectors. Even more serious, the man also saw Chiang with the head of Ch'ing Pang."

"The Green Gang, the most dangerous one. They are brutal, evil. So the Nationalists are now allied with Shanghai's financiers and underworld." Wei-chen's pulse spiked.

"The purpose of the April 12 attack was twofold. They wanted to purge the Communists and destroy the labor unions, including anyone associated with them. Over 300 people were killed that night. The surviving Communists and labor leaders are being tortured to learn the names of their supporters. That's why the killings continue. Chiang's forces, with substantial help from Ch'ing Pang, are working their way down the lists of names they're getting. International Settlement police are also involved in the round-ups."

"I attended some meetings with my friend." Wei-chen spoke in a hushed voice.

"My God. Did you sign any kind of support statement?"

"No, but I contributed some money. I tried to avoid being photographed. If they come after me, could something happen to the Romanovskys? Would they be implicated because I lived with them? Could I lose my job?" Wei-chen fought to remain rational but was losing the battle.

"Your involvement was probably too casual to warrant attention. If they were going to pick you up, it should have happened by now. But I think you should tell the Romanovskys about your involvement with the strike. They have every right to know the situation. You really should be more careful when people love you the way Mera and Jakov do."

"How do you know so much about the Romanovskys?"

"When I first met you three years ago, you made a very good impression on me. As I got to know you better, I was sure the American Consulate could use someone with your skills. I still have a close contact there but couldn't recommend you without doing some checking around.

"I can see what you are thinking. Please let me finish. I knew you wanted to work for a Chinese firm rather than a foreign one but, in case that didn't work out, I stopped by the bakery several times. Once I felt comfortable with the Romanovskys, I told them what I was considering. It was as if a floodgate opened. They praised you in every way possible, almost as if you were their son.

"It all worked out. Now I've become a regular customer, and you're working at the Consulate." Knight took a sip of beer and looked at Wei-chen.

"So you were spying on me." Wei-chen felt he had been played for a fool. "You probably talked to Mr. Cheng too."

"It isn't like that at all. If you advance in your job, which I predict you will, you'll be privy to confidential files. There is intense competition among the various foreign companies here, not to mention the Chinese firms. The consulate needs employees who not only have a good work ethic but who are also trustworthy."

Somewhat appeased, Wei-chen said, "Well, I guess I have done my share of spying on you too."

Knight laughed, then turned serious. "What do you mean?"

"It was all quite accidental, not intentional like it was with you. The first time I noticed you was only a few days after I arrived in Shanghai. I saw you walk out of Mr. Liu's porcelain shop with a package under your arm. I guessed you were an American resident, definitely not a tourist. Seeing you with that parcel made me decide to apply for a job there. The store front reminded me of my Uncle's shop, and I ended up working for Mr. Liu that summer.

"That July I saw you a second time. I was about to enter Jade Buddha Temple when I spotted Mr. Cheng sitting at the teahouse with a foreigner. Something about you looked familiar. Then I remembered having seen you at Mr. Liu's shop. Later, when Mr. Cheng came to the temple, I asked about you. All he would tell me was that you were a student of his.

"The third time was a year later. Again, I was on my way to meet Mr. Cheng at the temple. I looked across the street, in case he was at the teahouse, and saw you with a beautiful woman. When I mentioned having noticed you once again, he said it was not the right time for us to meet. That made me even more curious about this foreigner who appeared time and time again at the fringes of my life."

"That's quite interesting. I am fascinated with how people enter our lives. Why some stay and others move on. The loves we thrive on and the losses we endure." Knight looked somber.

Wei-chen was disappointed. This was not the response he expected. He wanted Knight to tell him about the woman. Had she disappeared from his life? Was she one of the losses he had endured? At that moment Uncle's face flashed in his mind.

"Are you all right? Sadness just swept across your face." Knight looked intently at Wei-chen.

"What you said made me think about Uncle. His death was a great loss to me. As for my parents, when they died I was too young to comprehend death. I have no physical memory of them but sometimes I have haunting dreams. Dreams about being young, alone and afraid. What about you? Who has departed from your life?"

"My grandfather passed away eight years ago. He taught me many things - a love of reading, chess, an interest in the larger world. The day he died a summer storm tore down a majestic oak behind his home, reconfiguring the landscape. In much the same way, his death transformed my heart. Not a day goes by that I don't think about him. I have come to understand all the things he taught me are part of me. So, in a way, something of him lives on in me."

"Were you closer to your grandfather than to your father?"

"That is a good question. And this isn't the night to discuss it." Knight looked away.

Wei-chen studied Knight's face. There was a veiled, faraway look about him. At that moment, a realization shot through him, an arrow from the future piercing his mind. Knight was the bridge to his future. One day he would cross that span.

Tonight he wanted to pursue something else. Wei-chen was determined to keep the conversation moving. Knight had never been so forthcoming. "What do you make of Mr. Cheng's ability to foretell events? Initially, when he knew I was curious about you, he said it was not the right time for us to meet. How did he decide when it was the right time?"

"He is mysterious, isn't he." Knight smiled. "I have given up trying to comprehend his psychic ability. Sometimes his predictions are unnerving. I have learned to accept that too."

So, Wei-chen thought, perhaps the tie between the Chinese scholar and Knight had initially been Chinese literature, but now it was much more than that. Perhaps it was even more than friendship, maybe something political. Wei-chen felt drawn to their world, like a compass aligning with the magnetic pole.

"Anti-foreign sentiment is stronger than ever. Do you ever think about leaving Shanghai?" Wei-chen asked.

"Things would have to get much worse for me to consider leaving. I will stay here as long as possible." Knight sipped his beer. "From the time I was quite young, I knew I wanted to live in China. When I started university, I was planning to teach here but, by the time I graduated, I wanted to work in the foreign service. After two tours of duty here, I was supposed to take another assignment but didn't want to leave China. Having a Chinese soul in an American body makes leaving difficult."

Knight's attempt to reassure Wei-chen failed. When Uncle's death left him unmoored, the Romanovskys provided him safe harbor and became like family to him. It was a life lesson, learning sometimes the thing you want most arrives in a form you aren't expecting. But, given what happened in the past month, if Chiang's government used those same tactics against foreigners, Wei-chen feared brutal conditions could force Knight and the Romanovskys to leave China.

Five

1932

Over the past five years, Wei-chen's career advanced at a steady pace. He now served as liaison to a segment of Shanghai's business community - a perfect front for his increasing involvement with intelligence operations.

Although work was demanding, he still managed to devote part of each weekend to painting. Through his art teacher, he established a connection with a small gallery in the French Concession. His street scenes of Shanghai sold quickly, both to tourists and locals. That morning the gallery rang him to say his largest piece just sold, one of Fuxing Park with its grand, leafy vaults.

Painting represented more than an additional source of income to Wei-chen. When he created, he lost himself completely in his work. It distracted him, at least for a few hours, from his deepening concern about Japan's designs on China. And there was another benefit. He saved all of his art income and was accumulating a substantial nest egg. He still wanted a woman to appear in his life and lay claim to his heart. Until this point, the better acquainted he became with a woman, the less time he wanted to spend with her. Now thirty years old, he was getting impatient for his true love to appear.

To celebrate the sale of his painting, Wei-chen rang Knight and offered to treat him to dinner at The Confucian. He arrived early to get a good table. Now August, the night air held a hint of fall. Sipping oolong tea, he took stock of the wrenching events of the past year. Dovetailing them with the information he accessed at work, he could draw only one conclusion. Japan intended to control not just Shanghai, but all of China.

He started thinking about an evening he spent with Knight and Dan McGuire, almost a year ago. Most of the conversation had focused on Japan's dominance in Shanghai. Besides having the largest foreign population in the city, the Japanese controlled two seats on the Municipal Council. They also insisted on patrolling Little Tokyo with their own police force. Technically Little Tokyo was part of the Chinese municipal city, not a legal concession, but Japan ignored that.

That evening Knight had commented there was more than one way to control a country. With Japan owning the largest number of foreign factories in China, he suggested their control could be commercial rather than military. Wei-chen disagreed with him, insisting Japan's goal was military domination of the country. Shortly after that, a small bomb was detonated on a Japanese-owned railway in Manchuria's capitol. Japan denied it, but there was no doubt their army set off the bomb.

When Japan used the incident to justify occupying the rest of Manchuria, Shanghai's response was immediate. The business community and political activists organized an anti-Japanese boycott. Wei-chen joined the groundswell, working on weekends to expand the boycott. Chinese businesses stopped selling Japanese products and serving Japanese customers. Dockworkers refused to unload cargo from Japanese ships. Westerners stopped patronizing businesses in Little Tokyo. The boycott exceeded anyone's expectations, forcing Japanese factories to shut down for lack of business.

But none of that stopped Japan. After occupying all of Manchuria in December, Japan proclaimed the new Republic of Manchukuo and turned its sights on Shanghai. This January another staged incident occurred. Five Japanese monks were attacked by a crowd in Chapei, the working class Chinese community adjoining Little Tokyo. It was a convenient place for a set-up. Most of Shanghai immediately recognized the duplicitous incident for what it was. The monks turned out to be members of the Buddhist Nichiren sect, a militant group that was directed to create a stir.

Within days the Japanese Consul General threatened to occupy Chapei unless the boycott was stopped and all anti-Japanese groups disbanded. When the boycott started last fall, McGuire had predicted a harsh response from Tokyo if it dragged on, and he was right. In January Japanese naval ships rode anchor in the Whangpoo River. Wei-chen remembered walking to the point where Soohow Creek flowed into the Whangpoo. Bracing himself against a bone-chilling wind, his chest tight with anger, he stared at the reflections of Japanese ships at Hongkew's doorstep.

By the time Shanghai's mayor called off the boycott at the end of January, it was too late. Japanese marines attacked the North Railway Station in Chapei. China's Nineteenth Route Army, a highly nationalistic corps, provided security for that area. Chiang Kai-shek ordered them not to resist, but they refused to abandon the station. Chiang fled to Nanking without ordering any reinforcements for them.

The strong resistance of the Nineteenth Army caught the Japanese off-guard. The naval commander ordered reinforcements from Japan to pound the Nineteenth Army into submission. That sent several hundred thousand civilians fleeing from Chapei to the International Settlement and the Old City. The decimated Nineteenth Route Army, heroes to Wei-chen, hung on until early March. By then eighty percent of Chapei's buildings had been destroyed and ten thousand civilians killed.

After the truce was signed in May, Wei-chen and Mr. Cheng had walked along the bank of Soochow Creek. At the crossing to Chapei, Chinese families streamed over the bridge, migratory birds returning home. Wei-chen remembered every word of their conversation and the scholar's advice.

> "Not even utter destruction deters them from going back. With eighty percent of Chapei leveled, it will take years to rebuild the town." Wei-chen watched people haul their belongings piled high in wheelbarrows and felt a smoldering rage.
>
> "These people have nowhere else to go. They migrated here because their villages held no future for them. By year's end most of those who fled to camps in the International Settlement will have returned." Mr. Cheng spoke without emotion.
>
> "Except for the ten thousand civilians who were killed in the bombing sorties."

"There is much resentment in your voice."

"I am furious. Under the demilitarization agreement Japanese troops have been withdrawn from Shanghai, but their garrison units are back in Hongkew, birds of prey, waiting for the right moment to attack."

"Beneath your anger there is fear, and it is justified. I am also concerned, but we must not let hatred and fear dictate our actions. We have to think clearly because Japan is not finished with its designs upon China. Tokyo claims the Republic of Manchukuo as Japanese territory, but this will not be enough. Their appetite for China's land is insatiable."

"My goodness, why the long face?" Knight said, sitting down.

Wei-chen snapped back to the present. "Thanks for rescuing me. I was thinking about the destruction and slaughter in Chapei earlier this year and what it really means. The current situation is only temporary. Japan will not tolerate this stalemate." Today's intelligence reports had confirmed his worst suspicions about Japan's designs on China. He still felt unnerved by them.

"We have been over this so often. There is a finite amount of what you can control in your life. Worrying about Japan's objectives will not change the situation," Knight said.

"I know you are right. There have been some changes in my job, more people reporting to me, so that should keep me occupied." He wished he could tell Knight about his promotion. In addition to gathering and assessing economic information, his responsibilities now included setting up a local network to gather intelligence on Japanese activity in Shanghai. Besides reporting directly to the head of the department, he had a major contact in the United States Department of Commerce who came to Shanghai twice a year.

"Still no special woman in your life?"

"Perhaps I have seen too many Western movies. I want a woman to capture my heart and my mind. I just have not met someone who holds my interest." Wei-chen evened his chopsticks with a sharp click. He knew Knight meant well, but the question annoyed him. Knight still did not have a wife, so why was he concerned about Wei-chen?

Changing the subject, Wei-chen handed Knight a letter. "I have some unexpected news."

That morning he had received a packet in the mail from Dr. Smith, his English literature professor. Before opening it, he turned an old, silver letter opener in his hand, something he found in the Ghost Market years ago. The characters for good luck were intertwined around the handle, making each use a wish for good fortune. He made a wish for something bright on his life horizon and then slit open the envelope. The contents threw a ray of light across the shadow cast by the Empire of the Rising Sun.

Knight set down the letter. "An offer to tutor English at the University of Shanghai is quite a compliment."

"Thank you. When I graduated Dr. Smith told me he intended to follow my career. When there was an unexpected opening, he thought of me. The class is only one night a week, which is perfect. It will be good to be back on campus again." He recognized it was unlikely, but the position might prove to be another way to sift for information.

———

After the fall semester, Wei-chen felt comfortable in his tutoring role. He enjoyed being on campus, and the position didn't require much preparation time. Dr. Smith told him his approach was a bit informal, but the results stood for themselves. The class was larger each month. Apparently he was quite effective at making English syntax comprehensible to students.

When he resumed tutoring in January, his self-assurance lasted until the second week. After class started, an attractive student entered the classroom and slipped into a seat at the back. She glanced down when she noticed Wei-chen staring at her.

At the end of class he glanced at her. "Next week we will study the confusing world of personal pronouns. I look forward to seeing all of you then." He couldn't keep his eyes off her.

The weeks between tutoring sessions couldn't pass quickly enough. Wei-chen found himself daydreaming, imagining conversations with her, seeing her eyes crinkle when she smiled at him. In class he forced himself not to regard her for more than a few moments at a time. One night he glanced up and noticed she was studying him. He quickly turned to another student but wondered if she was curious about him.

Her name, Hui-lan, meant virtuous orchid, an apt description for her delicate beauty. But Wei-chen sensed she possessed an underlying strength that was anything but fragile. He wanted to become acquainted with her but couldn't come up with any scheme that didn't seem bumbling. Besides, he still couldn't tell if she would welcome his friendship. Experiencing torment because of a woman was something new to him.

———

In early April, Wei-chen claimed an outdoor table at Le Papillon. When dusk fell, miniature lights in the plane trees glowed like fireflies. Wei-chen ordered tea and waited for Knight. He was impatient to talk to him but also nervous about it.

After they ordered their dinner, Knight said, "You have seemed preoccupied lately. Is everything all right at work?"

"Yes. My job is more demanding, but that is fine with me."

"What about your finances? If things are ever tight for you, you must let me know."

"It does not concern money. My financial situation is strong." Wei-chen's cheeks flushed. "I have been preoccupied, almost out of focus." He twirled his noodles.

"What about your artwork? Are your paintings still selling?"

"Yes, they are still selling. That is not it."

Knight looked closely at Wei-chen. "By any chance, is a young woman the cause of your preoccupation? Perhaps it isn't a lack of focus but rather a shift in your focal point." Knight ordered a beer.

After staring blankly at passersby, Wei-chen turned to Knight. "It is so farfetched I have not wanted to mention it. Sometimes you use the term blindsided so I looked it up. It is the field of vision where one cannot see approaching objects. I believe this has happened to me. There is a young woman in my class." Wei-chen rearranged the bok choy on his plate. "I have never felt an attraction like this. It is probably pointless." He set down his chopsticks and looked directly at Knight to see his reaction.

For just an instant, sadness flew across Knight's face. "When the heart is involved, it is not pointless. Perhaps irrational, but not senseless. I am certainly willing to listen, but I can't offer much advice. My first experience with love proved rather disastrous. I have just muddled along since then."

"You? A disastrous love affair? In all the years I have known you, not once have you ever mentioned it. You have always seemed satisfied with your life."

"It happened before I came to China, but my memories are still vivid. My sophomore year at Amherst, a friendship developed with a girl from a nearby college. Her name was Olivia. By the end of our junior year, we were madly in love. She was the realization of a dream I didn't know I even had."

Wei-chen sipped his tea and nodded, wanting Knight to continue.

"She didn't care that my family wasn't prominent, but her parents did. Our last year in school they threatened to disown her if she didn't stop spending time with me. By year's end, her duty to family won out over her love for me." Knight looked away.

He does not want me to see into his heart, Wei-chen thought. "You loved her very much. I hear it in your voice. Is that why you came to China? To leave your misfortune behind?"

"Not exactly. When I was young, missionaries visited our church each year, explaining their work, appealing for funds. Their stories fascinated me, especially those of the missionaries who worked in Asia. When I finished secondary school, my goal was to teach in China, and that didn't change while I was at Amherst.

"I made this clear to Olivia. She wasn't sure she could live so far away from family. Ultimately each of us recognized we would have to make sacrifices to be together, she to leave her family and me to forsake my dream of living here. I arrived in China with a broken heart but have never regretted the decision."

"But what about sharing your life with someone?"

"Frankly, the first few years after arriving here, I would not let anyone into my life. Friends at the Consulate kept trying to introduce me to eligible young women, but I just wasn't ready. Sometimes I wonder if I have become so selfish about pursuing my own interests that a spouse would make life too complicated."

"Did you ever see Olivia again?"

A distant look settled in Knight's eyes. "I am going to tell you something I haven't mentioned to anyone else. Something I have revisited many times."

Knight sounded detached, as if recalling something committed to memory, perhaps painful memory. Wei-chen paid close attention. He had never seen this side of Knight.

> "When I went home after my father's passing, I met an old college friend in Boston. During lunch I had the sensation someone was looking at me. I glanced across the room and noticed a woman who resembled Olivia, or at least resembled my distant memory of her. When our eyes met, there was no doubt. After her friend left, she remained at the table.
>
> "I asked for the check, hoping it wasn't obvious to my friend that I was rushing things. As soon as he left, I crossed the room. I told her I thought I would never see her again. When I bent to kiss her cheek, she turned her face and we kissed."
>
> "I'm not sure where to begin," I said.
>
> "You look remarkably the same, Gabriel. It has been almost twenty years since we've seen each other."
>
> "Yes. You still look lovely." She blushed.
>
> "The years have been good to you. You look good, and the silver in your hair gives you a certain gravitas. You're even more handsome than before."
>
> "Have you checked your eyesight lately?"
>
> "The last time I checked, it was fine. I see you quite clearly."
>
> "Where do you live?"

"After graduation I moved to Boston and married the following year. I have three children, a daughter and two sons. What about you?"

"Marriage? It never quite worked out. I'm still in China. Shanghai at the present."

"So, you followed your dream. It seems to have agreed with you."

"You mean you don't find my nose too big or my eyes too round?"

"No, everything looks quite right to me. Is it difficult to be a foreigner there?"

"Not really. Externally I may not look as if I belong in China but internally it has been a remarkable fit." After she peppered me with questions, I said, "I've often wondered if you became a writer."

She still held a cup the same way, forearms resting against the table while she reflected. "I consider myself a clandestine poet. Writing poetry is like being on an island, an escape from my children's schedules."

"When did you begin writing poetry and why do you need to be secretive about it?"

"About ten years ago, the children and I spent two weeks at the shore. While they were playing in the surf, some lines came to me, fresh and effortlessly. That evening I wrote down the poem, only changing a few words. It was a simple piece. Now I use poetry to express my deepest feelings. It helps me sort things out."

"And you prefer these writings don't see the light of day."

"Most definitely."

"Are you happy?" She clutched her napkin and looked out the window, blinking back tears.

It was a very direct question, but I needed to know the answer. From the little she said, I sensed her children provided the linchpin for her marriage. Her husband seemed to hover in the background, detached, like a flying mystic in a Tibetan painting.

"I don't allow myself to ask that question. It would open a door I have managed to keep closed for quite some time. I met my parents' wishes when I married Arthur, but it seems I didn't meet mine."

"I shouldn't have asked."

"It's all right. I can't help but wonder what kind of life we might have made together. How long will you be in the States?"

"I leave in two days, but I have to catch a train shortly. I'm staying with my mother and sister." I wanted to reach across the table for her hand. I thought about delaying my return to Shanghai, but realized instantly that would accomplish nothing other than fan the fire of a past love for someone who is married.

"I wish you didn't have to leave so soon." She placed her hand on my arm.

I placed my hand over hers. "This afternoon has been a remarkable gift, Olivia. I never dreamed I would see you again."

"It could get very complicated if you lived here."

"Yes, it could. We would be like two moths circling a flame."

We left the restaurant and walked to the corner, each needing to take a taxi in the opposite direction. "Contact me if there's ever anything I could do for you. I expect to remain in Shanghai but, should that change, my sister will know where to reach me. Hannah's address is here on the back of my name card."

She looked up at me and took the card. Standing on tiptoes, she kissed my cheek and said, "I don't want to say good-bye."

I folded her in my arms and held her close. "For now, we have to go our separate ways." I kept an arm around her shoulders and flagged a taxi.

"This won't be the last time we see each other." She leaned into me as a taxi drew to the curb.

"No, it won't." I pulled her to me and kissed her.

She stumbled into the taxi and looked back at me. Tears rimmed her eyes. I stood there until I lost sight of her, wondering if our meeting was coincidence or destiny.

That night, after Mother went to bed, Hannah and I sat on the front porch. Fireflies danced in the yard, miniature lanterns against the indigo night.

"Mother has aged a lot since Father's death. I don't know how she would manage if you weren't living with her, Hannah."

"It hasn't been easy. Losing Father and then Nathan was devastating. Some days I have very little to give to her. I don't want to become like her, living out my days in the past. Thank heavens my teaching keeps me engaged outside this house."

"I guess I've been selfish."

"Truthfully, I think you have been. It hurt me when you didn't return for a visit after Nathan's death. Did you think I didn't need you that first summer without him? Couldn't you have helped with Mother for a month or two when I moved here?"

"I apologize. I hoped moving back home would somehow help with your loss. Is there any way I could make it up to you, other than moving back here? Do you still want to live with Mother?"

"It isn't only duty that keeps me here. I want to care for her, but I could use some support from you, and I don't mean financial. I don't even know what to ask of you. I'm tired, Gabriel. I'll see you in the morning." She shot to her feet and slammed the porch door behind her.

Early the next morning I tiptoed down the stairs, walked to the cemetery and spent some time at Father's and Nathan's graves. I heard footsteps sliding across the grass and turned to find Hannah at my side.

"Why didn't you tell me you were coming here? I've been driving around town looking for you. You look exhausted."

"I didn't sleep well. I am sorry I've let you down." She moved to my side. I placed an arm around her shoulders, an attempt at long overdue consolation.

On the way back, Hannah pulled up at the town diner. "Let's have coffee before Mother gets up." A lone customer sat hunched over the counter with a newspaper.

We sat in a booth at the front window. "I remember sitting here when I was in high school. The menu still looks the same." I ordered a short stack.

"I'm not sure how pleasant this visit has been for you. Perhaps we don't know how to be together after living apart for so long," Hannah said.

"No, it's been a good visit in many ways, but there's something I want to confess. Through the years I have felt guilty that the responsibility for Mother and Father fell to you, but not guilty enough to leave China. I can't imagine not living there. I understand if you're angry with me."

"I don't know who's more selfish - you for being determined to remain in China or me for wanting you to forsake that life. You would probably be miserable here. Will you ever live here again?"

"I haven't really considered it, but life can take unexpected turns. Speaking of which, yesterday I ran into Olivia, my college girlfriend. Do you remember her?

"Of course, I do. You were devastated when she broke things off."

"I don't think I took it that hard."

"You did. You left for China and didn't return to visit us for years." She smiled.

"Well, we happened to have lunch at the same restaurant yesterday. After our friends left, we talked for a while. I told her if she ever needed to reach me, you would have my current address."

Her eyebrows arched. "Are you expecting to hear from her and, if I may ask, is she married?"

"To answer your first question, she writes poetry. I told her if she ever published any pieces, I would like to see them. And, yes, she is married."

"Is there more to this than meets the eye?"

"I don't think so, Hannah." I avoided looking at her.

"Be careful, Gabriel"

"I think returning to China is being very careful."

"There, Wei-chen, now you know more about me than anyone else. I expect you to treat this with confidence. Also, you should now understand why I am the last person to give you advice about women. I'm feeling chilled. Let's go into the bar. I would like a brandy. This is one evening when I'll answer any questions you have for me."

Stunned by Knight's openness, Wei-chen said, "I think I will have a brandy too." The room was smoke-filled. Foreign correspondents crowded shoulder-to-shoulder at the bar, trading information. Knight steered past them toward a small table at the back of the room.

After the waiter delivered the brandies, Wei-chen seized the chance to probe Knight's well-guarded privacy. "Have you heard from Olivia since then?"

"No."

"Are you still in love with her?"

"Until I saw her four years ago, I thought I was in love with the memory of her. But the truth is, I still love her."

"Do you want to see her again?"

"Not unless she's a free woman. If she is in a difficult marriage, I don't want to create further strain. I believe she will contact me if her situation changes. And, no, I'm not sitting here on tenterhooks waiting for that to happen."

"What happened to the beautiful woman I saw you with years ago, maybe around the time your father passed on?

"Ah, Liliana. Well, before I came across Olivia in that restaurant, I thought Liliana might finally be the right woman for me. There were many things I loved about her. She was bright, beautiful, passionate and determined to create a new life. She and her sister fled here from Armenia after their parents were killed.

"Anyway, when I returned from that home visit, she knew something had changed in me. She deserved to have someone love her with complete abandon. I no longer felt capable of doing that. It was not an easy decision to stop seeing her, but it was the right one."

"You are an honorable man. Not everyone would do that. Personally, I find your story about Olivia's parents most relevant. I have no family, no wealth, no social position. Who would want their daughter to marry me, especially if their family has any means? Until I met Hui-lan, I tried to avoid thinking about it. You have been here long enough to understand how Chinese society operates."

"I have two things to say. Several years ago you told me the Chan family story. At one time they held a privileged position. Yes, their fortune was lost, but your ancestors were educated and respected. Secondly, those long-held social mores are breaking down, especially with university students. Life moves at a faster pace in Shanghai. This will work to your benefit. Does she know you're interested in her?"

"I don't think so. She disappears right after class. I need to come up with a plan to run into her. Back to your meeting with Olivia. I have a question. The expression ming chung chu ting means fated or destined. Do you think some things are destined?"

"After encountering Olivia in Boston, I have given that a lot of thought. Until seeing her across the room from me that day, I would have said there is no such thing as something being destined. Now I'm no longer sure. But there is something I do know. If I see Olivia again, it will happen because it is meant to be, because she will have decided to be free. It isn't something I will force." Knight ordered another brandy.

"I believe some things are meant to be." Wei-chen wanted to believe fate had played a hand in his meeting Hui-lan. He wanted destiny to tear down any barriers society could raise between the two of them. "I have more questions. Americans use the expression, love at first sight. Do you believe in that?"

"I believe in attraction at first sight." Knight took a sip of brandy.

"Do both people have to feel this?"

"I don't think so. You ask this as if I'm some kind of expert, which I certainly am not."

"But I value your opinion. Do you remember the first time you saw Olivia?"

"Yes, of course. She was studying with friends at the library. Something about her went straight to my heart. I kept going to the library at the same time each day, facing her from a couple of tables away. It took three days before she acknowledged me and smiled."

"Uncle taught me the term learned revelation means to know someone's thoughts. It takes time to know someone well. One cannot know deeply personal things at first sight."

"That's true, but you can know instantly if someone intrigues you."

"Yes, that is exactly what happened with Hui-lan."

"This conversation reminds me of a verse I memorized years ago. It's from The Rubaiyat by Omar Khayyam. Are you familiar with it?"

Wei-chen shook his head no.

"Khayyam was a Persian poet and mathematician. His writings from the twelfth century are beautiful and still relevant. I have never forgotten these lines. 'The Moving Finger writes, and having writ, moves on. Nor all thy piety nor whit shall lure it back to cancel half a line, nor all thy tears wash out a word of it.'

"I think it applies to your situation. You have the chance to become acquainted with someone who has appeared in your life. Life will not hold still for you. Are you going to seize this opportunity? What have you got to lose? Your pride? I am not sure how you should approach her. Perhaps you could talk to Mera. She is wise when it comes to matters of the heart."

By late May, Wei-chen still had not found a way to talk to Hui-lan alone. Either she left class before he could catch up with her or she was surrounded by friends. Early on a Sunday morning, he went to Dongtai Lu Market. He had been out with friends the night before and wanted some time to himself.

He took a tram to the Old City and wandered around the market. When he sauntered past stalls with porcelain ware, it sometimes seemed Uncle's discriminating eye was guiding him to a certain piece. He was always on the hunt for fine pieces to add to his collection.

Wei-chen was examining a small vase when he heard, "Good morning, Teacher Chan." The familiar voice made him spin around. Seeing Hui-lan, he almost dropped the vase.

"Good morning. What a surprise to see you here."

"Oh, I am looking for a birthday gift for Mother. The piece you are holding is lovely."

"Yes, it is. It is difficult for me to resist such a beautiful piece, especially if the price is right. Feel the weight of this delicate vase. It weighs almost nothing."

Handing the vase to her, Wei-chen felt a charge as Hui-lan's fingers touched his. Was he imagining she rested her fingers on his or was it just wishful thinking? "I would guess it is about eighty years old. What do you think?"

"I have no idea of the age, but the painting is finely done. What a lovely miniature of willows draping over a river bank."

"It appears this will be Mr. Fong's first sale of the day, so the negotiation should not be difficult. An early sale would be an auspicious start to his day. I have spent many hours with him learning the finer points of old pieces."

The shopkeeper, who was reading behind the counter, stood up when they approached. "Good morning, Mr. Chan. I thought you might like that piece."

"Good morning, Mr. Fong. It is very nice. How old is it?"

"There is no chop, but I judge it to be over one hundred years old."

"It does not seem quite that old to me." Wei-chen began negotiating, offering much too little while Mr. Fong demanded far too much. Wei-chen was adept at bargaining and striking a fair deal. He always left enough money on the table to satisfy the seller. Wei-chen left the stall smiling, satisfied with the price he had paid for the vase and also because Hui-lan stood at his side. "Now, about the gift for your mother. Do you have anything in mind?"

"Yes, I would like to find a tea caddy for her. A friend mentioned one of the stalls has bamboo caddies."

"I know the stall your friend has in mind. It is just a little farther ahead." They ambled past vendors. He noticed she was not in a rush. "How did you decide to attend the University of Shanghai?"

"I am from Nanking and attended a Baptist mission school there." Hui-lan picked up an old ivory fan from a basket, fanned herself and set it back down. "One of my secondary teachers arranged for a scholarship at Aurora University, the girls college here. Mother would have preferred I stay in

Nanking, but Father supported my wish to come here. This past fall I transferred to the University, and that is how I arrived in your class. Word spread quickly on campus that you were a good tutor."

"That is kind of you to say." Heat flushed his cheeks. "Are you going home for the summer?" He hoped she would say no.

"Yes, I leave in two weeks and will be back in September."

"Are you planning to be a teacher?"

"Yes, I want to teach literature at the secondary level."

"I think you would make an excellent teacher."

"Why do you say that?"

Wei-chen held her gaze. "I have watched you with the other students. You have a pleasant manner. Also, you understood the nuances of English quickly. I think teaching comes naturally to you." Her smile pierced his heart. "Here are the tea caddies. This stall has the best selection."

"The painted bamboo ones are beautiful. I think Mother would like this one with the vine trailing across it. Look, here is the artist's chop. The signature makes it even more special."

Wei-chen turned the caddy in his hand. "This one should appeal to any woman. The painting is delicate." Personally he preferred an antique caddy that had double happiness characters painted around it. It had probably been a wedding gift for a young couple. Big dreams stirred in his heart that morning.

"Quiet Heart Teashop is around the corner. It is a charming old shop. Do you have time for a cup of tea?" Wei-chen asked.

"You were right. This is a charming place." Hui-lan looked at the birdcages suspended from rafters. "I heard there was a teashop where customers bring their birds. They are all chirping to each other."

"Or perhaps singing to the customers. At any rate, it is cheerful. You mentioned going home for the summer. Do you have any siblings?"

"I have a younger sister. When I am in Nanking, I work in the office at Father's trading company. I enjoy spending time with him. What about your family? Where do they live?"

"Well, I have an interesting family. I have a Jewish mother, an American who acts like an older brother, a Chinese uncle who is a scholar and another uncle who is married to my Jewish mother." It came out so spontaneously. He had wondered for months how to address this issue only to give such an inane answer. He was upset with himself but then she started laughing.

Tears shone in her eyes. "I apologize for finding your lineage amusing but, you must admit, it is a bit unusual."

"Actually, the Chan family owned land outside Soochow for generations. Unfortunately, my father lacked the wisdom of my grandfather. He put the family wealth at risk through bad investments. Before he could turn things around, bandits killed him when he was returning from Shanghai. The following year my mother died. A paternal uncle adopted my brother, and my mother's brother adopted me. I have not seen my brother since then. I searched for him several years ago but the family was no longer there. I have not been able to trace them."

"How sad. I am sorry."

"It is sad. However, there was an element of good fortune in all this. My Uncle and Auntie Lin raised me as if I were their firstborn, always wanting the best for me. Years after Auntie's passing, Uncle knew I wanted to attend university in Shanghai. He was supportive of me, all the while knowing I would probably never live in Chia-hsing again. He died just before I finished secondary school."

"That is where your unusual family comes in."

"Yes, I cannot imagine life without them. Your parents must be progressive, sending you to Shanghai for your education rather than keeping you close to home." He was fishing for family information and hoped it wasn't obvious.

"Teacher Chan, it is a long story. Perhaps I will tell it to you another time."

"First of all, when we are not in class, call me Wei-chen. And, if the time is ever right, I would like to hear that story."

"I should go back now. I have to study for an exam."

"Let me walk you to the tram. I know a shortcut."

When the tram pulled up, Wei-chen said. "Do you think we could we meet for tea before you leave?"

She hesitated for a moment. He held his breath.

"Yes, how about next Sunday at Quiet Heart Teashop? Thank you for your help this morning." She hopped on the tram, then turned, looking back to wave at him.

Wei-chen stopped by the bakery several days later. The scent of fresh baked bread enveloped him with an immediate sense of comfort.

"My dear boy, you must stay for dinner. Jakov will be home before long." Mrs. Mera swallowed him in a hug, leaving a smudge of flour on his cheek. Even though he was thirty years old, he still liked being called her dear boy.

"Thank you. I will stay, but before Mr. Jakov comes back, I would like to talk to you about something."

Mrs. Mera took off her apron and hung it behind the counter. "Please sit down. Is everything all right at work? You never talk to me about what you do." She sat down and studied his face.

"Everything is fine with work."

"And your financial situation is still good?"

"Yes. Better than ever."

"By any chance, does this concern a young woman?"

Wei-chen nodded.

"Son of my heart, I am out of practice at dispensing maternal advice, but I will try my best. Heaven knows you need some feminine balance in your life. You have been surrounded by single men since you were little - your uncle, Mr. Wong, Mr. Cheng, Gabriel Knight. Sometimes I think Gabriel regards you as family, but he is guarded about the ways of love. I believe someone broke his heart a long time ago."

Wei-chen sighed and dropped his guard, speaking about how he had met Hui-lan. He admitted his hopes and laid out his concerns. For the first time in months, the tension inside him eased a bit. When he mentioned finding Hui-lan at the Ghost Market, Mrs. Mera raised her eyebrows.

"You say she found you in the market. This is no accident. She is interested in you. Do you have plans to see her again?"

"Yes, we plan to meet for tea next Sunday. But there are some things that concern me. Hui-lan's parents might not want their daughter involved with a man who has no family. Family lineage is important to the Chinese."

"You must not think about that. You must reach out for life and take risks. How many times do you think she will come looking for you. Oy! I tell you, this girl likes you. Heaven knows you like her. We must think about some ways you could spend time with her."

"That is why I came here. I would like to hear your suggestions about how to pursue her."

"Maybe you could ask her to play chess. It may sound odd, but you can learn much about someone by observing how they play games. How you do anything is how you do everything." Mrs. Mera thumped the table with her fingers. She looked pleased with her suggestion.

"Let me ask you a question. What if her interest is piqued by this handsome young man? What if she wants to become acquainted with you? You must let her know you are interested in her. Are you quite sure of her family's reaction?"

"No, I am not. I will pursue her with all my heart if I find she is interested in me. Also, there is something else. I am not sure of her marital status. Perhaps her parents have arranged a match for her."

"Then you need to find that out. If they have done this, my intuition tells me she is not pleased with it. My dear one, I cannot advise you like a Chinese mother, but this Jewish mother wants you to claim your place in life. Jakov and I have made our way through very difficult situations, fleeing to Shanghai, separating from our sons. I have spent much time thinking about life and why things happen the way they do. Sometimes we want something so much we try to force it. If I have learned one thing, it is that we cannot force life. But we must also seize opportunities when they come our way.

"Let me tell you a story." She folded her hand over his. "This happened long ago in my village. The son and daughter of two families were matched from the time they were children. It was unspoken, but everyone assumed they would marry when they grew up.

"One day a stranger came to the village. His town was destroyed in a pogrom, his family killed. He almost died too. The young man went from shop to shop looking for work. Out of concern for the lad and because he sensed his resolve, the owner of the bakery hired him. Within a short time, he proved his worth and made some friends.

"One of his friends was the brother of the girl who was essentially betrothed. The brother started bringing his friend home for dinner. As I am sure you can guess, the young woman was attracted to him. In time, she grew to love him. Despite her parents' displeasure, she insisted he was the man she wanted to marry.

"B'shert is the Yiddish word for something that is destined to occur. People who are meant to be together will be brought together. Perhaps this has happened with you and Hui-lan. From the little you have told me, I think she is interested in you, perhaps fascinated with you."

Wei-chen wondered why anyone would be fascinated with him, but Mrs. Mera's statement resonated within him, planting a seed of hope. "Is the story is about you and Mr. Jakov?"

"Yes, it is." She released his hand. "No matter what situations we have encountered, I consider myself most fortunate to be with him. Life wanted us to be together. Now, about this young woman, do you think she found you in the market by accident?"

"Yes. It was just by chance we were there at the same time."

"Does she know you like antiques?"

"Perhaps. After class one night a group of us were talking about markets, and I recommended some stalls in Dongtai Lu."

"I am not so sure you met by accident." With the certainty of an experienced fortuneteller, she predicted, "If you see her walking towards you again, it will be more than just coincidence."

Six

1933

Wei-chen sat at a table outside Le Papillon waiting for Knight. A discernible coolness displaced the heat of the August day. The onset of autumn and Hui-lan's return were not far away. His internal alarm clock was going off, signaling possibilities of the heart.

After Hui-lan left for Nanking in June, Wei-chen resigned from his evening tutoring class. He wanted to be free to pursue her when she returned, which meant removing the obstacle of student-teacher involvement. Besides, if she didn't want to continue seeing him, facing her in class each week would be too difficult.

He studied the art deco buildings puncturing the skyline. The infusion of foreign investment after Japan's destruction of Chapei, the area adjoining Little Tokyo, struck Wei-chen as contradictory. How could anyone think Japan would remain satisfied with the status quo or think it was safe to make substantial investments again. In the past week the American Consulate General moved south of Soochow Creek to the center of the International Settlement. Being farther away from Little Tokyo and Chapei suited him.

"Sorry I am late." Knight said. "Let's go inside and get a table. McGuire will be here soon with Josh Ryan, a foreign correspondent who just returned from Nanking. I have wanted to introduce you to him for some time. He is fearless, about your age and a bit of a maverick. He left Texas several years ago and took a tramp steamer to Shanghai, determined to make his living as a reporter. His perseverance paid off. He is now a correspondent for *The New York Times*."

Wei-chen tried to imagine what a maverick from Texas might look like, perhaps big and tough, definitely exciting. McGuire and Ryan joined them a short time later.

"How are things in Nanking?" Knight asked Ryan.

Ryan took a sip of beer, then said, "Chiang Kai-shek is still obsessed with defeating the Communists. His fourth offensive against the Red Army met with some success but, as everyone knows, he has left China unprotected. When Japanese forces advanced from Manchuria and crossed the Great Wall, Chiang did not stand up to them. He should have demanded that they retreat. Instead he gave in to their demands and agreed to set up a demilitarized zone. The latest word is that Chiang is planning to conduct a fifth campaign this fall. He intends to blockade the Communist supply routes and choke them off."

Wei-chen studied Ryan. He was about six feet tall and lanky. A hank of red hair fell across his forehead, giving him a boyish look, but his deep blue eyes conveyed inner intensity and drive. Wei-chen wondered why Ryan wanted to leave Texas. He knew America's economy was in trouble. Maybe Ryan came to China out of desperation or maybe he was in search of adventure.

"I agree it is a mistake for Chiang not to confront the Japanese. They need to be stopped now. People want Chiang to take on the Japanese rather than the Communists. What do you think of Madame Sun Yat-sen's efforts to coordinate resistance to the Japanese?" Wei-chen directed the question to Ryan.

"I am convinced she cannot make Chiang change his course. He thinks the Communists are more of a threat to him than the Japanese, but that's because he is concerned about his political survival. On the national scale, he should be much more worried about Japan."

After Ryan and McGuire left, Knight made a proposal to Wei-chen. "There is something I want you to consider because the situation with Japan is getting very serious. You don't have to comment, but I want you to know what I'm involved in. My job gives me access to strategic information, some of it sensitive. I know you have a contact in the United States Commerce Department because sometimes I meet with him when he comes to Shanghai. I assume you have a local network tracking Japanese activity, both economic and military. I am not looking for intelligence from you. I am offering to be one of your sources."

After wandering through the Ghost Market, Wei-chen stopped at Quiet Heart Teashop and took his favorite spot at the front window. He lost all sense of time, staring at the tea leaves in his cup, trying to read them. Then he perceived a presence and looked up to see Hui-lan. He wondered how long she had been there.

"Hui-lan, what a nice surprise. I thought you were returning next week."

"I waved to you from across the street but you were lost in thought."

"I was trying to read the tea leaves but could not make any sense of them."

She laughed.

"Please sit down. How was your summer?" Wei-chen signaled for more tea.

"It is always good to be with family. I especially like working in the shop with Father."

They made small talk until Wei-chen could not stand it one more second. He needed to seize the moment, even if it did not come off right. "Hui-lan, there is something I want to tell you. I will not be tutoring English this fall."

She scrunched her eyebrows. "What happened?"

"The truth is, I want to spend time with you, and having a student-teacher relationship could get in the way of that. I am not making any assumptions about how you regard me, but I would like the chance to get to know you better."

She sighed. "Well, what a nice coincidence. I feel the same way. The only reason I was planning to take the class again was to see you."

"Really! There must be something interesting we could do. Would you like to go to a foreign movie sometime? We could learn some English we will never use again. Or we could go to Fuxing Park and watch old men play chess, although that is not very exciting."

"Well, if I were with you, perhaps it would be." She smiled, then quickly studied her teacup, blushing.

It seemed impossible they were having this conversation. How could life change so rapidly? Knight was right when he said life would not hold still, that Wei-chen should not let an opportunity slip away.

After lunch he walked her to the tram. When it pulled away, he remembered Mrs. Mera's prediction. If you see her walking towards you again, it will be more than just coincidence. His heart sensed the faint, steady signal of love.

———

Several days later, instead of heading to his apartment after work, Wei-chen searched the university library for Hui-lan. He finally found her in the research room, half hidden behind a stack of reference books. "Hello, Hui-lan." He pulled out a chair and sat across from her.

Her eyes blinked wide. Then she laughed and covered her mouth.

Completely forgetting the remarks he had carefully rehearsed, he stared at her, then blurted out, "Sorry to startle you. I wish I could say the library is on my way home from work, but we both know better than that. I will not keep you from your studies for long. I was just wondering if we might get together Saturday afternoon, maybe play chess and then have something to eat." It was a cool evening, and his palms were sweaty.

"That sounds nice. Sometimes Father and I play chess. But I have to warn you, I am no expert."

"We could meet in Fuxing Park. There are tables for people to play checkers and chess. It is a beautiful place to spend an afternoon."

When he left the research room, he turned around to see her one more time. She was staring at him with an indecipherable expression.

———

Wei-chen arrived early Saturday afternoon to reserve a table in the park. When Hui-lan joined him, she said, "We are surrounded by old men."

"Yes. Look at them, completely absorbed in their checker games. Before we start, I will show you some strategies I learned from Gabriel Knight."

Much to Wei-chen's surprise, winning the first match required intense concentration, and he lost the second. Humbled, he decided he had nothing to teach her. A bolt of illumination shot through him. Hui-lan knew quite well how to play chess. The lesson was simply a ruse for her to spend time with him. Like morning dew on grass, the knowledge of love condensed around his heart.

"I think we should leave now. Are you hungry?" he asked.

"I would like some noodles."

"I know the perfect place. There is a noodle shop a few streets from here."

"Last week you told me you had taken up painting. When did you start?"

"When I was growing up, the puppet maker across the street was Uncle's best friend. I spent countless hours in his shop with his dog wrapped around my feet. Once Mr. Wong realized how much I enjoyed watching him create puppets, he taught me how to capture the expressions on their faces. Eventually he hired me as his assistant.

"After I moved here, I did not paint again until I finished university. At that point I took classes from an artist who had studied in Paris. I still study with him when I have the opportunity and have had some success selling my watercolors. A gallery in the French Concession carries my artwork.

"I lose complete track of time when I paint. As the scorpion would say, it is in my nature. My grandfather was an accomplished calligrapher. I like to think I inherited some talent from him."

"What do you mean about the scorpion?"

"I will explain once we are inside. The shop is here."

Hui-lan sat down across from him, folded her hands in her lap and looked at him. Wei-chen wanted her to sit across from him the rest of his days.

"Now let me tell you about the scorpion. I never tire of listening to my friend Mr. Cheng tell this story."

"A Buddhist monk was walking from one village to another when he heard a muffled voice crying, 'Help me. Please help me.' The monk looked around but did not see anyone. Then he heard the voice again. It seemed to be coming from a well. He walked over, peered inside the well and heard the plea once more. Finally he saw a scorpion clinging to the wall deep inside the well.

'Please help me', the scorpion said. 'I wanted some water and slipped down inside the well. Now I cannot get out.'

'I would help you but you are a scorpion. If I help you, you will sting me.'

'No. If you help me out of the well, I promise not to sting you.'

'Since you promise not to sting, I will help you.'

"So the monk lowered the bucket, the scorpion jumped into it and the monk pulled the bucket back to the top. When he reached safety, the scorpion swung his tail around and stung the monk."

'How could you sting me? I helped you and you promised not to sting.'

'We must all be true to our nature. As a monk, your nature is to help every living thing. Being a scorpion, I am also true to my nature.'

"Hmm, I wonder what your nature is," Hui-lan said.

He wanted to tell her she was precious to him, that she inhabited his thoughts constantly, but all he said was, "You have nothing to worry about. Stinging is not in my nature."

His heart surrendered to her smile.

———

Later that week, upon arriving home from work, Wei-chen found a message from Mr. Cheng under his apartment door. He wanted Wei-chen to meet him at the Jade Buddha Temple. Wei-chen turned around and left for the temple.

The scholar was standing at a side altar, lost in contemplation.

"I came as soon as I got your message."

"I have some information for you, but it seems you have some positive news yourself."

"It is not exactly news. I played chess with Hui-lan on Sunday. I was going to teach her some strategies."

"Did she beat you?"

"We each won a game."

"And what do you think about that?"

"I think she pretended she needed a chess lesson so we could spend the afternoon together."

"I agree. You have met your match in more ways than one. I know you are concerned about the differences in your backgrounds, but your generation is rethinking many traditions. I see it in Shanghai, especially with the students. Couples walk hand-in-hand and reject arranged marriages. These are substantial changes. Time is working to your advantage."

The truth in these words fed the seed of hope already sprouting in his heart. "What kind of information do you have?"

"I have a letter to show you." Mr. Cheng opened his satchel. "It has taken a long time, but I finally received some information about your uncle. A monk from a monastery near Soochow searched temple records at outlying villages. He found the temple where your uncle was once registered, but his family no longer lives there. The monk walked through the town, asking if anyone remembered them. Finally, he found a shopkeeper who remembered that your uncle had moved south with his family. He did not know the name of the town but was sure they relocated outside Canton."

"Regardless of the distance between us, I will find them one day," he promised himself out loud. Before he left the temple, Wei-chen burned joss sticks. One part of his family puzzle was now in place. He resolved to complete it piece by piece, however long it took. The possibility of finding his brother one day darted across his mind. How would they recognize each other? Would they look alike? Would they be drawn together like lodestones?

—

In early October Wei-chen took Hui-lan to Le Papillon. "Is it too cool to sit outside?"

"No. It is a beautiful evening. What a charming place. The little lights in the trees look like glowworms."

For the first time, they talked openly about political issues. He was relieved to learn their political views were aligned. Among other things, she thought Chiang-Kai-shek was placing the entire country at risk by ignoring Japan's advances. Mr. Cheng often cited the four-character idiom - i chien ju ku - old friends from the first meeting. That was how he felt tonight, as if he had known her for a long time.

She asked him about his work, and he downplayed his responsibilities. "My position comes under the commercial attaché. This division develops trade contacts for American companies and provides a liaison to Chinese businesses. So we end up promoting the economic interests of both countries. A number of local employees report to me. I never lack for things to do."

When they left the cafe, she wrapped a silk scarf around her shoulders and stayed close beside him. At the dorm, he walked her up the steps. When she turned to him, he took hold of her scarf with both hands and tightened it a bit. Looking down at her, he brushed her forehead with a kiss.

He turned around at the bottom of the steps. She was holding her scarf where his hands had been. "I will not leave until you are safely inside."

Her smile was an invitation to the future.

In 1934 the Lunar New Year fell in mid-February. Before Hui-lan left to spend the holiday with her family, Wei-chen wanted to have an open discussion with her. After seeing her every weekend over the past months, he had no doubt about his feelings. He made reservations at a bistro in the French Concession where they would not come across any of her friends.

That afternoon he sketched along Soochow Creek, a convenient place to monitor Japanese activity on the other side of the creek. Just as he was about to pack up, several Japanese naval ships dropped anchor, ships he had never seen before. Instead of drawing he took notes. Before he knew it, the afternoon was gone. Not having time to change clothes, he dropped off his knapsack at the Consulate. This was one evening he absolutely did not want to be late for a dinner reservation.

When he picked her up at the dorm, she glanced quickly at him and raised her eyebrows.

"I apologize for my casual attire. I lost track of time when I was sketching and did not have time to stop by my apartment. I wanted to make sure we kept our reservation."

He placed a hand in his jacket pocket, and she linked her arm through his. "Well, with you I am never quite sure who is going to show up - the artist or the trade specialist."

After they ordered their food, he took a deep breath. "There is something I want to discuss with you. You have fascinated me since the first night you appeared in my class. I was not sure how to pursue you or even if I should. When you told me you were from Nanking, I thought perhaps you had a boyfriend there."

"Well, we have something in common because I have been attracted to you since that first night in your class. I thought perhaps you were involved with someone because you seemed unaware of my interest in you. Do you remember the first time we met in Dongtai Lu Market?"

"Of course I do. I remember how our hands touched when I passed the vase to you. I even hoped your fingers had intentionally lingered on mine."

"I have wondered if you have some concern about my family, if that is the reason you have been guarded. Even though we see each other a lot, you have been very proper." Hui-lan looked directly into his eyes.

"At one point my family had a substantial position, but that is no longer the case. I have enough of the old ways entrenched in me to be respectful, so I hesitated to move too quickly."

"Oh my, you have been so careful."

"I assume you have not mentioned me to your parents. I doubt they would be pleased with my social position. I am concerned about driving a wedge between you and your family."

"I think that should be my concern?"

"I agree, but I understand the cost of losing one's family."

"I think you should be guided by your heart rather than your mind." Her face flushed with emotion.

"I am trying to do that. I have tried to show my respect for you and wish to show my love for you. But I don't want you to hide this from your parents.

If you have any misgivings about our relationship, we must face them. Please consider this over the holiday. When you return, if you still feel the same way, you will make me an extremely happy man."

On the second night of Lunar New Year, Wei-chen spent the evening with the Romanovskys. They sat at a candlelit table near the front window. Because of the holiday, the bakery was closed for several days. Mr. Jakov seemed relaxed and even sipped a glass of wine. They could sleep late tomorrow.

"So how are things with Hui-lan?" Mrs. Mera asked.

"I will know more after she returns. I expect she will talk to her parents about me."

"If Hui-lan were only interested in family status, she would not have approached you. Obviously her values run deeper than that. I think she sees someone who has overcome losing his family at a young age, someone who has a quick mind, is well educated, has a good job and is also a talented artist.

"Personally, I think you have every reason to be hopeful. Many people recognize these qualities in you. Those are the very reasons Gabriel Knight took an interest in helping you find work."

Mr. Jakov concurred. "It is important to dream of possibilities, perhaps even impossibilities, and then trust in what life brings you."

Wei-chen studied the Romanovskys. The street lamp cast shadows over their shoulders, draping them in the peace that comes with old friendship. They were an inspiration for the life-long companionship he wanted with Hui-lan.

Later that evening he started a painting of her. Months ago he had committed the scene to memory - Hui-lan entering Quiet Heart Teashop, backlit by street lights, framed by the doorway. Each brushstroke expressed his love for her. He painted with belief in their future.

SEVEN

1934

Wei-chen went to Quiet Heart Teashop early and sat at their usual table. He stared out the window and waited for Hui-lan. She waved as she crossed the street, looking subdued, not excited.

After she sat down, he studied her for a moment. She looked happy to see him but appeared tense. He decided to dispense with any small talk about her trip home. "Over the New Year break, I thought a lot about our last conversation."

"I did too. I want to explain how I have arrived at my age without an arrangement for marriage. Four years ago I was engaged, but my fiancé died before we could marry. Actually, after he became ill his family sent the matchmaker to my parents. They still wanted us to marry, believing the wedding would drive away evil spirits.

"My father firmly said no to their request. He is not a superstitious man. He did not want to sacrifice my future, knowing I would soon be a widow and not be able to marry again. After that happened, some people called me an old maid. I told Father I wished to finish university in Shanghai, that I wanted to have a chance to make a future for myself. Mother was reluctant to let me leave, but Father supported me.

"While I was home for Lunar New Year, my parents invited the son of a family friend to dinner. Mother is still trying to find a suitable mate for me, but Father knows me well. He sensed my resistance. The following day at work we had a long talk about the changes in my generation. I told him about you and asked for his blessing to pursue our friendship."

"What was his response?"

"He asked about your family and your career. When I explained the circumstances of your uncle adopting you, he seemed to understand. He was impressed that you work for the commercial attaché and liked that you are involved with trade. But he had questions about your work I could not explain. I only have a vague idea of what you do. You seldom talk about your job."

"I have not talked much about my work because I think it would bore you. Developing trade relationships is not exactly exciting work. I have been with the consulate for seven years. Each year my responsibilities have grown. I now supervise a staff of ten employees, all of which is reflected in my salary. " He could never reveal his intelligence gathering operation or his close monitoring of Japan's commercial and military activities in China.

"I understand his protectiveness. If I had a daughter like you, I would want to know everything possible about a potential mate for her. But, tell me, did he agree to your spending time with me?"

"Yes. So here I am."

Caught off guard by her candor, Wei-chen dropped his usual restraint. "You cannot imagine how delighted and relieved I feel." His eyes locked onto hers.

"Oh, I have a very good understanding of what you are feeling." Hui-lan returned his gaze, then dropped her eyes, cheeks burning.

"When you walked into the teashop this morning, you looked tense. For a moment I thought things did not go well with your parents. It shocks me to think that your former fiance's family was asking you to sacrifice your future. It must have been frightening for you."

"It was very upsetting, but I was certain Father would never allow it. As for you, had you no idea how much I care for you?"

"Yes, but I was concerned your parents might not approve of my absentee family and would forbid you to spend time with me. Also, when it concerns affairs of the heart, I am inexperienced. I lack confidence in these matters."

The past year anxiety tracked him like prey, causing him to second-guess Hui-lan's affection. Now he was free to pursue her.

"If you could only understand how others see you. One of your most appealing qualities is your lack of convention. Perhaps it is because you have spent so much time around foreigners."

"How you perceive me is all that matters. Now I have something to tell you, but nothing nearly as dramatic as your story. Like your father, Uncle questioned the old conventions. When a family approached him about an arranged marriage for me, he turned them down. I discovered this only after I moved to Shanghai. Even though it would have kept me near him, he did not want me constrained in that small city. He always understood I wanted more and did not resent my desire to leave."

"How selfless of him, to set you free like a bird. It could not have been easy."

"No, I am sure it was not. But he did not want to limit my future. I will remain forever grateful to him because otherwise I would never have met you. I am quite sure fate is pleased with the match it has made. Come along with me. There is something I want to show you."

An hour later they stood in front of the Cathedral of St. Ignatius. "I want to show you the bell tower. One of the church caretakers allows me to go inside. The only condition is we must not ring the bells."

Hui-lan laughed, grasped Wei-chen's hand, and climbed the stairs just behind him. He looked back at her every few steps. Good fortune accompanied him today.

"This view is definitely worth the climb. I feel like a bird flying over the city, trying to decide where to land next." Hui-lan's face creased in a smile.

Wei-chen placed his arms around her and drew her close. She leaned against him. They kissed, giving in to their pent-up passion. When they finally walked down the stairwell, he said, "I want to show you one more thing. We will take a tram most of the way there."

When they stopped outside a building in the International Settlement, Hui-lan asked, "Is your flat here? Are you finally going to allow me see where you live?"

"Yes. I have something to show you."

"This sounds quite mysterious."

"From my viewpoint, it is either going to be quite gratifying or very disappointing." Wei-chen led Hui-lan to his flat and opened the door. Sunlight from the central courtyard spilled into the room, highlighting a draped easel.

"Come in but stay right there." He crossed the room and unveiled a painting.

"It looks like me."

"It is you. I will never forget the first time you entered my classroom. You stood in the doorway, trying to decide where to sit. I took a mental photograph of the scene. You have haunted my dreams since the first time I saw you."

"The same is true for me." Hui-lan looked straight into his heart.

Wei-chen remembered the old seer's prediction, a woman would enter his life and bring him happiness. How long ago was that? Five, maybe six years? He kissed her again and felt love, the master spider, spinning a web around them.

Two months later the Romanovskys invited them to dinner, along with Gabriel Knight. Hui-lan stopped Wei-chen before they arrived at the bakery. "I am nervous about meeting this acquired family of yours. I think we should have waited longer to do this."

"On the contrary, this is the perfect evening for you to meet them. They have wanted to meet you for months. Ever since Mrs. Mera found out Mr. Cheng met you, she has been insisting we come for dinner."

Wei-chen made introductions and guided the conversation, shifting between English and Chinese. He caught Knight studying Hui-lan, assessing the woman who had captured his friend's heart. When Mrs. Mera asked for help with dessert, Wei-chen took her cue and followed her to the kitchen.

"We are very pleased to meet your friend. It is obvious she is quite intelligent. Also very pretty, but you do not want a woman who is too attractive.

That could cause trouble. She is just right, except she should eat more food. She is thin as a bird."

Spoken like a Chinese mother, Wei-chen thought.

"Gabriel, what have you heard from the foreign correspondents?" Mr. Jakov asked.

"They say a groundswell is building against Chiang's obsession with the Communists. Even elements of the Chinese army oppose his position. They are concerned the Japanese army will take advantage of Chiang's reluctance to confront them. As for the Communists, the ones who survived the long march to Shansi Province are safe for now."

Mr. Jakov's question changed the tenor of the evening. Well aware of storm clouds looming on the horizon, Wei-chen did not want this evening to be marred by a discussion of Japan's desire to control China. He intended to be wed to Hui-lan before the storm broke.

Frantic rapping on the door made Wei-chen fly to his feet and open it. "Hui-lan, what is wrong?" He had never seen her so distraught, her face pinched from trying to restrain tears.

"I found out this morning I was not accepted for the teaching position. They want someone with experience. I will have to return to Nanking after graduation."

Shocked, Wei-chen's mind raced through possibilities. He wrapped his arms around her. "Perhaps another position will open up this summer. Are you sure no other schools have openings?" Neither one of them had expected her to have any difficulty finding work. Unlike the western world where depression stalked the economies, Shanghai's economy in 1934 was racing full tilt.

"I am not willing to look outside the city. If I cannot live near you, it makes no sense. Father consented to my staying here only if I could teach. It looks as if I will have to return to Nanking and teach there or work for father."

"That all makes sense, except to my heart." There was no question their love would survive the test of time but he wanted her near him. His mind scrambled for some kind of rationale. "If you have to teach in Nanking next year, it should make it easier to find a job in Shanghai the following year, but I will not give up on finding a way for you to remain here."

"Whether I teach or not, I am giving myself one year in Nanking. Then I will come back no matter what."

"Letters will be a poor substitute for your caresses. Somehow this will all work out."

"Yes, somehow it will work out." Hui-lan leaned into his shoulder and placed her hand over his heart.

Days later, just before leaving for Nanking, she pressed a coin-shaped butterfly charm into his palm. "I pray this symbol of joy and long life will reunite us soon."

Wei-chen slashed through each day on the calendar, marking time until Hui-lan's return, whenever that would be. Between work and painting, his days were full. The gallery sold his paintings quickly. He double-checked the total in his bank account and was satisfied he had accumulated sufficient funds to propose marriage.

A sense of urgency dogged him. In Hongkew, across Soochow Creek from the International Settlement, Japanese troops were staking claim to neighborhoods. Before they unleashed their growing force, he wanted to be under one roof with Hui-lan.

In July he posted several teaching openings to Hui-lan. Three weeks before school was scheduled to start, Hui-lan rang him. She said a position in the French Concession had just opened and she was accepting it. Wei-chen felt the force of destiny at his back.

Within the week, they were strolling along the Whangpoo waterfront. Claiming an empty bench, they held hands and watched the shifting reflections of boats. Her presence beside him dispelled the anxiety that had trailed him all summer. She was back, and he wanted her to never leave again.

After her return Wei-chen started searching for a larger flat. In November he found one in the International Settlement, an ideal distance between their work places. Before committing to it, he showed it to Hui-lan.

"Well, what do you think?"

"This area of the Settlement is lovely. I like that it is on the second story and on a quiet street."

"Now I have one more question." He paused for a second, then blurted out, "Will you marry me?"

When she hesitated, he said, "There is no need to answer this moment. My financial situation is quite strong. I have been saving for years. I promise to be a good husband all the days of my life."

Hui-lan gently covered his mouth with her hand. "Yes."

"Yes. Just like that?"

"Yes. And I will love you all the days of my life."

"What about your parents?"

"It is still several years away, but a marriage has been arranged for my sister. My parents are pleased with the arrangement, especially after the ticklish situation with me. With all your letters and phone calls this summer, they will not be surprised with our engagement. Mother no longer resists my being in Shanghai. When I finish teaching next May, I could spend a final summer with them."

"I really do not want to wait that long."

"Do we have to set a date today?"

Wei-chen twined his arms around her, like the double happiness character. "No, we do not have to do that today. I think we have already accomplished enough for one day, except for one thing. I would like to stop by the bakery."

"My dears, this is wonderful news." Mrs. Mera clasped her hands. We celebrate your love for each other. It is b'shert. It is your destiny to be together.

A month or so later Wei-chen met Knight at a teashop. "How is Hui-lan getting along with teaching?"

"Quite well. She is at the same school where she student taught so it has not been a big adjustment."

"How about you? I don't see much of you these days." An amused look played across Knight's face.

"You know very well how I am spending my time. Unless something comes up at work, Hui-lan and I spend our evenings together. For someone so young, she is strong and determined. I have never felt this depth of love before. I am fortunate to have her in my life."

"It has been many years, but I still remember how it feels to give your heart to someone. Have you two set a wedding date?"

"No. Her parents want us to wait until Hui-lan visits them after the school year. They would like her home for one more summer. I am trying to convince her otherwise, and I think I am winning the debate."

"I hope you will be able to marry before summer. She could still visit her parents. I think you two belong under one roof and see no point in your delaying it."

In late January 1935 Wei-chen and Hui-lan were married in a small civil ceremony. With that fait accompli, they traveled to Nanking for the Lunar New Year.

Eight

1936

Eleven months later, at the end of December, Wei-chen set out for Le Papillon. He joined Knight at the bar and ordered hot tea. It took several minutes for the warmth of the bistro to displace the chill in his bones. "I cannot stay long. Hui-lan and I are leaving early tomorrow to visit her parents. Today at work I learned that Chiang Kai-shek was kidnapped. Details were still coming in when I left. Do you know anything about it?"

"You just missed Dan McGuire. He left a copy of his piece that will run in tomorrow's *North China Daily News.* They have identified the group responsible for the kidnapping - Chinese troops the Japanese had forced out of Manchuria."

Wei-chen grabbed the proof and read it.

> ...Generalissimo Chiang Kai-shek, leader of the Nationalist Party, was kidnapped yesterday by a group of Chinese soldiers, led by a Manchurian field marshall. These troops had been driven from Manchuria by Japanese militarists. In a telegram sent to the government in Nanking, the mutineers made the following demands for Chiang's release: include the Communist Party in the government, stop the civil war against the Communists and unite with the Communists to resist Japan.

> Since the early 1930s Chiang Kai-shek has mounted extensive campaigns against the Communists. With the failure of each campaign, the outcry has increased for him to oppose the Japanese rather than the Communists. By ignoring nationwide appeals for resistance, Chiang has compromised his position of leadership...

"A couple of months ago Josh Ryan mentioned some Chinese troops were furious with Chiang for not standing up to the Japanese, but this kidnapping caught everyone off guard. Placing their lives in this kind of jeopardy means the soldiers felt there was no other way to bring about a change in policy.

"Before coming here this evening, I heard a radio report claiming the soldiers might kill Chiang. It may be the best bargaining position they have. I think it will be interesting to see how this is resolved. What do you think will happen?" Knight said.

"There has to be some kind of compromise. It is possible that, to save his life, Chiang will finally be willing to change his position. Although I don't know how the kidnappers could trust him."

In preparation for the 1937 Lunar New Year, red lanterns straddled the Jade Buddha Temple entrance. When Wei-chen passed through the temple gate, the January wind fanned incense across the courtyard. Nostalgia gripped him, and memories of simpler times flooded his mind. He climbed the steps to the main altar, lit three joss sticks, closed his eyes and entered a state of timelessness.

The sense that he was being watched interrupted his contemplation. He turned and spotted Mr. Cheng. "How long have you been here?"

"Not long. Your spirit was traveling. Would you like some tea? We could go to the small dining room."

"Yes, I would like that." Wei-chen tightened his muffler, and they walked to the main building. He had not seen Mr. Cheng since December. Wei-chen thought he looked older and, perhaps for the first time since he had known the scholar, tired.

"I see you have a new jacket."

"Hui-lan insisted I get it. It is much warmer than my old one." Wei-chen splayed his hands around the tea cup. The heat from the porcelain tingled his frigid fingers.

Mr. Cheng asked after Hui-lan, then said, "I have not seen you since Chiang Kai-shek's release by the kidnappers. What do you make of the situation?"

"I hoped there would be some kind of compromise, but I never expected Zhou En-lai would be the one to save Chiang's life."

"Yes, it is ironic. In 1927 Zhou narrowly escaped being murdered by Chiang's underlings yet, when the kidnappers wanted to kill Chiang, Zhou convinced them otherwise. He is an intelligent leader. I am sure he calculated that Chiang is still China's most powerful commander. The Communists know they cannot stop a Japanese invasion without him."

"Gabriel says politics makes strange bedfellows. I hope the unification of the Communist and Nationalist armies will provide an effective frontline. I am concerned it will not work, but what other alternative do we have?"

"If only this had happened sooner. China would be in a much stronger position if Chiang had not spent years pursuing the Communists."

Wei-chen studied Mr. Cheng's knitted brow. After years of observing the scholar, he knew this translated into a strong foreboding. "I believe you sense something unfortunate, perhaps even evil, is about to occur.

Mr. Cheng looked away. "I am getting to be an old man. Sometimes it is difficult for me to remain optimistic."

Wei-chen wanted the serenity within the temple grounds to spill over the walls, to spread over Shanghai and all of China. Whatever it was Mr. Cheng sensed, it was not good. On the way home, he tried to shake a vague unease. He felt his and Hui-lan's future was imperiled.

Before dawn he freed himself from a terrible dream. He was standing in a Shanghai side street, watching Hui-lan walk away from him. She no longer wanted him. A profound sadness gripped him. She wanted another man.

There was nothing he could do about it. He told himself it was just a dream but felt deeply shaken and profoundly sad.

Hui-Lan was sleeping on her side. He draped an arm over her. She sighed, took his arm and pulled him in close. He kissed her neck, and she turned to him. The urgency in their lovemaking followed him to work and stayed with him all day. But the dream's effects also lingered. He couldn't shake the apprehension of abandonment.

In mid-June Wei-chen and Hui-lan ate outside at Le Papillon. A breeze ruffled twinkling lights in the plane trees. It was a beautiful evening, but not beautiful enough to dispel the turmoil inside Wei-chen. The next morning Hui-Lan was leaving for Nanking. He left most of his food untouched.

"Do you wish I were not leaving tomorrow?" she said.

"No, but I think it is a mistake for you to be gone until school starts. Both Gabriel and Mr. Cheng think Japanese forces could attack this summer. I understand you need to spend time with your parents, but being gone until the end of August is entirely too long."

"What if I return the second week of August?" She grasped his hand. "To be honest, I do not want to leave you, but I must respect my parents' wishes. This will be the last long visit."

Wei-chen wanted to make her stay but knew not to force the issue. He admired Hui-lan's independent streak. She was a modern woman. Besides, the same loyalty she showed to family, she showed to him. He could not have wished for more, except for her to remain in Shanghai.

"I understand why you need to see your parents, but my heart does not want you to leave." He didn't want to end the evening with an argument.

When they returned home, Hui-lan brewed a pot of tea and sat across from Wei-chen at their kitchen table. "There are some things I want to say to you before I leave. You are very careful with what you reveal to me about your position at the consulate. I think you do that to protect me. I am quite sure you are involved with some kind of intelligence gathering. Perhaps it only involves finding ways to undercut Japan's expansion. Or maybe it includes sabotage. Whatever you are doing, I know it is very serious. I do not want to know what it is, but I admire you for the risks you are taking."

Wei-chen reached for her hand and kissed her palm. "Come here."

Still holding his hand she came around the table, sat in his lap and wrapped her arms around his neck. He kissed her cheek, her neck, her lips. Finally he gathered her up and carried her to the bedroom.

Afterwards, he held her in his arms until dawn.

Summer days moved at a torpid pace, as if humidity and heat were slowing time. In early July haunting dreams stalked Wei-chen. They always started the same way. He was a young boy again, eavesdropping on Uncle and Mr. Wong, frightened by their talk of Japanese aggression. Then, in an instant, images of ravaged villages and streets littered with charred bodies appeared. He always woke up covered in sweat, his stomach in a knot.

The last dream was so unsettling Wei-chen went to the temple after work. When he passed through the gate, Mr. Cheng was talking to the novices. Wei-chen nodded to him and continued to the main altar. He burned incense and then waited in the inner courtyard. The usual sense of serenity that pervaded this space was gone. He paced, waiting for his friend.

At last Mr. Cheng came across the courtyard. "Sit down with me. I can tell something is troubling you. What is the cause of your anxiety?"

"Dreams. Recurring dreams."

"Tell me about them."

Wei-chen described some of his dreams and then looked away from his friend. "Last night's was the most horrifying. A young woman was lying on the pavement, covered with blood. She had been slashed by bayonets. I cannot erase the image from my mind." He hunched over and stared at the ground.

"Dreams can mean many things. Sometimes they are an expression of fears," Mr. Cheng said.

"But can they not also foreshadow events?"

"Yes, they can. You fear for Hui-lan's safety."

"I am very concerned about her. I want her back now."

"Have you talked to Gabriel and your journalist friends about the new government in Tokyo? Although Prince Fuminaro heads the government, General Tojo is the driving power behind the throne. He has long had designs on China. The land of the rising sun desires to cast its shadow over all of Asia. When I meditate, I sense something dark and dangerous approaching."

"How soon? Perhaps in the fall?"

"No, before that." Mr. Cheng spoke with certainty.

"Hui-lan plans to return in mid-August. I will insist she come back sooner." Wei-chen walked home, apprehension dogging his every step. He rang Hui-lan that night. He told her the situation was deteriorating and he wanted her home by the end of July.

Several days later, Wei-chen waded through the smoky haze of Le Papillon and spotted Knight and Josh Ryan, the *New York Times* correspondent, hunched over a table. "I filed the report this afternoon. This is big," Ryan said, just as Wei-chen pulled up a chair.

"What is big?" Wei-chen asked.

"You're aware Japanese troops are guarding the railroad line they operate from Peking to Tientsin, right? On July 7 a large number of their troops conducted maneuvers north of Peking. During the operation, Japanese officers alleged one of their soldiers had been kidnapped.

"The next day Chinese troops found the soldier in a brothel. It was all a lie, an attempt to draw China into war. When that didn't work, Tokyo dispensed with a formal declaration of war. Japanese troops are storming out of Manchuria, heading across northern China," Ryan said.

"How effective do you think the United Front will be?" Knight asked.

"Before I left Peking, I talked to a Nationalist officer. He said the Communist and Nationalist armies are solidly united against Japan. But he admitted they are no match for the Japanese imperial army. Japan has substantially more troops, and they are better-armed and better-trained. Right now Japanese forces are massed north of Peking. If that battle is lost, the Chinese army will retreat toward Shanghai and set up a front in the Yangtze River valley."

Ryan just confirmed everything Wei-chen had learned at the Consulate before he left work. "If the United Front cannot defend Peking, why should they be able to protect Shanghai?" Wei-chen asked.

"I can't answer that. This is unfolding too quickly."

After Ryan left, Wei-chen said to Knight, "Hui-lan was planning to return in mid-August, but I do not want her to wait that long. I have asked her to come home by the end of July. But, having said that, I am not sure how safe Shanghai will be. Do you think she is safer remaining in Nanking? Mr. Cheng believes something will happen before September."

"After what Josh just reported, I would guess Nanking is the safer place right now. But if she is determined to return to Shanghai, she should do so before the end of July. In the twenty-five years I have been in China, this sort of danger has never been so imminent."

Already unsettled, Knight's advice rattled Wei-chen even further. As soon as he got home, he called Hui-lan and asked her to return within the week. She promised to talk to her parents and ring him the next day. Wei-chen did not mention his concern that he might not see her for months. He went for a long walk and tried to clear his mind. She mentioned her father was not feeling well.

Hui-lan rang him early the next morning. "I understand your concern about my return date. Whatever is going to happen, I want to face it with you. Please allow me two more weeks."

The slight hesitation in her voice alarmed Wei-chen. He sensed she was more concerned about her father's health than she was letting on.

After work the next day he met Knight at a teashop.

"You look upset. Has something happened?" Knight asked.

"Did you know Chiang Kai-shek ordered the evacuation of Peking today?"

"No, I only listened to the early morning broadcast. What else do you know?"

"The Japanese army is about to break through the United Front. Our forces are evacuating Peking and Tientsin and dropping south to defend Shanghai. Chiang hopes to gain the support of Western nations by staging an offensive from Shanghai." Wei-chen drummed his fingers on the table.

"You are on edge. Calm down. You need to stay rational."

"I asked Hui-lan to return by next week. She said to give her until the first of August. Her father is not well, and she is spending a lot of time in their office. But Chiang's retreat changes everything. She should not delay until August."

"With China's forces dropping back, do you think Hui-lan's parents will allow her to leave?"

"She is strong-willed. I am not so sure they could stop her." Wei-chen hoped they wouldn't force her to remain in Nanking. He wanted her by his side.

"I'll talk to McGuire tonight and get his assessment of the situation. Let's order some dinner. I'll ring you after I talk to him."

———

Two days later Wei-chen met Mr. Cheng at Jade Buddha Temple. "What do you hear from Hui-lan?"

"When I talked to her several days ago, I asked her to return this week. She hesitated and said she needed two more weeks. Her father has some kind of medical problem. They have not determined what is wrong."

"Her father is dying."

Wei-chen stared at Mr. Cheng. "She did not mention that. Are you sure? Perhaps it is someone else. Are you never wrong about these things?" Just once, he wanted his friend to be wrong.

"After we arranged this meeting, I meditated about Hui-lan and her family. The vision that came last night was vivid. Her father does not have much time, perhaps a few months. Hui-lan will soon know his condition."

"If that is true, I believe she will want to remain there until he passes. She is fiercely loyal to him, and her family is relying heavily on her." Wei-chen stood up and paced the courtyard. "There is another concern I have not expressed to anyone. What if the United Front cannot prevent the Japanese from overrunning Shanghai. If that happens, I expect the Japanese will attack Nanking next."

"Yes, they will. They intend to control all of China, perhaps all of Asia."

Mr. Cheng's somber tone rattled Wei-chen.

The first week in August Chinese troops massed on Shanghai's outskirts. The Japanese navy responded by forcing the International Settlement police out of Hongkew and declaring their authority over that area. The city district with the densest Japanese population, referred to as Little Tokyo, was located within Hongkew.

British, American and Russian patrols guarded the International Settlement with blatant force, especially along Soochow Creek, which separated the settlement from Hongkew. Municipal police patrolled the rest of the city. Wei-chen was working long hours, constantly evaluating information and checking his sources for new developments.

On the evening of August 5 Hui-lan rang him, sobbing. He could barely understand her. "Father is dying. He has lung cancer, and it is spreading. He is in terrible pain. I want to be with you but I cannot leave him right now."

"I understand why you need to stay in Nanking. My heart aches for you. I am so very sorry. But I want you to return soon, even if for a brief stay. Then you could go back to Nanking and be with your father again."

Wei-chen tried to console her but also convince her to come to Shanghai for a while. The window of time for her to return was about to close firmly. He wanted her with him before war broke out.

The cadence of foot patrols woke Wei-chen at dawn. Standing at the window, he looked at the street below. British troops were marching down the sidewalk. Last evening's radio broadcast confirmed the reports' they had received at the Consulate earlier that day. The Japanese navy was evacuating all Japanese civilians and doubling their troop presence in Hongkew.

By August 12 twenty-six Japanese warships were riding anchor on the Whangpoo River. When the Japanese military demanded that Chinese forces withdraw from their positions around the city, Chiang Kai-shek refused. Instead he increased troop levels and sent in the first-rate 87th and 88th army divisions.

Every morning Wei-chen listened to the news before heading to work. The breaking story on September 14 was that Chinese and Japanese troops had fired on each other the previous night. He rushed to the Consulate to learn the details. It turned out troops had exchanged fire in the northern districts, but it appeared to be an isolated incident.

He left work mid-morning to meet one of his contacts, then decided to check on the Romanovskys. Because of unusual traffic congestion, he took back streets. When he reached the bakery, Mrs. Mera was standing in the doorway, compassion etched across her face. "Come inside. Have you eaten?"

"I am fine, thank you. I just wanted to make sure you are all right."

Mrs. Mera brought tea to a table near the front window. Mr. Jakov joined them. A current of humanity streamed past the shop.

"We have been listening to the radio all morning. The gunfire was isolated, but these people remember the bombing of Chapei in 1932. They remember the destruction of their homes and are not waiting for it to happen again. It reminds me of the pogroms. My heart goes out to all of them." Mrs. Mera blinked back tears.

Wei-chen stared at the horrific scene outside. Terrified Chinese inched their way forward in the sweltering heat. Multi-generational families moved en masse. Babies peered out of baskets strapped to their parents' backs, grandmothers with bound feet straddled loads in wheelbarrows, children shouldered poles with bundled possessions swinging at the ends. Desperation delineated every face.

"The Shanghai Municipal Council is improvising temporary shelters in the International Settlement and the French Concession. I wonder how they can possibly find space for all these people." Mr. Jakov looked weary.

"I must leave soon. Do you feel safe? Would you like me to come back here tonight?"

"The emigré council is meeting this afternoon to organize its response. We will be fine. Do not worry."

Wei-chen met Knight at a noodle shop near his office. "I just left the bakery. Families are fleeing from Chapei with everything they can carry. They are all terrified. It is contagious. I am alarmed too."

"The news reports are extremely disturbing. I believe the battle for Shanghai has begun."

"Hui-lan was supposed to return this week. What if she had been caught in the middle of all this?" The unmistakable explosion of bombs cut off Wei-chen.

"That's close. I can't believe they are bombing the Settlement," Knight said.

Within minutes sirens wailed across the city. The owner of the noodle shop turned up the radio and silenced the customers.

> ...Minutes ago two bombs fell on Nanking Road near the Bund. The Palace Hotel took a direct hit. A second bomb exploded outside the Cathay Hotel. It is sheer mayhem. Cars are burning on Nanking Road. Clothing and body parts lie strewn over the street. Many business patrons as well as refugees were hit..."

When two more detonations went off, Wei-chen and Knight ran to the doorway. Smoke was rising from the direction of the Bund. Sirens blared from a different direction.

> Hold on. What's that?...Ambulances are being delayed because of bomb attacks on Avenue Edouard VII. They fell near the intersection where food was being distributed to refugees. There appear to be many casualties. There are some questions about the planes...

Everyone stood frozen, straining to hear the report.

"I had not expected anything like this. It did not occur to me the Japanese would attack the Settlement. I cannot stay here. I need to return to the Consulate."

"Be careful. I'll try to ring you tonight."

That evening, when Wei-chen turned the corner to his street, he noticed someone standing in front of his building. It turned out to be an old university friend who lived in Chapei. "I have been worried about you. Come inside." The teacher looked shell-shocked. Wei-chen made tea and tried to engage him.

Sitting at the kitchen table, his friend stared with vacant eyes at the street below. "When they heard gunfire last night, people started fleeing immediately. By the time I left Chapei this morning, the streets were clogged with people. Except for Garden Bridge, the Japanese closed all entrances to the Settlement. Thousands of people were forced to escape through one check point. Everyone was jostling each other. Some children and old people were trampled. I stumbled over a mangled foot. The bridge was slippery because of blood. I saw a Japanese guard bayonet an old man and throw him into Soochow Creek. And, just as they have done in other cities, troops forced attractive women from the line and pulled them into nearby buildings. I will never forget the screams. When their families tried to interfere, they were thrown back."

Wei-chen poured more tea. The porcelain pot clinked against the cups. Tears traced the contours of his friend's face. "You are welcome to stay here as long as you need to."

"Thank you. If it is safe, I will head for my village tomorrow. I want to leave before there is an all-out attack by the Japanese."

When Wei-chen turned on the radio, they learned Chinese pilots were responsible for the detonations. The first bombs were meant to sink the Japanese flagship, but the ship's antiaircraft barrage panicked the pilot, causing him to drop the bombs too early. The subsequent bombings on Avenue Edouard VII were also accidental. Estimated fatalities exceeded 1700, with roughly 1400 wounded.

"We are our own worst enemy." Wei-chen set out some food. "Please excuse me while I call my wife."

Hui-lan answered after the first ring. "Are you safe? What happened today?" She sounded tense, fearful.

He told her the day started with Japanese troops taking over Chapei, leaving out the horrific details his friend had related. She fired questions at him about the bombings and the refugee situation in the International Settlement.

"I am not sure how long this connection will last. In case we are cut off, there are a few things I need to say. The battle for Shanghai is underway. No one knows how long it will last. Our elite forces have surrounded the city and will fight bravely. When the fighting has ended, I will come to get you. I love..."

The phone line went dead. He stared at his painting of Hui-lan and tried to suppress the fear burning inside him.

The third week in September Wei-chen met Knight at a teashop near the consulate. "Listen to this from today's *Shen Pao.*" Wei-chen gripped the newspaper. 'If Japan thought they were going to take Shanghai as easily as they took Peking and Tientsin, they have had a rude awakening. Chinese forces are fighting with immense courage. A unit of six hundred soldiers held off Japanese troops for a week before being killed to the last man.'

"Do you want to know what I think about that?" Knight asked.

"Yes, because I do not like what is being left unsaid."

"That is exactly right. The Chinese army is fighting courageously in Chapei and Pootung. Their barricades are obstructing the Japanese advance, forcing them to fight street by street, making their soldiers targets for our snipers. But I think we are going to lose the battle for Shanghai. It's already late September. Before long Japan's troops will number in the hundreds of thousands. It might take a couple of months, but they will prevail. And when they do, Chiang will order the United Front to retreat and make a stand at Nanking."

"Everything I hear at work supports what you just said. Shanghai is hemorrhaging. Over five thousand Americans and British left in August, wealthy

Chinese are moving to Hong Kong and factory owners are relocating their operations inland. The city is still overwhelmed with homeless people, even though 350,000 refugees have headed to their home villages."

"Today's *North China Daily News* reported that the baby patrol of the Chinese Benevolent Association picks up hundreds of little corpses each morning. They're either cremated in large bonfires or crammed into coffins and buried at a temporary cemetery. There are layers of coffins." Knight took a sip of tea and looked away, staring at nothing.

"Hui-lan wants to know about the conditions here, but I cannot mention that. It is too horrific."

Later that week Wei-chen went to Jade Buddha Temple to meet Mr. Cheng. "How is Hui-lan?" the scholar asked.

"Her situation is still the same. She is managing the business. Her father's health continues to deteriorate." Wei-chen paced the courtyard. "To be honest, I wish her father would pass soon. It is difficult for her to watch him suffer. More than anything, I want to go to Nanking and bring her back here. But I know she will not agree to that until his death."

"And just how would you propose to break through the military cordon around Shanghai?"

"There are rumors our forces will retreat from Shanghai within the month. I could find a way to move out with them."

Before he fell asleep that night, he took inventory of Hui-lan's possessions. The books she used in her classes stood next to his on a bookshelf - together. The way the two of them were meant to be.

Nine

1937

In mid-October Wei-chen asked Knight and Josh Ryan to meet him at Le Papillon. He hadn't slept well for several nights and was having difficulty concentrating at work. Knight was already sitting a table in the back room when Wei-chen arrived. Ryan joined them a few minutes later.

"The drinks are on me tonight," Wei-chen began. "I cannot stand being separated from Hui-lan any longer. I am going to Nanking and want any advice you can give me."

"Do you have a plan?" Ryan asked.

"A friend at the Consulate knows a cart driver who can pick me up outside the city. Once we are well on our way to Soochow, he can drop me off at a train station. From Soochow, I will continue to Nanking."

"How are you planning to get out of the city?" Knight asked.

"When I leave the International Settlement, I will be dressed like a tradesman, seemingly headed home for the night. I should be able to avoid any suspicion when I pass through the checkpoints. Once I am well beyond the city perimeter, the cart driver will pick me up and take me to a point where I can safely catch a train. The trains to Nanking should continue to run as long as the United Front is defending Shanghai. What do you think?" Wei-chen looked at his friends to read their reactions.

Ryan, usually quick to respond, pursed his lips. Knight took a deep breath and said, "Josh, you go first."

"You had better have contingency plans. The United Front cannot hang on much longer. When they retreat from Shanghai to Nanking, several of us journalists are going to follow them. Could you delay until then? I hate to see you travel alone. The building rubble has provided excellent cover for Chinese snipers. The street-to-street fighting has been costly and humiliating for the Japanese. They expected to control all of China within months. They are enraged that they've been bogged down. You need to stay well clear of them."

"I plan to leave the day after tomorrow. I will not wait longer than that."

"What if Japanese planes strike the railroads? What will you do then? You need to be prepared for that," Ryan said.

"I hope Gabriel can help with that. Jardine Matheson built those railways. I expect they have employees at each station I could contact. If the rail lines are attacked, I will find carts to take me from town to town. It should just take several days longer if I have to do that."

"When did you last hear from her? Are you sure she is still in Nanking?" Knight asked.

"I have not been able to reach her for two weeks so no, I am not sure her family is still there. For my own peace of mind, I must try to find her. If she is still in Nanking, I want to face whatever is going to happen with her. If they have escaped, I will try to track them down."

"I will have a list of contacts for you tomorrow. If you think of anything else you need, let me know." Knight downed his brandy and ordered another one.

Two nights later Wei-chen slipped out of Shanghai dressed as a worker. At the arranged meeting place, a farmer hid him under burlap bags in the back of his cart. He was traveling with only the clothes on his back. Late afternoon the next day, he got off the cart at a train station several stops before Soochow. Amazed at the number of people jammed on the platform, he took a deep breath and forced his way into the crowd.

He managed to find a space standing at the back of a car, an old preference formed when he started taking city trams. It allowed for an easy exit. He conversed as little as possible with his fellow passengers. When he needed to speak, he dropped the Shanghai dialect and used that of his childhood. He did not want to be identified as being from a big city. He stood with folded arms, guarding the money sewn into the lining of his jacket.

When the packed train pulled out of the Soochow station, people were left standing on the platform. Chinese were fleeing to the interior in increasing numbers. He was on edge and could not help wondering how he would proceed if Hui-lan and her family had left Nanking.

About an hour outside of Nanking, as the train was approaching Chenchiang, a bomb detonated, sending a shock wave through the train. When the brakes were thrown on, bags flew from overhead bins and passengers were tossed over each other. Wei-chen managed to get his footing and rushed to the exit. He was the second one out of the car.

The sound of an airplane engine made him look up. A plane with The Rising Sun insignia on its wings was banking for a second pass, heading back to the train. He ran for cover in a bamboo thicket with two other men. People were pouring out of the train, scattering in their search for cover. His heart pumped hard and fast, his eyes riveted on the plane. The bombs seemed to fall in slow motion. Then everything went white.

When Wei-chen came to, he felt intense pain running through him. He placed his hand on his left thigh, and it came away wet. The person closest to him appeared to be dead. Wei-chen tried to get up but fell back. The other man who had taken cover with him sat on his haunches and looked at Wei-chen's leg. Without saying anything, he undid Wei-chen's belt. When he cinched it on his upper thigh, Wei-chen passed out.

Later, at the fringe of consciousness, Wei-chen became aware of a rocking motion and voices fading in and out. He was wedged in a cart with other wounded people.

"At last you are awake."

Wei-chen turned in the direction of the voice. An elderly woman bent over him and placed her hand on his forehead. "Your spirit has been traveling. I was not sure you would come back. My husband brought you here a week ago."

"A week ago! Where am I? What day is it?" Wei-chen attempted to sit up and dropped back onto the bed.

"You are just outside Chenchiang and have been with us seven days. Your leg was wounded and badly infected but our village doctor stitched it and applied poultices. It seems to be healing now."

Realizing it was now the first week in November, Wei-chen's heart raced. He had lost a week. "I must find my wife."

"Where is she?"

"In Nanking with her parents." It took effort for Wei-chen to speak. He was aware how weak his voice sounded.

"Are you sure she is still there? Perhaps her family has fled."

"No, I am not sure. I was not able to reach her before I left Shanghai." Then he panicked. "Where is my jacket?"

"It is here, folded under the bed. My husband and I are honest people. We assume money is stitched inside the pockets. It is all there. We have not touched it."

"I apologize for my rudeness. It is only because of your good care that I am alive." He wanted to leave immediately for Nanking but could not sit up, much less get out of bed. Ten days later, once he was able to get up and walk a bit, he asked the husband to deliver a message for him to Knight's contact in Chenchiang.

Several days later Mr. Chou, Knight's business associate, arrived in a mule-drawn cart. Before leaving the house, Wei-chen slit open a pocket in his jacket lining and extended the packet with both hands to the couple.

Then, relying heavily on a cane, he made his way to the cart. "I greatly appreciate your coming for me. I would like to leave for Nanking as soon as possible."

Mr. Chou hesitated for a moment. "Until that is arranged, I insist you stay with my family. A week ago Gabriel Knight sent a telegram asking if you had contacted me. Since then I have been hoping you would find me."

"What is the latest news with the war?" Wei-chen said. Mr. Chou insisted Wei-chen sit between him and the driver for greater stability. But, even with that, each jolt of the cart shot pain down his leg.

"Conditions are deteriorating. In early November three Japanese divisions landed at Hangchow Bay. They have been pursuing Chiang Kai-shek ever since he retreated from Shanghai. Many railway bridges between Shanghai and Nanking have been destroyed. Chiang's forces are now in Nanking but that will not last. It is rumored he will soon leave for Chungking and make it the temporary government capitol."

On the way to the Jardine Matheson office, they saw a crowd gathering at the main temple and stopped. "Stay here. I will be back as soon as I find out what has happened."

When Mr. Chou came back to the cart, he looked shaken. "A monk from Soochow just arrived here. He said the Japanese attacked Soochow last week. After plundering it they kidnapped thousands of women, probably to use as sex slaves. The city of 350,000 is nearly empty. Now Japanese forces are destroying rural communities between Soochow and here. Houses are being burned to the ground, villagers bayoneted. The earth is scorched from the ferocity of the attacks. They are headed this way."

After their son and daughter went to bed, Mr. Chou asked Wei-chen to join him and his wife for tea. He spoke in a hushed voice so the children could not hear. "Tonight many people are leaving Chenchiang to return to their native villages. My wife and I have decided to leave early tomorrow. It will take several hours to reach my parents' village. The hills surrounding their town are honeycombed with caves. We will hide there until the Japanese advance past Chenchiang. You are welcome to join us."

"Thank you but I need to leave for Nanking. I should be able to stay ahead of the Japanese forces. I must get to my wife before they attack Nanking."

"How do you plan to get there? It would take days to walk there and you are not strong enough for that."

"I will find a cart driver to take me there. I can pay someone extremely well."

"What good does it do to have money and not be alive to use it? I do not know anyone who would take that risk. This town is going to be deserted tomorrow. We want you to join us but you may stay here if you prefer to. We will talk again in the morning."

By morning Wei-chen knew he had no alternative other than to leave with the Chous. He still needed to use a cane and wasn't capable of walking any distance. He felt he was abandoning Hui-lan and was furious with himself for not having left Shanghai sooner.

After hiding in a cave for ten days, the Chou family returned to their ancestral village, which Japanese forces ended up bypassing. Several days later, having learned it was once again safe, they returned to Chenchiang.

Most structures were intact although many were badly damaged. "The imperial army must have been in a hurry to get to Nanking," Mr. Chou said, when they entered town. "After we stop at our home, I want you to come to the office with me. We will try to wire Gabriel Knight and let him know we are all safe."

Since leaving the cave, Wei-chen had practiced walking without a cane. His leg was getting stronger, but he knew Japanese troops would dispense with him quickly if he tried to enter Nanking. His only hope was that Hui-lan had convinced her family to leave. That evening, December 13, red-tinged clouds blanketed the western horizon. The color intensified at nightfall.

"Nanking is burning," Wei-chen said to Mr. Chou.

Mr. Chou nodded to him. He looked shaken. "I wish I could have done more to help you."

"You and Mrs. Chou could not have done more. I will leave for Shanghai tomorrow."

Anxiety pounded in Wei-chen's heart. Placing his hand around his wrist, he tried to slow his pulse so he could think clearly. There was nothing more to do here. He felt as if someone had punched him hard, taking all the wind out of him. He blamed himself for not traveling to Nanking in early October.

Before leaving the next day, Mr. Chou gave Wei-chen a list of contacts who could help him move from town-to-town until he was outside Shanghai. After insisting the Chous accept several packets of money, Wei-chen climbed into a cart. It took him four days to reach the outskirts of Shanghai.

With Japan now controlling all of Shanghai except for the foreign concessions, Wei-chen needed to re-enter the city through either the French Concession or the International Settlement. At his last stop he found a farmer who smuggled rice into the city and who agreed to guide him. On December 18 he slipped back into the International Settlement at dusk.

Wei-chen rang Knight when he got to his flat. "I wanted to let you know I am back. Maybe we could meet tomorrow."

"Can we meet tonight? Have you eaten?"

"I am too exhausted to go out." All Wei-chen wanted to do was sleep.

"I am coming over right now. I will stop at the noodle shop near your flat and won't take no for an answer." The phone clicked.

Half an hour later, when Wei-chen opened the door, Knight's mouth dropped.

"Do I look that bad?"

"Yes, I am afraid so. Thank heaven you made it back safely." Knight set the soup on the table and pulled out a chair for Wei-chen. "Tell me everything that happened. I'll make some tea."

"Your list of Jardine Matheson contacts was invaluable. Except for them I would not be here. Mr. Chou saved my life and the others helped me return here." It took an hour for Wei-chen to relate what had happened over the past seven weeks and to answer Knight's questions.

"I cannot forgive myself for not leaving sooner. If I had left just a few days earlier, I could have made it to Nanking."

"Perhaps, but there was still heavy fighting going on here. It is also possible Hui-lan and her family have fled Nanking. If they did, there was no way for her to reach you and let you know.

"Here is what I know. In November thousands of refugees fled to Nanking. Responding to this, some key individuals created the Nanking Safety Zone to protect non-combatants. Nanking's civilians are also fleeing to the Safety Zone. Also, before the Japanese attacked, a large number of civilians, maybe hundreds of thousands, fled Nanking. It is quite possible Hui-lan and her family are either in the Safety Zone or were able to escape." Knight said.

"Thank you for giving me some hope. Let's meet for dinner later in the week. I will let you know what I learn at the consulate."

Wei-chen was exhausted but couldn't shut down his mind. After finally drifting off to sleep, he shot up in bed at one o'clock. A chill swept into the room. He sensed something terrible had happened.

At daybreak Wei-chen walked to the consulate. He went through everything on his desk and then met with the head of the consulate's commercial section. Since the American Embassy was located within the Nanking Safety Zone, he was hoping Hui-lan - if she had not fled Nanking - had sought refuge there.

When Wei-chen asked about this, the commercial chief said, "It is impossible for us to verify that right now. All communication with the Embassy stopped on December 10 when Japanese forces started their furious assault on Nanking. I will let you know as soon as we re-establish any kind of connection.

"Japan wasted no time in setting up a puppet regime in Shanghai. You will need to be very careful. Wang Ching-wei, a former Kuomintang officer under Chiang Kai-shek, has agreed to head the new government. His secret services unit are running a brutal operation from a villa on Jessfield Road. They are torturing and executing individuals they have identified as threats. They are also extorting businessmen."

Wei-chen spent the afternoon with his staff and then left to meet Mr. Cheng. When he approached The Confucian, the scholar waved to him from one of the front windows. So much had happened since he had last seen his friend. Wei-chen felt exhausted.

"It is good to see you," Mr. Cheng said, gently patting Wei-chen's clasped hands. "You are limping. Tell me about your journey."

Wei-chen talked through dinner and ordered more tea afterwards. "If I had left sooner, I could have reached Nanking." He stared at his hands, studying his interlaced fingers.

"Yes, that is possible, but you are looking at the situation with hindsight. When you left for Nanking, you were acting on the information you had at that time. The battle for Shanghai was not over. You made the best decision you could. You must not punish yourself for not being able to read the future. You were and are caught in the tide of history."

"It took me a long time to fall asleep last night. I finally did, but around one o-clock a deep chill filled the room. It was impossible to sleep after that. I am afraid something terrible has happened to Hui-lan. I have never asked you to do this but could you please try to discern something about her."

"I tried this afternoon but I could not work through to an image of her. The scale of what is occurring is too large. All I see is red. I see the blood of China. I have an overwhelming sense of pain and death."

———

Two days later, Wei-chen went straight to the Foreign Correspondents Club after work. McGuire, Ryan and Knight were already there, hunched over a secluded table. Ryan had just returned from Nanking, and Wei-chen wanted to hear about everything he had witnessed. McGuire waved him over and called for a waiter.

Wei-chen ordered tea, then molded his frigid fingers around the hot porcelain cup. "Thank you for meeting with me. I assume Gabriel filled you in on my failed attempt to reach Hui-lan. I returned two days ago. It has been difficult to get information about Nanking. The consulate cannot reach the embassy there. Josh, I am hoping you might have some suggestions for me."

"Do you know if Hui-lan and her family fled or managed to reach the Safety Zone?"

"No. Her father might have been too sick for them to leave Nanking. As for her reaching the Safety Zone, I have no idea. It has been impossible to reach her, and the United States Embassy is not responding."

"Josh, tell us what you observed from the time you arrived there," Knight said.

"I will try to just state the facts, but it has been hard for me to cover this story objectively." Ryan took a sip of beer and continued. "In early November when I followed the United Forces to Nanking, the situation was chaotic. Refugees were pouring into the city from the countryside. In late November foreign residents were advised to leave Nanking, and most of them did. The first week in December Chiang Kai-shek flew to Hankou to set up a temporary capitol. The next day Chinese Air Force squadrons flew to airfields farther west, leaving Nanking without any fighter defense.

"Although most foreigners fled, some very significant ones remained behind. John Rabe, a German businessman who has lived in China for 30 years, heads the International Safety Zone Committee. The committee took over the civilian government when the Chinese cabinet fled with Chiang. The Ginling Women's College is also part of the Safety Zone. After most of the faculty left, Minnie Vautrin - an American dean at the school - became acting head of the college. She opened the school to women and children. The campus was flooded with tents.

"After three days of fierce resistance, the United Forces retreated on December 11. With five army divisions trying to escape across the Yangtze, the retreat turned into a rout. Nanking's citizens were left on their own. The Safety Zone already sheltered thousands of refugees but, after the Japanese attacked the city, hundreds of thousands more fled there. The situation was overwhelming. Minnie Vautrin did everything she possibly could, including helping wounded solders escape. She burned their identity papers and uniforms and disguised them as civilians.

"On December 12 the bloodbath began. Can you imagine what it's like to turn a corner and find a young woman bleeding to death, a bamboo cane shoved between her legs after she has been raped repeatedly? The streets were filled with scenes of mutilation. Of the thousands and thousands of women who were raped, most were killed afterwards and then mutilated - breasts cut off, sharp objects shoved into their vaginas.

"The ones who died quickly were better off than the women who faced massive gang rapes or were forced to be sex slaves. An older woman confided to me that young women were being tied to beds and raped for hours each day until they were too bloody or infected to be useful. Japanese troops went after Chinese men too, forcing them to commit sodomy, to have incestuous relations with their mothers, their sisters, and then killing the entire family. They chopped off a monk's penis when he refused to rape a woman."

Ryan stopped for a moment. He looked shaken. "There was a solider bleeding to death, his jaw shot away. He held out his hand to me. All I could do was hold it for a few seconds before he died. So many bodies were thrown into the Yangtze that it ran red with blood. The last evening I was there, I was walking along the river and came across a pool of water - only it was not water. What looked like mud was blood-soaked soil.

"The next day when two other American reporters and I were leaving, we saw soldiers executing Chinese men. I would guess there were about a thousand of them, made to kneel in small groups and then shot in the back of the head. It was horrific. Some of the Japanese soldiers were laughing while this was going on. There was nothing we could do except leave and try to get word out about the genocide."

Ryan called for another beer and stared at the table, his eyes glazed over. "All of this happened over the course of several days, and it still continues. After the foreign correspondents left, the city was sealed off. The Japanese want to squelch any further reporting of the massacre. I will never forget the savagery I witnessed."

Raw emotion traced Ryan's face. He was in his early thirties but the circles under his eyes made him look older. Wei-chen tried to be patient but could not wait any longer. "Do you know any way I could find Hui-lan?"

Ryan thought for a moment. "I know of one possibility but first the bloodletting has to stop. There is a courier I've used from time to time. When the carnage stops and it's safe to enter Nanking, I will see if he would be willing to trace her. I think the best place for him to start would be with Minnie Vautrin, assuming she managed to stay alive. Give me all the information you can think of - family names, friends, home address, business address. I will see what I can do."

Ryan shoved his notebook across the table, and Wei-chen started writing. His hand shook when he handed the pad back to Ryan. "I cannot thank you enough for helping with this."

"No thanks necessary. I hope my contact will be able to help you. We could all use a bright spot in this sordid world. I am leaving the day after tomorrow and am not sure when I will be back."

Ten

1938

In late January a group at the consulate met with George Fitch, an American missionary the Japanese had permitted to leave Nanking. Somehow Fitch managed to conceal eight reels of 16-mm negative film documenting the atrocities committed in Nanking. He and other members of the Safety Zone Committee were trying to publicize the crimes that continued to be committed. He said that, after seven weeks, the intensity of the massacre was finally diminishing.

After the meeting with Fitch, Wei-chen's concerns about Hui-lan's safety heightened dramatically. Fitch's horrific images haunted him. He tried to fight it off, but a strong foreboding accompanied him everywhere he went.

In early February John Ryan rang Wei-chen to say he had just arrived in Shanghai and wanted to meet with him and Knight. That evening Wei-chen and Knight hopped off a tram and walked at a brisk pace to Le Papillon. Hunching into the wind, Wei-chen tightened his muffler. A frigid chill blanketed the city.

What are you thinking?" Knight asked.

"If Hui-lan were all right, I think Josh would have told me. I am concerned that either his contact could not locate her - or something worse."

When they entered the cafe, the bartender directed them upstairs. Wei-chen heard Ryan ordering a pint of beer as them climbed the stairway. He was sitting in an alcove where two benches straddled a narrow table. Wei-chen and Knight sat across from him. When Wei-chen shook hands with him, he studied Ryan's face for any indication of what he might know and did not like the mask he saw before him.

Ryan flagged a waiter. "Let's get you something to drink." After ordering tea for Wei-chen and a brandy for Knight, he continued. "When I got back yesterday, there was a package waiting for me from the courier. You remember I mentioned Minnie Vautrin, the head of Ginling College."

Wei-chen nodded yes.

"Hui-lan's sister is at their campus."

"What about Hui-lan? Is she there too?" Wei-chen was concerned by the way Ryan glanced down at the letter.

"No, she isn't. Hui-lan's sister talked to Vautrin and her assistant. This letter contains everything her sister said. I can't find a good way to tell you this. Hui-lan died defending her family. I am so very sorry."

Wei-chen gripped the table to steady himself. "Please read it," he whispered.

Dear Mr. Ryan,

I am passing this letter through the same courier who delivered your inquiry. I trust somehow it will reach you. We have information about Lin Hui-lan, the young woman you are seeking. Her younger sister arrived at Ginling in late December. Her story follows.

When Lin Siu-lan arrived here, she was in shock. Two days passed before she was able to speak to us about what had happened. Before the attack on Nanking, her family made a hidden compartment in one of the wardrobes for their daughters. On December 18 they heard screams and gun shots on their street. Both daughters put on old clothes and rubbed ashes on their faces and arms to look as unattractive as possible. Hui-lan insisted her sister enter the compartment and commanded her to remain there for the day.

Within several hours, Siu-lan heard yelling and then pounding on the front door. With a loud crash, the door was broken open. She peeked through a slit in the wardrobe and saw Hui-lan place herself between her parents and the soldiers. Swinging a cleaver, she managed to strike one of the Japanese, causing him to drop his gun. That enraged the other soldiers. They bayoneted Hui-lan and her parents, slashing at them again and again, leaving only after ransacking the house.

Siu-Lan remained hidden in the wardrobe throughout the night. You can imagine her horror and terror. Early the next morning, she edged past the bodies of her family and fled to the house of a neighbor. It took them most of the day to reach the campus because they had to hide continually from foot patrols. Corpses littered the streets.

The carnage has now stopped for the most part, but Siu-lan continues to be haunted by the memory of the murder of her family and feels guilty about the lack of a proper burial. When bodies are gathered, they are buried at mass sites quickly and without ceremony.

I extend my sympathy to your friend and regret the loss of his loved one. I wish it were not so.

My best regards,
Minnie Vautrin

"She did it to protect her sister." Spasms rippled through Wei-chen. He looked at his hands, amazed they were steady. The surges pumping through him seemed to be invisible. He was not sure he could stand.

"Yes, I believe she attacked the soldiers to throw them off, to infuriate them. She was very brave," Ryan said.

Knight handed Wei-chen a handkerchief. Wei-chen was surprised, then realized his face was wet.

"I'm going to leave you two now. I regret being the bearer of such tragic news. I wish it could have been otherwise. I don't know what to say. I am so very sorry." Ryan handed the letter to Wei-chen. "I need to pack up. I will be leaving in a couple of days, heading off to follow the United Forces."

"Thank you for your help. I know this has been difficult for you too." Wei-chen's voice wavered, searching for footing.

"You need to keep telling the world about the massacre," Knight said.

"All the journalists I know are doing their best but Nazi Germany is taking more than its share of headlines right now." Ryan nodded to Wei-chen and walked to the stairs, his shoulders hunched.

"I need to leave now." Wei-chen stood up and walked down the stairs in a wooden gait, rigid, willing himself not to collapse.

Knight flagged a taxi and gave directions to Wei-chen's flat. While Knight was paying the driver, Wei-chen started into the building.

"Wait. We must talk." Knight hurried to catch up.

"Not tonight, my friend." Wei-chen closed the door to his flat and turned the key in the lock.

"I am not leaving. I will not leave you alone tonight," Knight said. "I will be waiting outside your door."

An icy chill filled the room but Wei-chen didn't light the briquet stove. He collapsed at his kitchen table, racked by sobs, and eventually fell into a fitful sleep.

Knight's rapping at the door jolted Wei-chen awake. "Please talk to me. Please let me in."

Wei-chen checked his watch. It was two in the morning. He opened the door and stared at Knight who looked rumpled and frigid.

"You can't be alone now. My flat isn't big enough. I am taking to you Mr. Cheng's," Knight said.

A bone-chilling wind whipped down the streets. When they finally arrived at the scholar's building, he was standing at the door.

"Come inside. I have been expecting you." He embraced Wei-chen and held him close, saying nothing.

Just after daybreak the scent of jasmine tea wafted from the kitchen and woke Wei-chen. His grief roared back in full force. The letter from Minnie Vautrin lay at the foot of the bed. He read it once, then again. Hui-lan's murder filled him with rage. He was angry with himself for not having been there to defend her, to die with her.

When Wei-chen opened the bedroom door, Knight and Mr. Cheng were sitting at the small kitchen table. Hot briquets glowed in the stove, and flickering shadows danced across the prayer rug.

"Come join us." Mr. Cheng motioned. He poured boiling water over tea leaves, swirled them and threw out the water before pouring more water into the teapot. Then he poured a cup of tea for Wei-chen.

Wei-chen grasped the teacup with both hands, willing warmth into his hands and limbs. He felt as if he were shattered into a thousand pieces. "I looked back at her." Tormented, he hunched over.

Knight touched Wei-chen's shoulder gently. "What do you mean?"

"It happened the first time I took Hui-lan to the bell tower at the Cathedral of St. Ignatius. I wanted to show her how beautiful Shanghai looked from the tower. While we were climbing the stairs, I turned around to look at her. She looked beautiful and so happy to be with me.

"But now I think it was like Orpheus looking back at Eurydice. I never should have done it. If I had not turned around..." Wei-chen stared at the table, unwilling to look at either of his friends.

"The story of Orpheus and Eurydice is a myth. It does not have any power to be recreated. I remember your being fascinated with that story when we talked about it because it is so different from Chinese mythology. But it is only a myth," Knight said.

"I understand myths are symbolic but they speak to something deep in our psyche and our humanity," Wei-chen said.

Mr. Cheng took Wei-chen's hands in both of his. "Look at me. You are trying to understand why Hui-lan died. You are looking for a reason. You are blaming yourself for her death. You think somehow you might have prevented her death."

Wei-chen lifted his head and looked into the scholar's eyes.

"What happened was beyond your control. This barbaric bloodletting is unparalleled in our history. We do not have the power to stop this ugly beast, not yet. I want you to stay with me for at least a week. Come here each evening after work." Mr. Cheng's firm tone left no room for debate.

"Thank you for your offer, but I would be very poor company for you."

"Which is precisely why you must stay here until you are ready to be alone again."

"Did you know Orpheus tried to follow Eurydice to the underworld? He waited for seven days but was not allowed to enter. He was only reunited with her when he died." Wei-chen looked out the window. "I am tired. Perhaps we could go to the temple this afternoon."

Wei-chen walked back to the bedroom but Mr. Cheng's advice to Knight penetrated through the door. "Do not be alarmed, Gabriel. It will take time but Wei-chen will heal. He does not know it yet, but he has a strong will to survive. Hui-lan's death will force him to grow in a new direction. Each one of us has lessons to learn and teachers to guide us. I believe he will help many people on his life journey."

Wei-chen remained with Mr. Cheng for ten days. Visits to the temple after work and the scholar's quiet companionship helped stabilize him. After he finally returned to his flat, Wei-chen forced himself to focus on work, but loneliness stalked him the moment he left the consulate each night. Hopelessness hid between the pages of books. He presented a mask to his co-workers, wondering if he would ever smile again without it feeling forced.

He didn't need to look in a mirror to know he looked wounded. Someday his eyes might reflect vitality again, but right now he could not imagine it. The heart cannot lie. Other than that, he was sure he looked the same - shock of black hair falling across his forehead, high cheekbones now more pronounced since he had lost some weight. Wei-chen decided to grow a mustache and goatee, similar to Uncle's, to mark the change in his existence, to demarcate his past with Hui-lan from his future without her.

Comfort eluded him except for one small ritual. Before he went to bed, he burned incense before a photo of Hui-lan and prayed for her spirit.

At the end of February, there was a letter for him at the mail drop. He stared at it, blinking several times. Hui-lan's handwriting. How could this be possible? His hand trembled. He walked upstairs, sat at the kitchen table and slit open the letter.

30 October 1937

My dearest Wei-chen,

A week ago I tried to return to Shanghai. My family, especially Father, agreed with my decision to be with you. I could not stand being separated from you any longer. I tried to time my trip to arrive after the battle for Shanghai had ended and before the Japanese could reach Nanking. The train was well beyond the city when the railroad was bombed. I managed to return to Nanking on a farmer's cart.

In early September I wondered if I might be pregnant. A doctor confirmed it two weeks later. Even with Father's illness, my parents knew I needed to be with you. We agreed I would return when the fighting stopped, and it would be safe for me to travel.

I have left some things unsaid in my letters, so I am writing them to you now, in case I do not make it back to Shanghai. I am heartsick about being apart from you and am afraid I will never see you again. I am usually not one to regret things, but I wish I had listened to you last summer when you asked me to return early. I think of you constantly.

Do you remember when we first met and talked about the ginkgo tree, how it has endured since prehistoric times? I believe we Chinese will also endure, no matter what foreigners do to our country. If something happens to me, my spirit will still carry my love for you. My love will endure, and so will China.

I have been having dreams, most of them about terrifying things. There are Japanese soldiers and dead bodies, many of them, all horribly mutilated. But I also have a recurring dream that brings me peace.

It always begins in a cemetery filled with freshly dug graves. People are standing near the graves, crying. Then the light changes, and a huge ginkgo extends its branches over everyone. The leaves screen the sunlight, changing it to a soft golden hue. The families stop grieving. The tree drops its leaves on them, and they feel the presence of their loved ones. I feel comforted when I awake from the dream.

I know I might not survive the Japanese attack on Nanking. Half the city has fled. Everyone has heard of the atrocities the soldiers are committing on their way here. If I die - if it is possible - I will always watch over you, my dearest love.

Your devoted wife, Hui-lan

Wei-chen spent the evening in darkness and silence. They had created a child. His sense of loss weighed even heavier, something he had not thought possible. He felt numb. Maybe his mind was protecting him. Maybe his heart could not bear any more pain. At last fatigue rescued him, bringing him sleep until dawn. He read the letter again when he woke, then set it on the rattan basket beside his bed. He studied a photo of the two of them, taken days before Hui-lan left. Like a pond reflecting the arching willows on its bank, their eyes reflected the deep love in their hearts.

After work that day he stopped by the bakery. "Come in. I have been hoping you would stop by." Mrs. Mera embraced Wei-chen. "Jakov and I were about to have tea. You must join us." Her gaze penetrated his eyes. "I think you came here to tell us something."

"I brought this for you to read."

Mrs. Mera gently unfolded the letter. Heads bent together, the couple read Hui-lan's letter.

"When did you get this?" Mr. Jakov asked.

"Yesterday."

"Ah, son of my heart." Tears rimmed Mrs. Mera's eyes. She grasped Wei-chen's hand.

After a few moments, Mr. Jakov said, "What do you make of this?"

"I am amazed the letter got to me. She must have sent it with someone who fled Nanking before the attack. She was well aware she might die. It is as if she were preparing me for that, almost consoling me. I cannot stop thinking about the burden she carried, knowing she and our child would probably not survive. It will always haunt me that we were not able to reunite and that I could not protect them."

Mrs. Mera held Wei-chen's gaze. "She was very strong. Hui-lan was trying to give you some of her strength. Tell me, do you feel guilty?"

Stunned for a moment, Wei-chen responded in a hushed voice. "Yes. I think I should have been with her. I should have died with her."

"Mein Gott." Mrs. Mera gripped Wei-chen's hand more tightly.

Mr. Jakov placed an arm around Mera's shoulders. "Death's scythe is indiscriminate. In Russia during the pogroms we saw this many times. Often the youngest and most talented were taken. One cannot make sense of it. Mera and I were fortunate. Our family made it to safety. This was not true for many of our friends. I believe you were meant to survive."

Mrs. Mera insisted Wei-chen stay for dinner. When the Romanovskys described their desperation after the revolution, Wei-chen realized their story was a parable for the current of history now sweeping across China. He left the bakery feeling less alone and promised to return the next week.

On the way home, Wei-chen clamped his jacket to his chest, a shield against the biting wind. Remembering the day Hui-lan convinced him he deserved a warmer coat, tears blurred his vision. Then, out of nowhere, he thought about the seer he met years ago in the old Chinese quarter. What was it the old man said when Wei-chen asked him if he would every marry? He picked up his pace. Where were his notes from that unexpected meeting? Wei-chen emptied two rattan boxes before he found them. The memory of that afternoon floated back to him, the seer sitting in a shaft of light, reading a tattered book. He found the response to his question about finding a mate.

"I believe you have been reluctant to become acquainted with young women. This is going to change within the next few years. I see a great love coming into your life. A lovely young woman will bring you happiness, and you will do the same for her."

Why didn't the sage look further ahead? Did he foresee something tragic? Wei-chen returned to his notes and read the comments about China's future.

"I cannot make exact predictions, but I sense life will become extremely difficult. Although there is much fighting between the Communists and the Nationalists, I see a larger war with Japan." Wei-chen set down the notes. Perhaps it was not a gift for someone to see into the future.

Then he read the answer to his final question, which was if he thought Wei-chen would remain in Shanghai. "It is interesting you even pose that question. Perhaps you sense you will not always live here. Many years from now you might decide to leave Shanghai, but that should not concern you now.

Wei-chen lit the small brazier, made a pot of tea and stared out the window. Stars peeked through bare branches. The celestial light was cold tonight. He felt unsettled. What about the seer's rather vague comment that Wei-chen might decide to leave Shanghai one day. Did he see something he didn't want to reveal?

The next evening Wei-chen met Mr. Cheng and Knight at a quiet teahouse. After reading the letter to them, he looked up to gauge their reaction. Knight, looking stunned, was at a loss for words.

Mr. Cheng took a deep breath. "I can say nothing that will ease your pain, but it is a gift this letter somehow made its way to you. You were both trying to reach each other at the same time. It is a terrible tragedy you were not reunited, that you could not defend Hui-lan and your child. You risked your life to find her. You did everything possible to be with her. I know you do not believe that right now, but it is true. You both loved each other very deeply, more deeply than other couples I know. I have no doubt her spirit will watch over you.

Several days later, the department head called Wei-chen into his office and shut the door. "I need to talk to you about something that is going to run in the afternoon papers. The editor Tsai-Diao-tu was decapitated last night. This morning his head was found on a lamppost in the French Settlement. A piece of cloth attached to it said, 'Look, the result of anti-Japanese elements.'

"For years Tsai-Diao-tu was outspoken about his opposition to Japan. His murder sends a clear message to anyone who opposes the quisling Wang Ching-wei. His puppet regime will do anything the Japanese tell them to do. Their Kempei Tei is an ruthless as Hitler's Gestapo. Its secret service agents are working with local gangsters to squelch opposition. Either the Kempei Tei or Chinese gangsters are behind Tsai's execution.

"The underground Chinese resistance appears to be run by Tai Li, head of the Kuomintang secret police in Shanghai. He is supported by secret service agents and a different set of gangsters. You need to tread carefully. I want you to re-evaluate every one of your sources."

Eleven

1938

In early March, with a deep chill blanketing the city, Wei-chen hurried to meet Knight after work. When he entered The Confucian, Knight was reading a newspaper. An inveterate bookworm, Knight read more than anyone else he knew. He felt tenderness for his friend who interpreted the world through words.

"Listen to these statistics from one of Dan McGuire's pieces," Knight said. "Of the nearly one million refugees who fled to the International Settlement and French Concession last summer, about one-third have managed to leave. The rest are struggling to survive in temporary shelters and, when those are full, they sleep on the streets and in parks.

"He says there's a new class of homeless. When the Japanese army flattened areas of the city and the outer districts, they escalated the number of refugees. Peasants who streamed in from the countryside for decades are now without shelter. In the statistics for 1937, the Municipal Council said it removed 20,000 corpses from Shanghai's streets." Knight put down the paper. "It's worse than I thought."

"Every night when I walk home, I step around collapsed figures. Chinese life is cheap, expendable." Wei-chen's tone cut a short edge.

"It has been somewhat busy at Jardine Matheson. How are things at the consulate?"

Wei-chen recognized the diversion for what it was. "Sorry for the abrupt response. Some days are more difficult than others. More reports came across my desk today that detailed the crippling effect of last fall's battle. Trade has dropped because of the damage our port sustained. Before the Japanese attack, fifty percent of China's imports came through Shanghai. The decline in trade makes it more difficult to provide assistance to the homeless. It depresses me to see them sprawled on the streets.

"So far the puppet Wang Ching-wei is respecting the neutrality of the foreign concessions, but that will not last. The Japanese will not rest until they control the entire city. Whenever I pass outside the concessions, I am on guard. I only go to Hongkew if it is absolutely necessary. When I cross Garden Bridge, Japanese sentries on the Hongkew side require all Chinese to bow to them when they enter or leave. They also require trams to stop so they can force Chinese passengers to bow. I have seen guards attack Chinese whose bows they did not consider deep enough. I smolder inside when I see this. It is difficult for me to veil my hatred for them."

"I'm concerned about you not being able to mask your anger. Japanese sentries won't hesitate to attack you," Knight said.

"There is no need to worry about me. I know the rage I feel is intertwined with my grief over Hui-lan's killing. I also think my hatred of Japan's occupation somehow prevents my grief from completely overwhelming me. My days at work pass quickly but the evenings can seem interminable. I cannot stop thinking about Hui-lan. I wonder if she attacked the soldiers not only to protect her family but also to provoke them to kill her quickly. In the initial weeks of the massacre in Nanking, Japanese troops sometimes eviscerated pregnant women." Wei-chen looked down at his food, unable to take another bite.

"I don't know how to console you."

"I will find a way to get through this. I will not do anything self-destructive. I have set a goal to document the killings and abuses that Japan is committing as an occupying power. I am vetting every one of my sources and have found some new people to work with. I have also removed a few from my prior list."

"You need to be careful. There are lots of spies cooperating with Wang Ching-wei's regime." Knight looked around the room.

"I am well aware of that. I survey the crowd every time I enter a place. Even this little shop, which I have always considered safe. I arrange meetings in nondescript places - out-of-the-way teahouses, the back rooms of noodle shops - and try to stay within the international concessions."

After they finished dinner, Knight would not leave until they arranged another meeting. Wei-chen understood his friend's concern but didn't want to be held accountable to anyone. On his walk home he sidestepped lifeless forms huddled on the sidewalk. These specters of the night haunted him. After making their pilgrimage to Shanghai in hopes of a better life, the result of their efforts was solitary death on the city streets.

Other than wealthy Chinese and foreigners who had managed to leave Shanghai, most residents in the foreign settlements were somehow carrying on with life. Schools were open and commerce continued to function, but at a lesser level. The excesses and frivolity of the early 1930s had disappeared. It seemed to Wei-chen that a dull veneer covered Shanghai.

Just ahead of him an old man lay on his side, curled around a small bundle of belongings. When he passed by, Wei-chen thought he heard a moan. Impossible. He continued to walk but slowed his pace. Could the man still be alive? It had to be too cold for him to survive in such threadbare clothing. Wei-chen looked back at the figure, stopped short and retraced his steps. He needed to know if the man was alive.

Bending down on one knee, he looked into the old, wrinkled face. Yes, he was still breathing. I have no choice, Wei-chen thought. From his jacket pocket, he removed the jade piece Hui-lan had given him when they became engaged. He stripped off his jacket - the one she had chosen for him - and laid it over the man, tucking it around the hunched shape as best he could. A sigh escaped from the bundle of humanity.

Clasping the jade piece, Wei-chen ran the rest of the way to his flat. Rushing into the room, he grabbed his old jacket off a hook and wrapped it around himself as tightly as possible. He felt chilled to the bone and utterly alone.

That weekend he met Knight at Le Papillon. After they ordered dinner, Wei-chen noticed Knight staring at his hands and quickly slipped them under the table.

"Those chilblains are getting worse. You need to soak your fingers in warm water each night or those raw spots will become infected."

Wei-chen looked away. He understood Knight's concern but felt so very tired.

"You must soak those chilblains and protect your hands from the cold. Would you please do that for me."

"Yes, I will do that for you." Wei-chen cast a sidelong glance at an adjoining table.

"And why aren't you wearing your other jacket? Wasn't it warmer?" Knight asked.

Wei-chen focused on a corner of the table. "Oh, yes, it was warmer."

"Where is it? You need to take care of yourself in this freezing weather."

"I found someone who needed it more than I did."

"You gave away your jacket?" Knight looked incredulous, eyebrows raised.

"I gave it to a man who lay dying on the street. I could not ignore one more homeless person freezing to death. The unremitting death in this city overwhelms me." He rearranged vegetables with his chopsticks, then stared at a young couple across the room. Absorbed in conversation, they were oblivious of anyone else. Their happiness created a glow in the dimly-lit corner.

"Wei-chen, are you all right?"

He looked at Knight, but his mind held a vision of him and Hui-lan. "I feel as if part of me has been cut away. When I am absorbed at work, I feel all right for a while. But the torment always returns. Have you ever known emotional pain so deep that it actually feels like physical pain?"

Knight closed his eyes halfway, searching distant memories. "I was devastated when Olivia broke off our relationship, but it does not begin to approach your anguish. I am at a loss as to how to comfort you. I am worried about you."

Wei-chen separated the various vegetables into little piles. "I cannot take one more bite."

"At least take it home with you."

"Yes, I will do that." Wei-chen intended to offer it to the first hungry person he met. When they stepped out onto the street, he said, "Good night. It may not appear so, but it was good to see you."

Several days later Wei-chen received a message from Mr. Cheng, asking him to meet at a teashop the next afternoon. He went there directly from the consulate, worried that something was wrong. When he walked in, Mr. Cheng waved from across the room, having claimed a small table near the briquet stove.

"An excellent choice of tables. It is raw outside." Wei-chen shivered.

"Are you too cold to take off your gloves?"

"No, not at all." Wei-chen set the gloves aside and placed his hands under the table.

"May I please see your hands." Mr. Cheng gently extended his hands across the table.

"I think you have talked to Gabriel Knight."

"Yes, he asked if I would have a conversation with you. He mentioned your chilblains and your weight loss. He is extremely concerned about you." The scholar's sturdy hands formed buttresses with his interlaced fingers. "He cares for you as if you were his son. He did not say that, but it is easy to discern. Because you gave your jacket away, he fears you are losing your will to live.

"I am concerned about you too, but my intuition tells me you will come through this. Grief is your constant companion these days, but that will change. I admire your act of compassion in the face of the enormous desperation that haunts our city. You are not letting your rage consume you. You are forging it into something else. You are being true to your nature."

Wei-chen sat in silence, trying his friend's words on for size to see if they fit.

Warm air seeping through the open window stirred Wei-chen. He felt a surge of energy and left his flat while it was barely light, making his way around the bodies of those who had died during the night. Would this nightmare never end? Mindless of which street he was on, he wandered through the International Settlement and unexpectedly found himself in Fuxing Park. His heart stopped when he looked at the bench where he and Hui-lan once played chess. An old couple was sitting there now. He envied the tenderness in their glances. Finding it too painful to stay in the park, he walked to the Old City.

When Wei-chen was approaching Yu Yuan Garden, something caught on the sole of his shoe. Repeatedly scuffing his shoe against the sidewalk, he tried to dislodge whatever was stuck there, perhaps a scrap of paper. Finally, exasperated, he lifted his foot and was stunned to find two entwined ginkgo leaves. He gingerly dislodged them and held the little fans in his hands. Most of their golden color remained. How had they survived the winter? He looked around. There were no ginkgo trees nearby. Then he remembered Hui-lan's final letter. "My love is strong, like the ginkgo tree. If something happens to me - if it is possible - I will always watch over you." He tucked the leaves in his jacket pocket, safeguarding them. I love you too, he thought.

Skirting the garden, he walked to the Ghost Market, something he had not done in months. When he turned the corner and saw Quiet Heart Teashop, he hesitated, then crossed the street and looked in the window. No one was sitting at their favorite table. A good omen he decided, letting thoughts of happier days draw him inside. The clink of porcelain cups against teapots comforted him and jasmine tea warmed him, steeping him in pleasant memories.

Bright sun shafts spilling across the table enticed him back outside. He wandered through the Ghost Market. Little treasures from the countryside flanked the side streets. Wei-chen walked in rhythm to the market sounds - the haggling between sellers and buyers, the touting of vendors, the chirping of bird in their cages.

He continued to Dongtai Lu. When he entered his favorite porcelain shop, Mr. Liu's face creased in welcome. "Good morning. I have not seen you in months."

"Good morning, Mr. Liu. That is so. Much has happened since the last time I saw you."

"Your wife. How is she?" Mr. Liu stopped, frozen by the expression on Wei-chen's face.

"She was not able to leave Nanking before the attack."

"I am so sorry," Mr. Liu said.

Wei-chen understood Mr. Liu was not sure what else to say. He wasn't exactly sure either, so he just blurted it out. "I have not come to see you because these past months have been difficult for me. Hui-Lan was killed shortly after the Japanese attacked Nanking."

"That is terrible. I offer you my deepest sympathy." Mr. Liu bowed slightly.

Wei-chen felt a breach in the defensive wall that he had constructed after Hui-lan's death. Relenting, he related everything Josh Ryan found out for him and the content of Hui-lan's final letter. In turn he listened attentively when Mr. Liu described how he learned to carry on with life, even though devastated by his wife's death.

"When you respect and care for someone, they become part of you. You are changed by them. So, even when they are gone, in some way they are still with you. They are part of you. Sometimes when I am troubled, I sense my wife's spirit is with me. It may not be true, but that is what I believe."

Before Wei-chen left, Mr. Liu said, "I have missed your visits. There is no need for you to purchase anything when you stop by. Abundance can also be found in friendship. Please return soon."

Wei-chen left the shop and circled back to Yu Yuan Garden. He sat on a bench and leaned back against the undulating dragon wall, letting the warm sun cauterize his wounded heart.

In late April Wei-chen went to Le Papillon. Now twilight, strings of lights blinked in the plane trees. Earlier that day Knight rang him to say Josh Ryan was back in town and would probably be at Le Papillon tonight. When Wei-chen stepped inside, Ryan was standing at the bar with colleagues.

Ryan noticed him and motioned for Wei-chen to meet him at a small table. "It's good to see you. How are you?"

"Much better than the last time you saw me. I was wounded and upset that evening. I came here to thank you for discovering what happened to Hui-lan."

"I have never had to deliver news like that to anyone. I left a bit abruptly because I didn't know how to comfort you. I knew you weren't upset with me on a personal level. Besides, it's quite usual for the messenger to be killed. It's been happening for millennia." Ryan touched Wei-chen's teacup with his pint of beer.

Wei-chen smiled. That was beginning to happen again. Within the past week or two, he had found himself smiling spontaneously when something pleased him. The first months after Hui-lan's death, he wondered if his heart was like a well run dry, that he might never feel a hint of joy again.

"I came back to gather a few belongings. The United Forces are moving their capitol to Chungking so I'm heading there. Maybe that line will hold firm," Ryan said.

"Do you think you will ever return to Shanghai?"

"Not as long as Wang Ching-wei's regime is in control. Life is becoming dangerous for the press. Ever since Japanese agents decapitated Tsai Diao-tu for his anti-Japanese stance, we have all been wary. He was a prominent editor, and he ended up with his head on a lamppost in the French Settlement. Did you know that goons are sending severed body parts - fingers and hands - to Chinese businessmen and journalists who oppose the Japanese regime? How's that for intimidation? Right now they are leaving the foreign press alone but that won't last. The Kempei Tei is like the Gestapo. Are you aware of what is happening in Germany?"

"Yes, we get reports at the consulate, and the Romanovskys talk about it every time I see them. Jews are fleeing here, just like they fled from Russia. What do you think is going to happen?"

"There are brutal years ahead for the world. I think the Germans and Japanese will seize as much territory as they can. Japan isn't going to stop with China, and Germany won't stop with Poland."

"Whatever happens, I know you are determined to be in the middle of it." Wei-chen understood the intensity in Ryan's tone reflected more than his desire to pursue the forces of history. He was also documenting monstrous violations of human rights.

"I can't imagine not chasing a story, especially this one. When I took that freighter to Shanghai, I never dreamed I would be covering Japan's invasion of China."

"The first time Knight mentioned you, he said you were a maverick, which I now fully understand, but you are also brave." Wei-chen glanced over at the bar. "I think some of your friends want to talk to you. I will leave now. It was good to see you again. I wish you safe travels. Be careful."

Ryan stood and shook hands with Wei-chen. "Whether you call it fate or luck, I think our paths will cross again."

"I hope you are right." He also prayed the gods would protect Ryan.

That evening Wei-chen thought about Ryan's comments. He fell into bed, troubled, and decided to have a long talk with Knight the following weekend. The next morning he glanced at his wall calendar, surprised he had forgotten to cross out yesterday's date. After Hui-lan's death he started making a slash through each day. Crossing out the date was a ritual, marking time, marking his grief. Maybe this break in the ritual was a sign his heart was beginning to heal, that happy memories of their love would eventually override his sorrow.

On Sunday morning Wei-chen met Knight at Public Garden, which ran along the Bund. "Good morning. How about taking a walk? I saw Josh Ryan two nights ago. He mentioned something I would like to discuss." Walking, rather than sitting on a bench, made it impossible for their conversation to be overheard.

"A walk sounds good. Afterwards we can get lunch from one of the street vendors."

"How much do you know about the murder of Tasi Diao-tu?"

"It's complicated. I have talked to Dan McGuire several times about it. He is working on a long piece for the newspaper. He said Tsai's murder was committed by the Kempei Tei, the network of gangsters and secret service types who work for Wang Ching-wei's regime.

"Even though Japan doesn't control the foreign concessions, it's their way of retaliating for any opposition to their regime. Prominent Chinese who oppose them are being threatened. The inspector who is investigating Tsai's death said several journalists have received packages containing bullets and decomposing hands."

"There is nothing subtle about that. Ryan also spoke of an underground network of Chinese resistance." Wei-chen was seeking confirmation of several things Ryan had mentioned.

"Yes, secret agents and gangsters who work for Tai Li, one of Chiang Kai-shek's aides, are involved in it. The gangsters have assassinated several nationals they considered traitors to Chiang's government. They're ruthless, but the Kempei Tei is much worse. Did Ryan mention Villa 76 and what is going on there?"

"We did not get into that."

"According to McGuire, agents are torturing businessmen and regime opponents at the villa. In exchange for their lives, business executives are required to turn over money and members of the resistance are required to join the regime. Those who refuse to cooperate are eliminated behind the building. The campaign to intimidate the press is also run from Villa 76. Some publishers have already left for Chungking."

"That is where Ryan is headed. He said he will not return here as long as the Japanese are in control. The regime is tightening their stranglehold on Shanghai. Collaborators are on the watch for any opposition to the government. Speaking of people leaving, do you ever think about moving from here? Maybe to Hong Kong? The American government has insisted women and children leave Shanghai, and a number of American businesses have relocated their head offices to Hong Kong and Manila."

"Jardine Matheson is committed to their presence in Shanghai. Besides, even if I wanted to move to their Hong Kong office, it's fully staffed. So the answer is no, I am not planning to leave. I intend to remain here."

That evening an idea dancing at the edge of Wei-chen's consciousness formed into a plan. It felt as if Hui-lan were guiding him. He couldn't distinguish his thoughts from the sense of her presence. After work the next day, he met Mr. Cheng at the temple. "There is something I have decided to do, and it involves you. I hope you will be willing to help me."

"Now you have peaked my curiosity. I cannot remember the last time you asked for my assistance." Mr. Cheng raised his eyebrows.

"Before Hui-lan and I were married, I saved a considerable amount of money. Instead of spending it, we continued to grow the account for the time when we would have a family.

"I want this money to be used to rescue children who have been orphaned in Shanghai. Because of your association with Jade Buddha Temple, I am hoping you can convince the head of the temple to accept these funds and allow you to oversee them on my behalf. I am not sure what should be done. Perhaps some children could be reunited with extended family, perhaps assistance could be given to orphanages. Whatever it is, I trust you to do this. I do not want my name mentioned."

"I will do as you wish. You are walking an enlightened path. I an honored to know you," the scholar said.

"I have chosen to do this because of Hui-lan. I am a better person because of her.

Four months later, on a Sunday afternoon in mid-July, the Romanovskys asked Wei-chen to meet them at Soochow Creek. He found them sitting on a bench along the bank. Across the creek, Hongkew bristled with Japanese foot patrols, beasts stalking at the boundary of their territory.

After they chatted for a while, Mrs. Mera said, "Have you been painting?"

"No, I have made some sketches, but that is all. The gallery that carries my work has asked for some paintings, but I have no new work for them to sell."

"We have something to give you," Mr. Jakov said. Mera nodded, impatient for him to continue. "There is an old Russian who comes from our village. Perhaps you remember him - Professor Zill, a long-time customer. He has bushy black eyebrows and a goatee that is almost white. Anyway, he was admiring the watercolor you painted of our shop several years ago. He asked who painted it and said it was quite good."

"Jakov, please tell him." Mrs. Mera clasped her hands.

"Yes, my kleine kugel."

Wei-chen smiled. Whenever Mr. Jakov referred to his wife as his little pudding, she beamed.

"The professor taught at an art school outside of Kiev. Since coming here he teaches art classes in his flat. Mera and I have talked to him. He would be pleased to teach you. We would like to pay your tuition to study with him."

"That is very gracious, but I cannot accept. It is too much."

"Yes, you can. All you have to say is yes. The professor says you have talent. We know you have the gift of painting. And, really, it is a way for us to also support him. He is a good customer. You simply must say yes." Mrs. Mera's insistent tone left him no other choice.

"Then, yes. Thank you very much." Wei-chen understood the Romanovskys were trying to help him as much as they were supporting the professor, killing two flies with one swat as they sometimes said. He did not want to insult them by refusing their generous offer. They knew finances weren't any issue for him. They were trying to help him heal. Besides, spending Saturday afternoons painting would provide a good counterbalance to his work.

The next weekend, armed with a sketch pad and graphite, Wei-chen took a tram to the French Concession for his first class. When he reached the third floor of Professor Zill's building he hesitated, unsure which door to approach. Part of him wanted to turn around and leave.

Just then, from behind the door on his right, he heard, "Let me see your drawings from last week." Spoken in a heavy Russian accent, the Chinese words were difficult to understand but the voice was gentle. Wei-chen knocked on the door, aware he was entering a new dimension.

A great Russian bear, Professor Zill filled the doorway. "You must be Mr. Chan. Come in. Welcome to our class."

Wei-chen walked in and quickly assessed the students. All were Chinese, ranging in age from a young girl in pigtails to an older gentleman. A young man motioned to an empty seat near him. Pleased with this courtesy, Wei-chen joined several students at a table. Everyone's attention was focused on a draped object perched on a small pedestal.

The professor crossed the room and removed the fabric in a swirl, revealing a skull. "You have one hour to draw this. You may begin now."

Wei-chen struggled to control his breathing and remain calm. Memories of Hui-lan's death seized him. Where had Professor Zill found this skull? It reminded him of the half-decomposed bodies that washed ashore along the waterfront. Death presented itself in many forms these days. Burial boats, sent to sea with the bodies of the dead often returned with the evening tide, still carrying their wretched cargo.

The skull embodied all Wei-chen had been struggling with since Hui-lan's brutal killing. The other students started drawing immediately. After what seemed like a long time, he forced himself to regard the object as a rock with interesting fissures, then started sketching.

Professor Zill wandered around the room, making suggestions to the students. When he saw Wei-chen's drawing, he nodded approvingly. After a short break, class resumed. The skull was no longer on the table. "Now, my artists, you will draw the skull from memory. You may begin now."

Wei-chen was completely caught off guard. The exercise was difficult. Before class ended the professor assigned exercises for them to do before the next session. As soon as Wei-chen arrived home, he placed the skull drawings side by side, determined to sharpen his observation skills.

Deep sleep brought vivid images that night. A young man was searching for the doorway to his future. He looked tense, afraid of passing through the wrong door and having it slam permanently behind him. The man, who was now Wei-chen, became lost in a forest. The leaves of a massive ginkgo tree sighed as the wind swept through them, and a doorway appeared in its trunk. Wei-chen opened it and climbed steps that spiraled inside the tree. Finally he reached an opening high above the ground. A panoramic view - a time continuum - spread before him. In the direction of the future, a large island appeared, its peaks wreathed in clouds.

Rain pounding against the window dissolved the image. Throughout the day the island's image persisted in his mind. It would not let him rest until he sat down and drew it. Even though he didn't understand it, he knew the dream was significant. A sense of calm pervaded the flat.

For the remainder of the summer, Wei-chen drew the visible and invisible. He sketched several studies of Hui-lan as references for future paintings. He sketched in teahouses, gardens and cafes, repeating the skull exercise again and again with different objects. When inspiration seized him, he drew on whatever type of paper was available at the moment. His eye, hand and mind became one. Stacks of drawings carpeted his flat. On a steamy August morning, he looked at the piles of artwork and realized that not only his flat was filling up but also his life.

That fall Wei-chen continued to study one night a week with Professor Zill. One of the professor's home exercises involved copying drawings of the old masters. Wei-chen immersed himself in line and form and learned to capture the essence of a subject. He could create a litchi shell that looked thin and brittle but gave a hint of the succulent fruit within. His favorite image was a porcelain teapot glistening with moisture from its contents.

Wei-chen recognized his obsession with art stemmed from the sense of peace it brought him. He never stopped thinking about Hui-lan. The pain was just not as intense.

Nine months later Professor Zill asked Wei-chen to remain after class one evening. "You have not shown me the drawings you do outside of class, but I know you do this because it shows in your work. I think perhaps you are ready for a new instructor."

"I am sure you have much more teach me. I want to continue working with you. I cannot imagine studying with someone else."

"Thank you. I also enjoy working with you." The professor thought a moment and smiled. "A possible solution is for you to study privately with me. You will now paint in oil, and we will meet each month to review your work. The Romanovskys believe in you, and I do too." The Russian bear embraced Wei-chen.

"Thank you, and from now on I will pay for your instruction rather than the Romanovskys." On the way home, Wei-chen stopped in a teashop and mulled over the evening. Although it was out of focus, a new pathway was stretching ahead of him. Something in his life was changing.

Several days later he went to the bakery to tell the Romanovskys about his new study arrangement. When he reached the shop, he paused outside the door. A young European man, perhaps in his late teens, was sweeping the floor. There was a new shop boy. Many years ago Wei-chen had done that same work. Ridiculously, he felt displaced, perhaps a little threatened.

"Come in, Wei-chen," Mrs. Mera said. "You are standing outside like the first time you came here."

Hug. Smudge. Yes, everything was still in order. Wei-chen felt reassured.

"Chan Wei-chen, I introduce you to Max Weissman," Mrs. Mera said. After they shook hands, Max continued sweeping. While the tea steeped, Mrs. Mera explained, "Max and his mother arrived in Shanghai two months ago. They are from Vienna. Jakov and I know a little German and Max knows Yiddish, so it works all right. We did not know much Chinese when you started working here, did we." After setting out pastries, she asked Max to join them.

Wei-chen studied Max. He was thin, shoulders bent as if carrying a heavy load. Sadness filled his eyes. Mrs. Mera and Max conversed briefly in Yiddish, and Max left for the day.

"Max and his mother fled from Austria several months ago. In November of last year, the Nazis destroyed Jewish communities in Germany and Austria.

They refer to it as krisstallnacht, night of crystal. Such a misleading term for a rampage of destruction, murder and rounding up of Jews." Mrs. Mera clenched her apron.

"They live in an area of the International Settlement where most of the German and Austrian Jews live. Not many Jews have sufficient funds to live in the Settlement. When a person leaves Germany, they are permitted to leave with only twenty Deutsche marks. People arrive with only the clothes on their backs and one valise. Can you imagine containing a lifetime in one valise?"

"How did you find out about them? How did they find a place to live?" Wei-chen wanted to know more about Max but was concerned about Mrs. Mera. Sadness had stripped her eyes of their usual vitality. Perhaps she was reliving their flight to Shanghai.

"One of the Jewish relief committees contacted me to see if we could employ anyone. Surely you have heard of Shanghai's prominent Jews - the Sassoons, Kadoories and Hayim."

Wei-chen nodded.

"These families are directing the relief effort for refugees. Of course, the most affordable flats are in Hongkew because it is still devastated from the Japanese takeover."

"What about Max's father?"

"He stayed behind to sell the family business and will leave as soon as he can. It is not easy to arrange departure tickets. When two places became available on a ship heading to the Far East, he insisted Max and his mother leave without him."

"Do you think he will be able to get out?"

Mrs. Mera shook her head no. "I think it is very unlikely. That is why a cloud of sadness hangs over Max. He needs rachmones, he needs compassion." Mrs. Mera swiped a tear away. "Memories of leaving Russia still haunt me."

Losing Hui-lan was devastating for Wei-chen, but at least he still had his country. He was not persecuted. He felt chagrined about his initial reaction to Max. Just then Mr. Jakov came into the shop. His presence dispelled the shadows of his wife's remembrances. Wei-chen watched her face brighten, as if a cloud has passed by, unblocking the sun.

"The reason I stopped by is to thank you for my art lessons. It was a wonderful gift. From now on I will meet with Professor Zill once a month to review my work. Also, I am going to start painting in oil." Wei-chen opened his satchel and took out a thin package wrapped in old silk. "I brought something to show my appreciation."

Mrs. Mera accepted his gift with the anticipation of a child. "Such beautiful old fabric. Did you find it in one of the antique markets? I will save this."

"Meine Schoene, please unwrap it," Mr. Jakov said.

Carefully unfolding the fabric, she spoke in a hushed voice, "Jakov, it is the Wushingting Teahouse. Look at the reflection in the pond. This is a beautiful drawing."

"I am glad it pleases you." Wei-chen wanted the drawing to displace some of the sadness she felt today.

As he was preparing to leave, Mrs. Mera walked Wei-chen to the door. "When you came to the shop today and saw Max, your face dropped. I want you to know you will always be the son of my heart."

She saw through him, just as a mother would. He felt immensely grateful.

Twelve

1941

A somber November sky reflected the mood in Shanghai and Wei-chen's growing apprehension. When he arrived at the teahouse, Knight and Mr. Cheng were sitting at a table near the heater. Deep in discussion, they didn't notice his arrival.

"I feel as if I am interrupting something," said Wei-chen.

"Not at all. Sit down. We've only been here a short while." Knight poured tea for Wei-chen. "We were discussing the campaign that Wang Ching-wei's regime is running against the press. Decisions about which journalists to kill and which newspapers to bomb are implemented from Villa 76, but Japan is pulling the strings behind the scenes. Until this fall they made a pretense of recognizing American authority, but now their troops freely enter the concessions. With the Vichy government controlling the French Concession and the evacuation of British troops to Singapore, there is no one to stop them."

"Japan no longer respects the right of the settlements to self-police. As soon as their encroachments within the foreign concessions started to occur, the consulate reported their non-compliance to the Department of State. Japanese troops have begun to restrict the freedoms of foreign residents. Everyone at the consulate is on edge, including me."

"Paired with the war in Europe, none of this bodes well," Knight said.

"Most foreigners have left Shanghai in anticipation of worse things to come, and they are right to do so. There will be a massive attack by the Japanese - and soon. All of Asia will be drawn into war. America too. Perhaps you should consider leaving before this happens." Mr. Cheng looked intently at Knight.

Knight studied his tea cup.

When Knight didn't respond, Wei-chen said, "In the past three years Germany has devoured western Europe, and Japan is about to do the same here. After extending their reach through most of China, Japan is now poised to move through the rest of Asia. Mr. Jakov compares Japan to a gigantic bird of prey, hovering, biding its time before it strikes. It is only a matter of time until they attack."

"That is an apt analogy," the scholar said. "And it is going to happen."

On December 8 what sounded like staccato bursts of firecrackers startled Wei-chen before dawn. Once fully awake, he realized it was distant gunfire. He turned on his shortwave radio and learned Japanese troops had attacked a British gunboat in the harbor and seized an American one. He rang Knight. They agreed to meet mid-morning near the consulate.

"I just walked past the consulate. Japanese soldiers are posted in front of it," said Wei-chen.

"Let's go to the small French cafe near my office. Alain, the owner, is one of my sources. He should have a good idea of what's going on."

When they walked in, the owner nodded and seated them off by themselves back near the kitchen. After the waitress brought their drinks, he came over and sat down.

Knight introduced Wei-chen and quickly got to the point of their visit. "We just came from the American Consulate. Japanese sentries are posted in front of it."

"They are also posted at the British, Belgian and Dutch consulates. Japan is seizing control of the International Settlement. There is talk of a Japanese attack on Hawaii. That is all I know right now."Alain spoke in a hushed tone. "Come back later today, and I might have more information for you."

When Wei-chen and Knight returned that evening, Alain stopped by their table. "I am sure you know by now the Japanese Air Force was very busy today. Besides striking Pearl Harbor, they also attacked Guam, Wake and Midway Islands, Hong Kong, the Philippines, Singapore and Malaya."

"Yes, they accomplished a lot over seven hours, and all without any declaration of war against those countries. God help us all," Knight said.

"I will stop by before you leave. Mind that table near the front window. They are collaborators."

"The last radio report I heard said the United States Congress is expected to declare war tomorrow. Europe's survival depends on this and so does Asia's, but I am not sure America has the resources to fight a massive war on two fronts. Japan's domination of Asia and the Pacific will be brutal. We have only seen the beginning of it. I am afraid we will see a repeat of Nanking's massacre across the region." Anger interlaced with fear roiled inside Wei-chen.

"I share your concern, but Japan has awakened a sleeping lion. The attack on Pearl Harbor will resonate deeply across America. The big question now is how quickly America can get on a wartime footing. As for Japan, they are wasting no time in taking over the International Settlement and the French Concession. When I got to work today, a notice on the front door said the property is now under Japanese control. The same notice was posted at all foreign businesses. No employees may enter the firms without Japanese permission. I had to wait an hour before I could get into the building. They'll keep the company running as long as they can strip income from it.

"There's one more thing. By Saturday all Allied nationals have to register at the Enemy Aliens Office. We will be photographed, issued a registration number and given an armband we'll be required to wear in public," Knight said.

"So they are going to keep track of you? I am extremely concerned about where this is heading. Do you think the Japanese got the armband idea from the Nazis? They require Jews to wear armbands with the Star of David on them. I hope they will not force that on the Jewish community here. As for me, the Japanese have seized and shut down all the Allied consulates, which means I am out of a job. Diplomats are being held under house arrest somewhere in the French Concession."

"Let me see where things stand at work by the end of the week. A couple of people I know want to get out of Shanghai while they still can. With your trade expertise, you should be able to land some kind of position."

—

Through December Wei-chen looked for work and kept his expenses to a minimum. His one indulgence was stopping at a teahouse each day. He carried a small notepad with him. Besides maintaining a list of those killed by the regime, he documented the changes taking place.

Changes under Occupation

December 1 - British, American and Dutch shipping companies order their vessels to bypass Shanghai.

December 3 - Swire Shipping orders its ships to leave for Hong Kong.

December 8 - Japan attacks the Philippines, Guam, Hong Kong, Singapore and Malaya hours before the strike on Pearl Harbor. The Union Jack is struck from Hong Kong and Shanghai Bank and replaced with Japan's red-and-white Empire of the Sun. Allied nationals are given five days to register with the Enemy Aliens Office.

December 9 - Foreigners are forbidden to go to nightclubs, hotels, movie theater, bars and restaurants.

December 10 - All banks in the International Settlement are ordered to abide by regulations issued by Wang Ching-wei's regime. Foreign banks may operate only two hours a day and foreign bank accounts are frozen. Foreigners are not allowed to withdraw more than two thousand Chinese dollars a month from their accounts.

December 15 - Foreign-owned cars are confiscated.

December 23 - All supplies on hand - rice, cooking oil, automobiles, medicines, fuels - must be registered.

December 28 - Residents may no longer move from one place to another without permission. Transient Chinese must return to the countryside.

December 31 - Public transportation is cut back drastically.

Wei-chen surmised it all dovetailed into one thing. By placing constraints on all elements of daily life - supplies, transportation, finances - the Japanese were using what they forcibly acquired to underwrite their extensive war effort.

In early January 1942 Wei-chen joined Jardine Matheson as a trade assistant. The pay was adequate, and he was thankful to have a job. At work he kept his private life to himself. He and Knight had no contact. Friendship with an Allied national would cast suspicion on him.

Over the Lunar New Year holiday, Wei-chen met Knight at Quiet Heart Teashop. They had started this weekly ritual in December. After Hui-lan's death Wei-chen mostly avoided the teashop but now, after four-and-a-half years, remembrances of their happy moments outweighed his grief. It was the perfect place to meet Knight because it provided a safe location to rendezvous and talk openly. The shop owner sympathized with the Chinese resistance. When Chinese collaborators came in, he signaled his patrons. Japanese troops seldom came there but when they did, conversations shifted to innocuous topics.

During the week they gleaned information from shortwave broadcasts and the Chinese and American communities. On the weekends, they traded facts and talked for hours as the the warmth of the teashop provided a respite from the cold and the grimness of Japanese occupation.

Looking across the table Wei-chen noticed the fine lines around Knight's eyes had deepened and his hair had grayed considerably. The war was taking a toll on everyone, including foreigners since the government had seized control of their bank accounts. The withdrawals of foreigners were now restricted to one thousand Chinese dollars per month, reducing their standard of living to the subsistence level of poor Chinese families.

"With everything that has occurred, do you ever think you should have left Shanghai while it was still possible?" Wei-chen asked.

"It's too late for regrets. And, to be honest, I knew that if I left, I might never return. Besides, do you think I would be required to wear such a fashionable red armband in America? It has been almost a month since they required the Allied nationals to register. I think it's interesting how they stamped the armbands - A for Americans, B for British, N for Dutch and X for all the others."

"How can you be so glib about it? This is not the end of it. I am worried about what they will do next." Concern flashed across Wei-chen's face.

"I should have seen it coming, but I never expected to be declared an enemy alien. And I certainly didn't expect to see American prisoners of war paraded through the streets of Shanghai. They are the ones I am really concerned about - captured on Pacific islands, put on display here. Where will they be sent next and how will they be treated?"

"I understand that but I am concerned about you."

Knight spotted a Japanese soldier in the doorway and dropped his voice. "I do feel more conspicuous these days, perhaps even targeted."

"I am a little less concerned about the Romanovskys. Since the Soviet Union and Japan have a treaty protecting Soviet nationals, Russian Jews fall into this protected category. Max should be okay too. Jewish refugees from Germany are considered German, so the Japanese grant them the same privileges as German nationals. Today the BBC reported the German government does not want the occupation government protecting Jews here, but the Japanese disagree. They respect Jews for their business acumen and their access to international finances. They want to tap into that talent," Wei-chen said.

"Bizarre world, isn't it, these decisions about whom to hate, whom to destroy."

"In case you have not noticed, Americans are at the top of the Japanese destroy list."

"I have noticed lots of things. It looks as if Japan is having its way throughout Asia and the Pacific, but something else is happening. I think the Japanese forces are overextended, like Napoleon's troops in Russia. Right now the situation looks bleak, but I believe America's involvement will turn the tide. I wear my armband with pride."

"We still need to be careful. The soldier is gone but the owner signaled there are collaborators several tables away." Wei-chen spoke in a hushed tone. "I rely on my bicycle for transportation. Because of auto restrictions, the wealthy are forced to use rickshaws. I am sure the Japanese are diverting fuel to support their expanding war."

"That's my guess too. They are grinding life to a halt here. They shut down over two hundred factories in January. A British banker told me the regime is draining the bank accounts of foreign businesses. He also said they are appropriating any factory machinery that can be used in the war effort. Remember the holes we saw in the walls of the British mills? Japanese troops looted the machinery and sent it to Japan."

"And how about our rice? Japanese forces are eating China's good rice. The rationed rice we are forced to make do with is terrible. The black market rice is too expensive for me, but I find it interesting the regime cannot stop entrepreneurial peasants from sneaking it in. My neighbor saw peasants crawling under the barbed wire fence surrounding the International Settlement. They stuff bags of rice under their clothing and sell it from house to house," Wei-chen said.

"Other than the wealthy, no one can afford the rice sold on the black market."

Wei-chen glanced around the room and continued in a quiet tone. "Every time I see a Japanese soldier, I think about the price their occupation is exacting from China. I think about Hui-lan's death and how the Japanese are raping China - our women and our land. Mr. Cheng counsels me not to feed on hatred, that there is a law of cause and effect, that the future bodes ill for Japan. When hatred lurks at the edges of my mind, it is difficult but I try to remember his words."

Thirteen

1943

On the first day of the Lunar New Year, Wei-chen bundled up and walked to The Confucian restaurant for dinner. Candle light, framed by windowpanes, spilled onto the sidewalk. When he entered, Mr. Cheng and Knight were already sipping tea.

Greetings finished, the scholar filled Wei-chen's tea cup. "Gabriel, I understand some Allied nationals are being exchanged for Japanese prisoners of war. Did you apply to repatriate with your countrymen?"

Knight thought for a moment. "I think you must be referring to the Gripsholm, the ship that just left for Hong Kong. The answer is no, I did not. There are plenty of women and children and older people who should be given the chance to leave before I do. I just learned that John Powell, the editor of the *China Press*, managed to clear out on the ship, but he departed in a terrible state. Did you hear what happened to him?"

"The last I knew, he was being held at Bridge House." Mr. Cheng looked somber.

Wei-chen sucked in his breath. "That is serious. Max walks past Bridge House when he crosses Garden Bridge into the International Settlement. Mrs. Mera said Max has mentioned hearing horrifying screams coming from that building."

"The Kempei Tei use age-old methods of coercion - water torture, shoving metal spikes under fingernails, burning men's private parts. Many of the prisoners are released when they are close to death. This happened to a monk's brother," the scholar said. "The Kempei Tei thought he was a member of the resistance. He was not, but that made no difference. They are not held accountable to anyone."

"All I know is that Powell was in ghastly condition when he left. A friend of mine knows the American doctor who treated him. The Kempei Tei must have realized they had gone too far and called the doctor in. By then Powell's feet were black and flesh was peeling off his toes. He was hospitalized and treated for beriberi. He went into Bridge House weighing one-hundred-sixty pounds and came out weighing seventy-five pounds. He is not expected to recover, but at least he is heading home. Even with all this, I still believe Japan will be defeated. And I am not ready to leave," Knight said firmly.

"Much more will come to pass before the Japanese leave China. I think you two celebrated a bit prematurely last fall."

"Do you mean when we treated ourselves to dinner at Le Papillon?" Wei-chen asked. Mr. Cheng nodded. "Perhaps Gabriel and I were overly optimistic at that time but the battles of the Coral Sea and Midway were a turning point. They left visible chinks in Japan's armor. For the first time in years, I felt a glimmer of hope."

"You see something, don't you?" Knight stared at Mr. Cheng.

"Life is going to become much more difficult for all of us - especially you, my friend. I am not exactly sure what will happen, but you will survive. Wei-chen, do not look so worried. We will all survive." Mr. Cheng focused on the teapot and poured more tea for the three of them.

Less than a week later Wei-chen paced the temple courtyard, waiting for Mr. Cheng to finish a session with the novices. Finally, shadows shifted past the second-story windows as young monks filed from the classroom. When

Wei-chen entered the room, the scholar stood at a window overlooking the courtyard. He appeared tired, something Wei-chen seldom witnessed.

"I have been waiting for you, Wei-chen."

"I could not leave work early. Gabriel was not there today. When I walked past his desk, his secretary seemed upset. I was supposed to meet him last night but he never came to the noodle shop. He is not the only one missing. I think he was rounded up. I only heard part of the BBC report."

"When I arrived at the temple this morning, I learned the Japanese are rounding up enemy aliens and sending them to internment camps. The men are being taken first. Women and children will soon follow. Let me see what I can find out. Meet me at the teahouse in three days. By then I will know where he is. Do you have access to a shortwave radio?"

"Yes, I have one. When the survey of personal property was ordered last fall, no one I know turned over their radio sets or cameras to the government."

Three days later, between sips of oolong tea, Mr. Cheng spoke in calm, measured tones. "Seven internment camps have been set up. Gabriel Knight is at Lungwha, near the airport where a bombed-out college has been converted into one of the camps. The friend who located Gabriel said visits will be allowed but you should wait several weeks before going there. You will not be allowed into the camp but you will be able to approach the barbed wire fence surrounding it."

"Thank you for locating him. Did you learn anything about conditions in the camps?"

"No, I did not. I expect they are grim."

When Wei-chen left, he felt too unsettled to be alone so he walked to the bakery. Usually Mrs. Mera was delighted to see him but this day she appeared distracted.

"Hello, Wei-chen. Come in. I will make some tea." She gave him a quick hug.

"Has something happened? Where is Max?" He looked around the shop.

"He found a job in Hongkew. When the Japanese ordered Jewish refugees from Eastern Europe to move to Hongkew, he had to quit. Now they live in a bombed-out tenement. Refugees who arrived before 1937, like Jakov and me, will be allowed to remain in the International Settlement and French Concession.

"Did you know the puppet government refers to these refugees as stateless persons? Twenty thousand of them are being forced into an area less than two square kilometers, an area already densely populated by Chinese. People are living on top of each other. Hundreds of these families set up successful businesses outside of Hongkew - grocery stores, coffee houses, pharmacies. Now they have been forced to close them. Their investments are lost. It is all so very wrong." Mrs. Mera's gaze dropped to her folded hands.

Wei-chen wasn't used to seeing Mrs. Mera this upset. She seemed shaken to the core. "You are right. It is unjust, but I believe they will find a way to survive. Several streets in Hongkew are already referred to as Little Vienna. We all need to remain strong until Japan is defeated." Still watching her, he continued, "I think there is something else you have not said."

"At the Jewish community meeting, they reported the Nazis are uprooting Jews across Europe and sending them to death camps," Mr. Jakov said, entering from the back room. "And they want the Japanese to kill all the Jews here."

"That is madness."

"Hitler is a madman. Shortly after Japan invaded China, Heinrich Himmler - the head of the Gestapo - made it clear the Nazis wanted Japan to begin exterminating Jews. When the Japanese did not comply, Himmler sent Josef Meisinger, a Gestapo officer, here last summer. Meisinger became known as the Butcher of Warsaw after he ordered the extermination of one-hundred-thousand Jews in that city.

"He was sent here to do the same thing." Mr. Jakov's voice carried restrained anger. "His plan was to round up Jews on Rosh Hashanah when we would be in synagogues. Then he proposed to dispose of us by various means - sending us out to sea on boats without food or water, working us to death in salt mines or forcing us into concentration camps. None of it has been implemented. It seems the Japanese believe Jews have global influence because of their international finances. They have not wanted any part of Himmler's designs for us."

"At least for the moment," Mrs. Mera added.

In October Wei-chen biked to the Lungwha internment camp. Mrs. Mera always sent bread to supplement Knight's daily ration of congee and water. Today Wei-chen also carried a moon cake. In their few years together, he and Hui-lan always celebrated the Moon Festival by themselves. After her death, Knight and Mr. Cheng made sure he was never alone. They always went to dinner at The Confucian, where Wei-chen always gave Knight a moon cake, even though Knight didn't like them. The little ritual had become an ongoing joke between them.

Approaching the fence, Wei-chen heard one of the Americans call, "Knight, your friend is here."

Knight shuffled across the compound, collarbones protruding sharply above the neckline of his tattered shirt. Wei-chen had lost weight too, but his daily regimen of rationed rice and stale vegetables still kept him relatively healthy.

"It is good to see you." Wei-chen shoved the moon cake and some bread through the fence. He tried to hide his alarm. Leaning against the fence for support, Knight was noticeably weaker since Wei-chen's last visit.

"Say, what is this? A moon cake. I am so hungry I just might eat it." Knight smiled and examined the cake.

"What do you do with the bread Mrs. Mera sends you? Do you give it all away?"

"No, not all of it. Besides, sometimes I get extra food when wealthy Chinese visit their children's former teachers. They frequently bribe the guards to give food to the inmates. Why do you ask?"

"You are losing weight. Each time I see you there is less of you," Wei-chen said.

"Your clothes hang on you too."

"I know, and Mrs. Mera's dresses droop on her. There used to be a surplus of bread in the bakery, but now the shelves are mostly empty. I wonder how much longer we will have to live this way."

"Cooper, an acquaintance who says he's a former GI, has smuggled in a shortwave radio. Last night he picked up a BBC report. The Americans have dealt Japan some major defeats in the Pacific."

"It cannot happen fast enough. Mrs. Mera saw Max at a funeral. Because the cemeteries are outside Hongkew, Jews may obtain permits to attend funerals. Anyway, Max told her disease is rampant in Hongkew because of the overcrowding, especially for the poor who live in public housing centers. Max has a girlfriend who is also from Austria. This makes Mrs. Mera happy. She believes love is the grand solution."

"Perhaps it is."

"Yes, perhaps it is." Wei-chen resisted thinking about Hui-lan and why things had happened the way they did. He could do that on the ride back to the city. But something Knight said flagged his attention. "What do you mean, this Cooper says he is a former GI? It sounds as if you do not believe him."

"I think he's an American spy. He seems to have underground contacts. More than several times I have seen him talking at the fence with a Chinese man. Afterwards, Cooper always knows more about the war effort. I would wager the Chinese fellow is in contact with agents who travel between Shanghai and Free China. At some point the Japanese are going to be driven out of China, and the masters are assembling the pieces for a grand game of chess."

"You are being obscure. Which masters?"

"I am still piecing things together, but let's start with the foreigners who dominated Shanghai for most of the last one hundred years. After the war they will try to reinstate their former businesses and reoccupy their villas, but they will be in for a rude awakening. The old order is being uprooted. Once the Japanese are out of the way, the Nationalists and Communists are the real masters who will go head-to-head for ultimate control of China. That will be the grand game. Perhaps you should see what Mr. Cheng thinks about it."

On the long bike ride back to Shanghai, Wei-chen mulled over his conversation with Knight. Over the past six years he had witnessed Shanghai's beautiful women wither, camouflaging themselves in drab clothing, hiding themselves from the predatory stares of soldiers. But now, looking back over the past six months, he could see the city was deteriorating at an increasing pace. With Japan's military position collapsing, rotting garbage filled the streets. Instead of being picked up each morning, corpses were left to decompose for days. Rationing of basic staples and escalating prices starved the poor on an ever larger scale. Hunger gnawed constantly at Wei-chen. The Empire of the Rising Sun was disintegrating.

Then he thought about Knight's grand game theory. Not withstanding concerns about corruption, Wei-chen was sure Chiang Kai-shek would be reinstated as head of China's government. Western countries would continue to back him. But he agreed with Knight that it was only a matter of time until Mao Tse-Tung challenged Chiang. Wei-chen wished he could have faced whatever was coming with Hui-lan.

When Wei-chen talked to Mr. Cheng, the scholar's face turned somber. A soft breeze stirred leaves in the temple courtyard, sending them skittering across the stone. Wei-chen concentrated on the scratchy sound and remained silent.

Mr. Cheng's eyelids dropped halfway. "Gabriel Knight is right. When this war ends, the Communists and Nationalists will resume their struggle for control of China."

"Who do you think will eventually win?"

"We must finish with the Japanese occupation first. Within two years they will be gone. Then we can consider China's future."

Wei-chen knew his old friend saw more than he was willing to discuss. With a deep sadness registering on his face, the scholar looked away.

Springtime, borne on gentle winds from the south, caressed Wei-chen's face. He prayed they were the harbinger of summer winds carrying American planes to the north. When he got off his bicycle at the camp fence, Knight broke away from a small group. Although gaunt and covered in tattered clothes, the group still struck a defiant air. Concern dropped from Wei-chen's shoulders. His friend and his Yankee compatriots were going to survive.

"The camp guards look nervous today." Wei-chen passed a food parcel through the fence.

"We've noticed the same thing. And there is something else. The young soldiers have been pulled from the camp. Now most of the guards are older or disabled. Our rations have been cut again, but so have those of the guards. We are heartened by it because it means Japan's war machine is imploding."

Wei-chen stared at a little boy near the British dormitories. "What is wrong with that child?"

"It's rickets. Not enough calcium in his diet. Beriberi is becoming more prevalent in the camp because of the lack of vitamin B. Lack of treatment for malaria is a problem too."

Wei-chen took a hard look at Knight and decided that, other than malnourishment, he wasn't suffering from any disease. "Is mail still being delivered?"

"Yes. Some food packages are still being received too, but we think the guards keep most of the food for themselves. I wrote Hannah and suggested she start sending mail through you. I didn't think you would mind being our courier. I expect the mail system will break down as things get worse."

"Of course, I am glad to do that. Do you need writing paper?"

"No thanks. I still have some left. I have a letter for Hannah. Would you please mail it." Wei-chen nodded and Knight continued, "Have you had any difficulty biking here? I mean, does anyone try to take your bike or the small packages you bring?"

"No. Look at my clothes and this rusted bike. I am in the same straits as most Chinese."

"Some very desperate peasants have been gathering outside the gates. I am concerned about your safety, biking all the way out here."

"I appreciate your concern, but I am not worried. I have noticed the people across from the gates. Everyone needs more food."

That summer Wei-chen noted each time he saw silver glints sparkling in the sky. Dreams of freedom returned on the wings of American planes flying high overhead. In November bombers began delivering their payloads on the streets of Shanghai and its outskirts. The sorties both exhilarated and terrified Wei-chen.

In mid-February 1945 Wei-chen biked to the camp to mark the Lunar New Year with Knight. Ever since the the bombing runs had started, Wei-chen biked to Lungwha only once a month. Everyone he knew vacillated between desperation and hope - desperation about avoiding death during the air raids and hope that the raids would finally bomb Japan into submission.

"May prosperity be with you," Wei-chen called to Knight, leaning his bike against the fence. He radiated hope, knowing this Lunar New Year would bring liberation from Japan.

"I wish you the same. Next year we will celebrate in a free Shanghai."

"Yes, we will have dinner at The Confucian." Looking across the camp to the airfield, Wei-chen noticed new piles of rubble. "There have been many bombing runs since I was last here."

"Yes, it's no longer a quiet neighborhood."

Wei-chen smiled, relieved Knight's sense of humor hadn't been starved out of him.

"They use captured Chinese to fill in the craters, but they can't keep up with the frequency of the bomb drops. There are fewer fighter planes on the airfield now."

"You should see what Shanghai looks like - sandbags banked around buildings, trenches lining the streets. There is a curfew from sundown to sunrise. The city looks scarred and gashed - like its people. They are bombing Hongkew too."

"Have you heard anything about resistance personnel coming into the city? Cooper said resistance troops, both Nationalist and Communist, have been drifting back to this area."

"He is right. Some collaborators have been killed on the streets. Mr. Cheng heard resistance units are responsible for the killings. Wang Ching-wei's regime is breaking down. Oh, I almost forgot. I have a letter from your sister." Wei-chen removed a crumpled envelope from his jacket.

"And here is one for you to send her. I have asked her to stop writing. It's becoming too dangerous for you to continue biking here."

"I am still fine with it. I like bearing messages for you. It is the least I can do. In fact, it is about all I can do."

"Well, I think the life of the message bearer is more important than what he is delivering. Really, the situation is becoming more unstable. Late at night people are moving through the countryside and they are armed."

"You mean you want me to stop coming here completely?"

"Yes. Heaven knows I look forward to your visits, but it is time to stop them. Resistance forces aren't the only ones moving about at night. There are profiteers who are setting themselves up for postwar life. They are armed and ruthless. Cooper said they will kidnap people and make them fence goods. I don't want you coming across them."

"So when will I see you?"

"I will find you when the war is over and it's safe to come into the city. You must not return here again." Knight stretched his fingers through the fence and interlaced them with Wei-chen's. "Good-bye for now."

"I had better leave before it starts to get dark. Stay safe, Gabriel."

Wei-chen couldn't stifle his concerns. What if a bombing raid hit the camp? How would Knight make his way to the city? How long it would be until he could see him again?

In March Wei-chen biked to Lungwha. When he reached the fence, he saw Knight stumbling towards him.

"You had better have a good reason for coming here. I told you it isn't safe anymore."

"Of course, I have a good reason. You sound angry with me." Knight's brusque tone caught him off guard. Worn out from the ride and worn down from life in a war zone, Wei-chen looked at the ground.

"I am not angry. It's just that I am concerned about your safety. My God, I don't know what I would do if something happened to you. You are family to me."

Wei-Chen pulled out an envelope from his jacket. "This came in the mail. It was enclosed in a larger envelope with a note asking me to deliver it to you. Because it's from your Olivia, I decided you should see it."

Seeing the return address, Knight tore open the envelope. When he finished reading the letter, he crumpled to the ground, tears streaming down his face. "Here, Wei-chen. You may read it."

Sitting on his haunches, Wei-chen pulled the letter back through the fence. He took another look at Knight and began reading.

December 15, 1944

My dear Gabriel,

Since this horrible war began, I have followed events in Asia and hoped you left Shanghai while you still could. Finally I contacted Hannah. I have been worried about you ever since she told me you were in an internment camp. I suppose I should have known you would never leave China, but I wish you were in a safer place.

The past year has been an extremely difficult one. After our two sons enlisted in the military in 1942, Arthur followed them within six months. There has been a tremendous demand for medical personnel on the various fronts, and he felt compelled to serve our country.

This past May our elder son James was killed near Salerno, Italy. I can't tell you how difficult it has been knowing he will never return home. Of the three children, he was the most like me. I feel as if I am missing a piece of myself - a limb, an eye, my heart. If it were possible I would give my life in exchange for his.

I think James' death was equally as devastating for Arthur. It seemed to increase his determination to wipe Nazism from the face of the earth. In late July, two months after James' death, Arthur was killed by a sniper in a French village. Even now, nearly a year later, I believe the loss of them has not fully registered. Thank God my two other children are all right. My daughter lives nearby with her family, and my younger son has a safe assignment with the Navy in Hawaii. At least he assures me he is safe.

I know I am not alone in my pain. Families across North America, Europe and Asia are reeling from the same sense of loss. I take some comfort in believing their deaths will help destroy the darkness of Nazism. I have to believe there was a reason for them to die.

Because the war effort has culled people from all walks of life, doors have opened for many of us left at home. The past three years I have been working as an editor at a publishing firm. The job has been a godsend, forcing me to focus on something other than my sorrow.

Hannah assures me of your safety, but I can tell she is quite concerned about you. She is afraid the Japanese will retaliate when they ultimately leave Shanghai. They will not accept defeat gracefully.

I pray for your safekeeping. Over the years I have thought about you but, until these past months, did not feel free to write you. I also pray to see you again one day.

With love,
Olivia

Wei-chen refolded the letter and passed it back to Knight whose face glistened. Overwhelmed himself, Wei-chen sought for words to console Knight but came up with nothing. Finally he said, "I brought some paper in case you want to write a note."

"Thank you." Hands shaking, Knight took the pencil and paper from Wei-chen and leaned against the fence. He tried to write but then stopped. "My handwriting is too unsteady. Please write for me." Stopping every few words, Knight dictated to Wei-chen.

Dear Olivia,

I send my deepest sympathy to you. I cannot imagine the depth of your sorrow and am at a loss for words to comfort you. Actually it is you who comforts me. Even with everything you have been through, there is an underlying strength in your words.

You and Hannah must not worry about me. It is quite apparent Japan is losing the war. Ultimately, they will abandon the internment camps. When that happens, I will write again.

Japanese control of the countryside is breaking down. It is too dangerous for Wei-chen to continue coming to the camp. I have told him he must not return here. The next time you hear from me, I will be writing from Shanghai.

I will keep you in my thoughts and prayers.

With love,
Gabriel

"Wei-chen, you have to leave now. There have been bombing runs each afternoon. They keep pounding the airbase near the camp. I can't imagine what there is left to destroy. One more thing. When I last wrote Hannah, I told her I was getting enough food. If she writes you and asks about me, please confirm that I am fine. I know I look terrible. Your eyes can't lie. They have cut our rations again, but I will survive. Mr. Cheng said so, and he is always right.

"You took a risk bringing me Olivia's letter. I thank you for that but, if she or Hannah writes again, you must hold the letters for me. It might be months before the camp is liberated. I do not want you harmed. I truly have missed you." His fingers grasped Wei-chen's through the fence.

"I promise to wait for you in Shanghai. I have missed you too." When Wei-chen got on his bike, the road blurred in front of him. Knight's halting walk, gaunt face and projected bones alarmed him. He prayed Knight would have the strength to make it back to the city.

Wei-chen usually managed to suppress the thought of Hui-lan's last days, but Olivia's letter brought back with full force the immense loss of Hui-lan's death. Deep sadness accompanied him back to the city.

After the Allied victory in Europe, Wei-chen expected Japan to capitulate but they continued to fight on. Each day seemed interminable, as if the Empire of the Rising Sun were in some kind of time warp. Honoring his promise to not visit Knight became increasingly difficult.

Japan's refusal to surrender after atomic bombs were dropped on Hiroshima and Nagasaki astounded Wei-chen. Finally, on August 12, he listened while Radio Shanghai announced Japan's surrender. City residents were ordered to restrain themselves until the formal declaration by Emperor Hirohito on August 15.

Wei-chen forced himself to wait three more days and then went to Mr. Cheng's flat. "Japanese troops have been leaving the past several days. Why hasn't Gabriel returned? I think I should go to the camp."

"He said he would return when it was safe, and he will. Civil authority still has not been established. He will come to the city when the time is right."

"What if he is too weak to leave the camp? I am going there."

"That would be unwise - an act of friendship but also one of foolishness. I insist you have a cup of tea with me," Mr. Cheng ordered.

The insistence in Mr. Cheng's voice made Wei-chen relent. Just as he lifted the teacup, there was a knock at the door.

"Come in." Mr. Cheng opened the door and stepped aside.

There in the doorway stood Knight. Almost dropping the teacup, Wei-chen ran across the room. He embraced Knight, unashamed of the tears streaking his face. When Knight staggered, Wei-chen quickly released him.

"Please sit down, Gabriel. A cup of tea will do you good. I am pleased to see you, my friend." Mr. Cheng tried to hide it but shock registered across his face.

After they finished with their tea, the scholar said, "I think you should stay with me for several days. You could begin to restore your health and get some rest."

"That is kind of you, but I am sure I could find somewhere to stay through Jardine Matheson."

"I think Mr. Cheng is right. I will stop at the office and let them know you are here. I will bring back any paperwork you might need."

"Do I really look that bad?" Knight asked.

Wei-chen nodded in agreement with Mr. Cheng, presenting a firm barrier against Knight leaving the flat.

Fourteen

1948

Wei-Chen was meeting Knight and Mr. Cheng mid-afternoon, so he took his time walking to Jade Buddha Temple. The warm breeze ruffling the plane trees foreshadowed the moist summer winds soon to come, but that was not the only change underway. The lack of activity in the streets unsettled Wei-chen. Since the Lunar New Year, Shanghai's pace was noticeably less frenetic. For many families, the New Year's visits to ancestral homes differed from the usual reuniting of family. They became a time of farewells before relatives fled China. After three years of fighting since 1945, the civil war was coming to a head. The Communists were gaining control of the country.

When Wei-chen arrived at the courtyard entrance, he stopped short. His friends sat riveted in discussion. Gusts of wind collected persimmon blossoms at their feet. They took no more notice of the blossoms than they did of Wei-chen. He felt like an intruder.

Finally Mr. Cheng looked in his direction. "How long have you been standing there? Come join us."

The scholar's casual tone rang false. Wei-chen winced. For as long as he could remember, his friend had always been straightforward. "What are you talking about?"

"Just the latest twists in the political situation," Knight said. "I have forestalled this as long as possible, but it's time for me to consider leaving China."

Wei-chen's chest tightened. He forced himself to breathe evenly. For the past two years he was concerned it would come to this. Knight had been a fixture in his life for more than twenty-five years. Once he left, Wei-chen was sure he would never see him again. In an instant all of the losses he had endured - his parents, brothers, Auntie, Uncle and, above all, Hui-lan - hammered at his heart.

"The Nationalists are losing control of China. Western organizations are already pulling their people out. I will stay until the end of the summer, unless the government collapses before then."

"Foreigners will not be welcome here when the Communists take over, and those who have had close ties with them will be regarded with suspicion. At some point, the borders will be sealed and no one will be able to leave China. Those who can afford to are getting out now. Hong Kong is being deluged with refugees." Mr. Cheng looked directly at Wei-chen.

"I am well aware of that. Yesterday a friend at the consulate came to say good-bye. He and his wife finally secured enough money to move the family to Hong Kong. His wife was forced to sell family heirlooms."

"Have you thought about leaving?" Mr. Cheng asked.

"No. Why do you ask that?" Caught off guard, Wei-chen reacted more sharply than he meant to. Now he understood what they were discussing before he arrived. "I cannot imagine leaving here."

The old sage looked away with half-closed eyes. "It may take some time, but there will be drastic changes in China. Your long association with Westerners will make the Communists question your allegiance to their new government. Perhaps you do not realize it, but part of you has become quite westernized. Your thinking reflects this. You have many more years to live, years that could be lived freely."

"But what about you? What will happen to you?"

"I am an old man, too old to start a new life. Like bamboo that bends with the wind, I will survive. My connection with the temple will help me. Jade Buddha Temple has protection at the highest levels within the Communist Party."

"I cannot think about leaving now. I am still coming to terms with Gabriel's decision."

"It will be several months before I leave. We still have plenty of time to talk this through." After a moment Knight added, "If you decide you want to leave, I am quite sure I could arrange your passage to Hong Kong. St. John's football team will play there in a tournament this September. I know the head coach very well. I think he would let you travel as some sort of assistant for the team. It would afford you legal entry into Hong Kong."

"When the time is right, you will know the path you must take." Mr. Cheng spoke as if he already knew what Wei-chen's decision would be.

Wei-chen walked to the Romanovskys, blanketed in a cloud of emotion, too overwhelmed to think logically. Before he entered the bakery he stopped abruptly, stunned by the sign in the front window - Building to Let.

"Hello, Wei-chen. We have been hoping you would stop by." Mr. Jakov held open the door.

"What does this sign mean?"

"I will get Mera so we can explain this together."

When Mrs. Mera embraced him, Wei-chen stood transfixed, a wooden figure.

"Son of my heart, you seem to carry a great weight."

"My heart is heavy today. I came to tell you Gabriel Knight will return to America this summer. And I think you are about to tell me you will also be leaving."

"Please sit down. What you say is correct." Mr. Jakov pulled out a chair. "We will be joining our sons in the new country of Israel. We have three grandchildren we have never seen. We have no future in Shanghai. It is time for us to go."

Mrs. Mera was unusually quiet. She placed her hand over Wei-chen's and kneaded it.

Wei-chen swallowed hard and compressed his lips, forbidding tears to form. "Mr. Cheng and Gabriel think I should leave China. They believe the future will be harsh for many Chinese, especially for those like me who work for the United States government."

"I agree with them. We have been talking to our customers. Most of them are planning to leave. They expect a difficult restructuring of society when the Communists implement their grand designs. We experienced this in Russia. Once was enough," Mr. Jakov said.

"I understand."

When Wei-chen returned to his flat, he had no appetite for dinner. His virtual family was disintegrating. He stared out the bedroom window at the central courtyard. Two sparrows flitted about the persimmon tree building a nest. He wondered if a sole sparrow would go to all that work for just himself. How would he make a life for himself in Hong Kong?

Days before the Romanovskys left for Israel, Wei-chen went to the bakery to say good-bye. For the past twenty-eight years, they had provided constancy in his life. The thought of never feeling Mrs. Mera's hand smooth away his worries, never hearing Mr. Jakov's wise counsel, never seeing them again slowed his step. He dreaded having this emotional foundation stripped away.

As soon as he entered the shop, Wei-chen extended a gift to Mrs. Mera. "When you look at this, please remember me. I will never forget the two of you and how you treated me like a son."

"How could we have done otherwise? I still remember the first day you set foot in our shop. There has always been something endearing about you." Mrs. Mera slowly removed the silk remnant wrapped around the package. She gasped and bit her lip when she saw the small, delicately painted blue-and-white vase.

"I remember the day you bought this beautiful piece, perhaps twenty years ago. We will treasure it." Mr. Jakov swallowed Wei-chen in a bear hug. The baker blinked quickly, unable to say more.

The embrace startled Wei-chen and forced him to comprehend this farewell was equally as difficult for Mr. Jakov. The threesome sat at the front window. After the Romanovskys detailed their plans, Wei-chen told them he intended to leave for Hong Kong in September.

When he stood up to go, Mrs. Mera folded her arms around him. "I will always love you. I will think of you each day."

"I will do the same." Wei-chen returned her embrace.

"Wherever you are, I hope you will continue to paint. I believe in your talent," Mr. Jakov said.

Wei-chen walked halfway down the block and then turned around. The Romanovskys were still standing in the doorway, Mr. Jakov's arm around Mrs. Mera's shoulder. Wei-chen gave a final wave and willed his feet to walk home. He knew he should feel happy for the Romanovskys, but the pain of separation consumed his heart. This first significant leave-taking left him exhausted. He sank onto the chair at his kitchen table and stared out the window at nothing.

The following week Wei-chen stopped by Mr. Liu's porcelain shop and gave him a small painting he had finished earlier in the year, months before entertaining any thought of moving to Hong Kong. The decision to leave Shanghai had frozen his desire to create. Shoved in a corner, his brushes and canvases gathered dust.

"Thank you for this painting. You have captured the market with its lively, little stalls. I understand your reasons for leaving, but it saddens me. Perhaps one day you will return. Perhaps you will miss Shanghai too much." Mr. Liu looked down, pretending to study the leaves in his teacup.

Wei-chen looked away. "Time will tell. Perhaps I will return one day." Mr. Liu had been a staunch friend in the dark years after Hui-lan's death. Wei-chen tried to shut out his concern about being friendless in Hong Kong while competing for survival in a sea of refugees.

After customers came into the shop, Wei-chen left and took a tram to the Cathedral of St. Ignatius. He wanted to view the city from the tower one last time. Like rows in a garden, tree-lined streets radiated through the French Concession. The wind, shape shifting the leaves, held the promise of an evening rain. Wei-chen looked in each direction, committing the scene to memory.

He recalled the first time he took Hui-lan to the bell tower. She had looked radiant taking in the panorama. It was now eleven years since her passing. Over time the profound sadness of her death had distilled into an abiding sense of their love. Thinking about Hui-lan comforted him. Lost in the moment, he felt as if he could turn and talk to her.

When he descended the stairs he felt better, any doubts about fleeing to Hong Kong now erased from his mind. Stepping outside the cathedral, he remembered his conversation with the seer in the Chinese Quarter some twenty years ago. The sage predicted Wei-chen might leave Shanghai one day, and it was happening. How could he possibly have known this, Wei-chen wondered.

In early August Wei-chen rushed down the streets of the International Settlement, pushing through the sultry evening air, racing against the impending storm. When he reached The Confucian, rain cascaded in opaque sheets, rebounding from the sidewalk. Wei-chen rushed inside and scanned the candlelit restaurant.

Gabriel Knight, the only foreigner there and a head taller than the other customers, waved to him from the back corner. Wei-chen stared at his friend. The sadness piercing Knight's eyes mirrored the sorrow in Wei-chen's heart. It was their last dinner together. Knight was leaving in the morning. They ordered their favorite dishes, then spent the meal shoving food around with chopsticks, mounding little stacks on plates.

"I want to go over the details one more time. Everything is in place for you to travel with the football team. You will leave the first week of September," Knight said.

"Are you sure the coach is comfortable with being part of this ruse?"

"Yes, quite sure. Many years ago he was given a new lease on life by someone he didn't know. A benefactor he never met paid for his education. I think the coach considers this a favor returned, helping you begin a new life."

"What about your friend in Hong Kong?"

"Mrs. Sterling left Shanghai in 1937, just before the Japanese took over the city. She is expecting you to contact her at St. John's Catheral, the Episcopal church in Hong Kong's Central District. We will pass letters through her until you establish an address. Do you have any questions?"

"No. I am nervous, but I know this is the right thing to do."

"Here is something for you." Knight handed an envelope to Wei-chen.

"You cannot do this. I will not take money from you."

"Then look at it as an insurance policy. Don't use it unless you have to. I'm not sure how soon you will find work when you get to Hong Kong. I have no doubt everything will be fine in the long run. It's the short term I am concerned about. I want you to have a financial cushion. Please accept this for my peace of mind. If you don't use it, then give it to someone who needs it."

"All right. Thank you. I have something for you too." Wei-chen reached into his satchel and placed a small, finely-woven rattan container in front of Knight.

Knight smiled when he lifted the lid. "This is wonderful. I remember the day you found this celadon piece in the market. You always had your uncle's discriminating eye." Knight's smile faded. A veil of sadness swept across his features.

Wei-chen struggled to maintain his composure. He shared Knight's reluctance to express emotion but Knight had befriended him since his early years in Shanghai. Before the evening ended, Wei-chen was determined to tell Knight how much his steadfast friendship had meant.

"I still remember the first time I saw you. You were coming out of a porcelain shop in Dongtai Lu with a package tucked under your arm. Knowing that a foreigner patronized the shop made me decide to investigate the store. It reminded me of my Uncle's shop, and I ended up getting a job there. I like to think that fate played a hand in it because you have become like family to me, helping me through the most painful times of my life. I know you are too young to be my father, but I feel a filial connection with you. I never dreamed what a journey we would have together."

"Yes, we are family. You have shown me a loyalty that many parents don't experience. I regard you as the son I never had." Knight looked away for a moment. "Once I'm back in America, it's unlikely Olivia and Hannah will let me out of their sight. I am well aware I haven't fully recovered from the years in the internment camp."

Wei-chen nodded. The camp had taken a physical toll on Knight. Deep lines etched his face, his shock of black hair was completely silver, his once sinewy frame now gaunt. "I understand what you are trying to tell me. We will not see each other again. After all these years, there is no easy way to say good-bye. I will always carry you in my heart."

"As will I. But we cannot stop the flood tide of history." Knight signaled for the bill.

"Could we pretend we might see each other again one day? Perhaps you will marry Olivia and spend your honeymoon in Hong Kong."

Knight laughed until tears filled his eyes. "Yes, let's leave it at that. That is a wonderful way for us to end the evening. Walk with me to the taxi queue."

They sidestepped puddles in tandem, walking in the rhythm of long-held friendship. Glistening streets reflected strung lights dancing in the plane trees. Wei-chen didn't find them charming tonight.

When they reached the queue, Knight placed his hand on Wei-chen's shoulder. "You mentioned coming to the ship tomorrow but there is no need for that. You know how the crowds are. There will be lots of jostling."

Knight's hand steadied him these last moments. Wei-chen nodded non-committally, studying Knight's face, memorizing it.

"I will write when I'm back in Massachusetts. Let me know how you get on. I will miss you terribly." Knight gave Wei-chen a final embrace.

"And I will miss you." Wei-chen compressed his lips. Knight had never been one for displays of emotion. When he stepped into the taxi, Knight looked back with liquid eyes.

Wet streets mirrored the taxi's taillights. Wei-chen followed the red streaks until they disappeared in traffic. He felt empty inside. He walked home, shoulders hunched.

Early the next morning, despite Knight's advice, Wei-chen took a tram to the shipping pier. Cargo ships, junks and fishing boats negotiated the Whangpoo River in wild choreography. After jockeying his way to the end of the pier, Wei-chen studied the passengers lined against the ship railing and spotted Knight. Flinging his arm above his head, he willed Knight to look at him and finally succeeded. They waved to each other until the liner turned the bend in the Whangpoo.

———

On his last day in Shanghai, Wei-chen delivered his rattan scholar's basket to Mr. Cheng. Over the past week, he had condensed his belongings. All that remained in his flat were the valise and satchel he was taking to Hong Kong.

"What is this?" Mr. Cheng asked when he opened the door.

"The Romanovskys gave me this small chest years ago. It is filled with books. I cannot throw them away."

"Of course not. I will find appropriate homes for these little treasures. Come in and have some tea."

"The past weeks have been an exercise in detachment. All I have left are Uncle's Kuan-Yin statue, my paintings of Hui-lan, a few family photos and some clothes. Leaving possessions behind is one thing, but walking away from friends has been incredibly difficult." Wei-chen, dry-eyed and weary to the bone, slumped in a chair and watched the scholar pour tea.

"Do you remember a conversation we had many years ago, soon after we became acquainted?" Mr. Cheng asked.

Wei-chen smiled. "When you told me I might leave Shanghai one day?"

Mr. Cheng nodded. "Yes. As soon as I said it, I realized I should have kept my impressions to myself."

"Your prediction concerned me enough that I consulted an old seer in the Chinese quarter. At first, when I asked him about your prophecy, he was reluctant to comment. Finally he said that, after many years passed, it was quite possible I would leave Shanghai."

"Would you like to know what I think now?"

"Yes. Very much."

"Throughout your life, you have lost those most dear to you - parents and brother, your auntie and uncle, then your beloved Hui-lan. Now the Romanovskys and Gabriel Knight have departed, and my days are numbered.

Your heart has sustained many losses. When you arrive in Hong Kong, you will be more than a political refugee. You will be a refugee of the heart.

"One of our adages says, keep a tree in your heart and perhaps the singing bird will come. I have no doubt one day the singing bird will come to you and fill your days with harmony. There will be some difficulties while you establish a new life, but you must persevere. Do not despair. You are making the right choice."

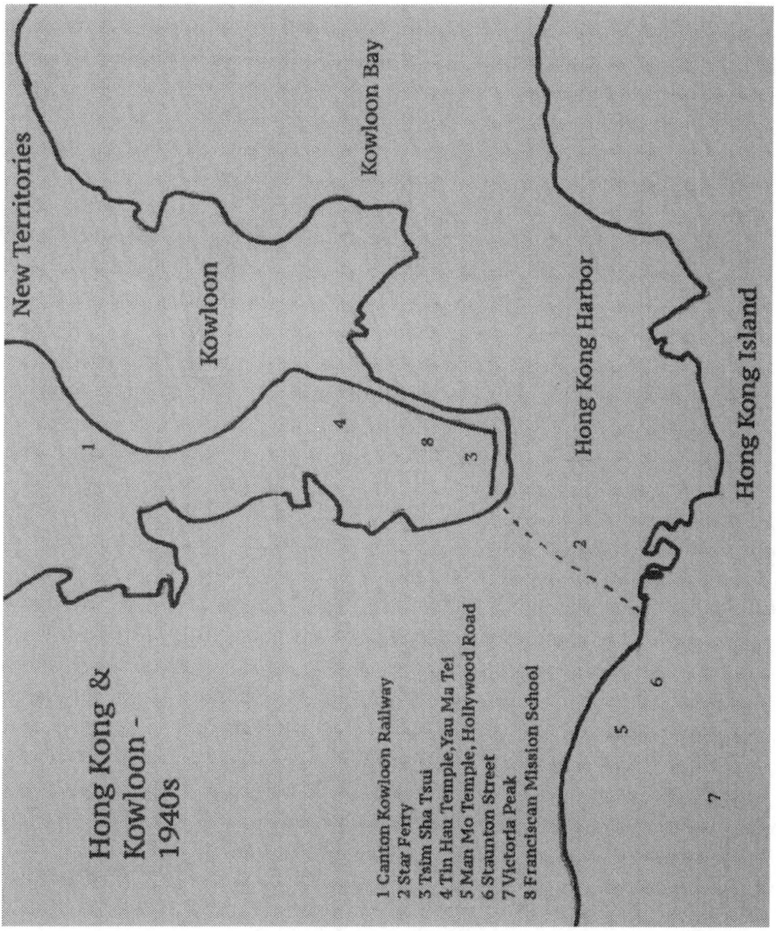
Hong Kong & Kowloon - 1940s
1 Canton Kowloon Railway
2 Star Ferry
3 Tsim Sha Tsui
4 Tin Hau Temple, Yau Ma Tei
5 Man Mo Temple, Hollywood Road
6 Staunton Street
7 Victoria Peak
8 Franciscan Mission School
New Territories
Kowloon
Kowloon Bay
Hong Kong Harbor
Hong Kong Island
1
2
3
4
5
6
7
8

HONG KONG

Fifteen

1948

Wei-chen stood at the railing until the Bund disappeared from view, then ensconced himself in a deck chair. For hours he endeavored to read a book about Hong Kong, poring over street maps of Hong Kong Island and Kowloon.

He tried to focus on the future but his mind played tricks on him. Faces of co-workers he enjoyed and friends he would never see again shape shifted above the pages. Doubt hovered at the edge of his consciousness, making a pest of itself. Like a concerto theme, Mr. Cheng's comment about his being a refugee of the heart played repeatedly in his thoughts. During the short voyage Wei-chen ate little. Adrenalin fueled his days. His sweat carried the scent of it, just as it had after Hui-lan's death. He was battling for survival, leaping into the unknown without loved ones near him.

Sultry, soporific air clung to the ship as it neared Hong Kong. When the first of the territory's small islands emerged above the horizon, Wei-chen packed away the book. The serenity of the scene captured his emotions, calming him. A fishing village curved along a bay. Boats lined the piers, nets strung like spider webs across the sterns. An old temple stood on a promontory. He had read most of the temples were dedicated to Tin Hau, the patron of fishing people. New gods for a new country.

After passing Lamma and Lantau islands, the large sentries outside Hong Kong, the ship plowed into the harbor. The view mesmerized him. Kowloon's steep hills - the nine dragons that gave Kowloon its name - marched in ascending ridges to the New Territories. On the harbor's south side, Hong Kong's Victoria Peak ascended steeply. Like incense smoke, clouds spiraled into the sky.

The scene seemed familiar to him. Then it all flashed back to him. After his first class with Professor Zill, Wei-chen went to bed tormented by the drawing exercise with the human skull, which had reminded him of the horror of Hui-lan's death. In the middle of the night, a vivid dream revealed an island wreathed in clouds. He had awakened with a profound sense of security, sensing the island was the pathway to his future. Because of the intensity of the image, he sketched the island that night. Now, along with several rolled-up paintings, that sketch was packed in his suitcase. It seemed providential. He took it as confirmation that he was on the right path.

Shanghai's Whangpoo riverfront was frenetic, but it paled in comparison with the activity that now sprawled before him. Thousands of junks maneuvered between the ferries crisscrossing the harbor. Ocean-going vessels disgorged passengers and cargo at the piers. A ship officer pointed out the typhoon shelter at Yau Ma Tei that safeguarded the small junks of the Tanka people, boat people who spent their entire lives on the water, their young children secured with tether lines to the boats.

After clearing customs Wei-chen hired a runner in the rickshaw queue, directing him to St. John's Cathedral. Colonial buildings and godowns - old commercial warehouses - lined the harbor's edge. Not as imposing as the Bund, Wei-chen thought, but an intense energy of unbridled enterprise charged the air. The church lay just uphill from the harbor, near the base of the Peak Tram Line.

When he walked through the gate, he stopped and gazed at the verdant grounds behind the church. Just then a door opened in a small building on his left.

"Nei hou. May I help you?" a young Chinese woman asked.

"Nei hou." Wei-chen tried to mimic her Cantonese. "I am looking for Mrs. Sterling. My name is Chan Wei-chen."

"Please come in. I will find Mrs. Sterling for you."

The young woman had responded in Mandarin. He felt grateful. It would take time to master Cantonese. He paced the front room, nervous, telling himself not to expect too much from this meeting.

"Good morning, Mr. Chan." Mrs. Sterling entered the room and extended her hand.

British accent. He didn't remember Knight telling him the family was English. "Good morning, Mrs. Sterling. I am a friend of Gabriel Knight. I believe he wrote to you about me."

"Yes, of course. Come back to my office. We'll sort things out over a cup of tea." After a few pleasantries about his voyage, Mrs. Sterling got down to business. "I assume you need a place to live and some sort of work."

"Yes. I would appreciate any advice you could give me." Wei-chen tried to strike the right tone and not give any hint of the desperation tugging inside him.

"I have no doubt you will manage to build a new life in Hong Kong. Hundreds of thousands of people have done it over the past decade. However, having said that, refugees have overwhelmed Hong Kong. At the end of the war, half a million refugees were sleeping in the streets. Now most of the homeless live in squatters' quarters on the hills above the city. Did you notice them on your way here?"

Wei-chen shook his head no. He didn't like the drift of the conversation.

"Shanties cover the hillsides above Wan Chai District, not far from here. It is a precarious way of life. Heavy rains, especially the black rains we have here, cause devastating mudslides. I assume you have money for lodging."

"Yes, I have enough to last a while but I hope to find work quickly."

"Gabriel Knight mentioned you worked at the United States Consulate General for quite some time. An acquaintance of mine works at the Consulate General here. The last time I spoke with her, she mentioned they were turning away job applicants. So I am not sure you would have any success there. You are going to think I'm all gloom and doom, but I want to warn you the influx of mainlanders has stymied Hong Kong's economy. Because of this you might encounter some resentment from local people as you search for a job. If the consulate doesn't work out, do you have any other skills?"

"I worked for Jardine Matheson's Shanghai office during the war. Perhaps a trading company would hire me. I am willing to do almost anything to get a toehold." Even if the Consulate General were hiring, he was in Hong Kong on a temporary visa and couldn't apply for a position.

"Do you have a place to stay?"

"No, I was hoping you could recommend someplace safe and inexpensive."

"Here is the address of a boarding house on the Kowloon side. It's in Jordan District, not far from the Star Ferry terminal."

"Thank you. Before I leave, I have a request. Gabriel Knight said he would write to me in care of St. John's Cathedral. Is that all right?"

"Yes, of course. I'll write down our office hours. Please stop by any time. One of those looks rather heavy." Mrs. Sterling pointed to Wei-chen's larger bag.

"Yes, it is a bit heavy. It holds some family belongings I want to keep."

"If you wish to leave that valise, I would be glad to store it in my office. I wish I could do more for you."

"Thank you. I would appreciate that. Until I find a proper place to live, it will be a relief to know these things are in a safe place."

"When you come to check for mail, please ask for me. I am interested in following your progress."

Apprehension trailed Wei-chen onto the ferry, crowding him at the railing. Mrs. Sterling's comments unsettled him, but he was determined to succeed in building a new life, just as he had in Shanghai. He didn't feel desperate, not yet.

By mid-October, Wei-chen still hadn't found work. Mrs. Sterling was right about the hiring situation. Only local hires were being considered. The hotels, restaurants and laundries had a surplus of workers. He felt invisible in his new homeland. For the fifth week Wei-chen left the church office empty-handed with no letter from Knight. Not since Hui-lan's death had he felt this forsaken. Why did Knight and Mr. Cheng ever advise him to come here. His new existence was like a bad dream.

On the ferry back to Kowloon, Wei-chen counted his remaining money. He stopped at the train station and looked at the schedules, debating whether to return to Shanghai. He decided to give himself one more week to find work. The only way he could manage to stay another week and still have return fare to Shanghai was to rent a bed space.

Stopping at several buildings with bed spaces was a baptism in despair for him. The conditions appalled him - stench, filthy cages enclosing the beds, managers with eyes like birds of prey. Exhausted and discouraged, Wei-chen walked to the Tin Hau Temple in Yau Ma Tei. After making an offering at the main altar, he sat outside on a bench. Several men were playing checkers nearby. He envied them their comradeship and sense of normalcy. While his mind raced through possible solutions, always running into dead ends, his pulse spiked.

Hours passed. The checker players left the temple grounds. Wei-chen felt someone watching him and looked over at the side altar. A man, whom he assumed worked at the temple, nodded to him. Wei-chen nodded in response, and the man walked over to him.

"Nei hou." The man spoke in the dialect of Wei-chen's village.

"Nei hou," Wei-chen responded, studying the man. It was the first time anyone had approached him since his arrival.

"Forgive my impertinence, but there is a look of desperation about you. Judging from your clothes and that small bag, I assume you need a place to stay."

The man's eyes were those of an honest man. "You are right. I need a place to sleep tonight. The bed spaces I looked at today did not appear safe."

"I know a place where you and your belongings will be secure. Other refugees stay there. Follow me."

Wei-chen fell in behind the man and followed him through Yau Ma Tei's crowded streets. The man turned around every so often to make sure

Wei-chen was still behind him. After several blocks, they turned into an alleyway. Clusters of people were hunched over open fires, cooking their evening meals.

The man pulled up short at a doorway. A shop sign hanging beside the door said Canton Laundry in bright red letters. "The laundry is on the ground floor. The upper two floors are filled with bed spaces. You will be safe here."

Wei-chen looked at the man's kind face. It was difficult to gauge his age. "Many times, thank you."

"You are welcome."

Wei-chen rang the buzzer. When he turned around, the man was gone. He looked up and down the alley. Other than families hovering over their small fires, no one was there. How the man could have disappeared so quickly puzzled Wei-chen.

"Nei hou, may I help you?" An elderly man speaking in Cantonese held the door partially open.

"Nei hou. I understand there are bed spaces in this building. I would like to rent a space if one is available."

The man assessed Wei-chen head to foot. "Yes. Come in. We have room for you."

Wei-chen trailed the old gentleman up to the first floor. When he entered the room, relief washed over him. The wire cages were stacked two high. The room was clean and fresh air wafted in through windows on the back wall.

"There are two spaces available. Perhaps you would prefer the one near the window?"

"Yes, thank you."

"Your bag will be safe in the wire space. Here is the key for the lock. I am Mr. Kwan. I live on the ground floor and manage the building for the owner. Do you have any questions?"

"I am Mr. Chan. I arrived from Shanghai over a month ago and need work. If you have any suggestions for me, I would be most appreciative." Wei-chen kept his voice steady, trying to give no clue as to his desperation.

"Let me think about it. We will talk in the morning."

Wei-chen unlocked the wire door, climbed in and shoved his bag to the back of the space. He still had ample room to stretch out full length and sit up without hitting the limits of the wire mesh enclosure.

The next morning Wei-chen waited near the building entrance. Within an hour Mr. Kwan came outside.

"Good morning. Will you join me for tea? I have some possibilities to discuss with you." Mr. Kwan led Wei-chen to a teashop around the corner and ordered jasmine tea for them. "Last night I wrote a letter of introduction for you to carry. I know the managers of these businesses. They might be looking for workers." He handed Wei-chen a list of restaurants and hotels.

"I cannot thank you enough." Wei-chen felt the wind at his back for the first time since his arrival.

"As for that, when you find work, you may take me to tea."

Wei-chen spent the better part of the day pursuing Mr. Kwan's suggestions. The leads evaporated like morning mist. Late in the afternoon he went to the Tin Hau Temple, looking for the man who led him to the cage home. He sat on a bench until dark, but the man never appeared. He walked back to his bed space, fighting despondency and hunger.

That night Wei-chen shot up in bed around three in the morning, completely disoriented, heart racing. After several moments he got his bearings but couldn't shake off the intensity of the dream. He lay back down and recalled every detail.

He had been walking in the Ghost Market and then abruptly found himself packed into a dimly-lit hall with hundreds of other people. Caught in the middle of the crowd, he peered through the men and women in front of him. At the far end of the room, two men sat behind a long table. A scale stood on the table, pans suspended on either side of its center beam.

Wei-chen looked around. People stood immobile with clenched jaws. His gut tensed, sensing danger. He tried to escape but his feet were frozen. One of the men behind the table called out names from a list, and the other man tended the scale. An old man stumbled forward when his name was called and stood before the table. The scale tipped to the right when the man's good deeds were recited and tipped to the left when his bad deeds were detailed. Eventually his good acts outweighed the bad, and the right side of the scale remained lower. Looking immensely relieved, the old gentleman left the room through a door on the right.

After watching several more such reckonings, Wei-chen comprehended this was Judgment Day. Damned individuals were forced to leave through a door on the left. When he heard his name called out, Wei-chen tried to back away but the crowd pushed him forward. He stood before the table, hands trembling. When the judge weighed his deeds, the left side of the scale tipped. Acid burned the pit of Wei-chen's stomach.

At that moment a loud scraping noise came from the back of the room. Wei-chen turned around. A destitute man was pushing open a large wooden door and slowly approaching the table with something draped over his arms. The man stopped at the scale and held out a jacket.

Wei-chen recognized the jacket. It was the one Hui-lan convinced him to buy, the one he wrapped around a dying man in the streets of Shanghai. The bitter cold of that evening, the brutality of the occupation and the despair he felt after Hui-lan's death coursed through him. He looked at the scale and watched it shift to the right side.

Now fully awake, Wei-chen looked through the wire mesh. The hotel sign across the street cast red light through the window, splaying an arrow shape across his mattress. His heart rate slowed. The dream's message was one of deliverance. He believed the arrow pointed to his future, that the bitter days were gone and the sweet ones had arrived.

The next morning when Wei-chen was leaving the building, Mr. Kwan stopped him in the doorway. "I have some good news for you. The manager of a small hotel on Nanking Road told me one of his workers left. He needs someone to work the night desk. I recommended you. What do you think?"

"When could I start?"

"Tonight."

A month later, Wei-chen moved out of the wire bed space to a small flat on Reclamation Street. Living in a neighborhood teeming with refugees, all seeking to reclaim their lives, comforted him. The next day he took a ferry to Hong Kong island to retrieve his bag from Mrs. Sterling.

"Good morning, Mr. Chan. I've been wondering when you would stop by. I have a letter for you."

The return address was Knight's. Relief and anticipation seized Wei-chen. "Do you mind if I open it now?"

"Not at all. Here's a letter opener. I will get some tea for us."

Wei-chen raced through the letter, then reread it a second time, savoring it.

October 5, 1948

Dear Wei-chen,

I apologize for not writing sooner. Hannah and Olivia thought I looked abominable when I arrived. It has been their mission to restore me to their perception of what I should look like. I don't know if this sixty-five-year-old body is capable of meeting their expectations, but I am trying. It has taken a while but I finally have my affairs in order. Over the years I wired money to a bank account here, so my financial situation is sound.

I hope things have come together for you. Your last letter concerned me. I didn't expect it would be so difficult for you to find work. Perhaps you have resolved that by now, but I have an opportunity for you.

A friend of Olivia's owns a toy company and would like to import some dolls from Asia. When Olivia asked if I had any suggestions, I remembered the doll you made for the Romanovskys. Mera treasured it. If you are interested, send a sample doll - or several for that matter - to me. If her friend likes the dolls, Olivia will negotiate the contract terms. She is protective of you, and she hasn't even met you.

I am enclosing a bank draft. It's a gift. If you don't need the funds, give them to someone who does. Let me know how you are getting on. Not a day passes that I don't think about you and wonder how your new life is proceeding.

With best wishes,
Gabriel Knight

"Is everything all right?" Mrs. Sterling asked.

"Yes. It's from Gabriel Knight. I am touched by his generosity." Wei-chen looked out the window, eyes glistening. "I appreciate your kindness too - storing my bag, receiving my mail. I am not sure how I would have managed without your help."

"I wish I could have done more." Mrs. Sterling poured tea, and they discussed Knight's business proposal. "What did the doll you made in Shanghai look like?"

"I sewed the little doll out of muslin, then used silk remnants for her jacket and pants and black yarn for her hair. My favorite part was painting her face. She had a sweet expression."

"If you go ahead with this, I would like to see your creations."

After depositing the bank draft, Wei-chen headed down Hollywood Road to Man Mo Temple. The dark, smoky interior enveloped him like a cloak. He burned joss sticks at the main altar and, for the first time in months, felt a hint of serenity. The pungent scent of a century's worth of offerings imbued the temple with a sense of timelessness. Disengaging from the physical world, he drifted into a cloud of contemplation.

When he finally stepped outside, shadows bled across the courtyard into the street. He hurried down the hill to the fabric shops in Sheung Wan. By the time he finished selecting fabrics and notions, an indigo sky framed Hong Kong's peaks. Crossing back to Kowloon, he stood at the ferry stern. Choppy waves fractured the reflections of bobbing junks. Like strung lanterns, streetlights twinkled against the flanks of Victoria Peak.

On the Kowloon side, he stopped at a teashop and ordered jasmine tea. The scent triggered the memory of the first time he and Hui-lan went to Quiet Heart Teashop. Nostalgia kept him company while he sipped tea and composed a note to Knight.

Dear Gabriel,

I was pleased and relieved to hear from you. With your sister and Olivia hovering over you, there is no question you will recover from your years in the internment camp. As for me, it took longer than I expected to find work. By now you should have received my letter telling you about my job and giving you my new address.

I cannot thank you enough for the bank draft and your continuing support. Your letter was a source of inspiration for me. This afternoon I bought supplies to make some doll samples. Please thank Olivia for this opportunity. If things do not work out with her friend, I will pursue the business here. Mrs. Sterling thinks it is a good idea.

It was good to hear from you and know the women are remaking you to their specifications. Please write soon and tell me about the new life you are building.

With best wishes, your faithful friend,
Wei-chen

*F*or two weeks Wei-chen worked on the samples in every spare minute, dreaming of his future. With the last stitch, his hope of making a livelihood from the dolls crystallized into the belief that it was possible. He decided to name his company W. C. Chan Creations Ltd. Before shipping the samples, he showed them to Mrs. Sterling.

"They are wonderful." She carefully lifted the dolls from the packaging. "I can't decide which one I like better. The Star Ferry man with his blue uniform and white hat is charming, and the little Chinese girl with her thick black braids is adorable. If the American company isn't interested in your dolls, I think they would sell very well in Hong Kong." Her brow scrunched.

Wei-chen knew she was thinking about potential customers. Like a butterfly flitting above a flower, hope hovered in his heart.

He regarded the enthusiastic responses of Mrs. Sterling and her staff as a harbinger of success, but the fear of rejection shadowed him. He struggled to practice detachment, to not get too attached to his vision that sparkled like a shooting star against the midnight sky.

Six weeks later Wei-chen tore open a letter from Knight.

Dear Wei-chen,

Congratulations! Olivia has reached an agreement with Mr. Daniels, the owner of the toy company. I have enclosed his order for 100 Star Ferry Men and 100 Chinese Girl dolls. Assuming they sell as expected, you will receive future orders.

Also, she set up a bank account for you. Enclosed is a draft from that account. Mr. Daniels has paid half down and will pay the rest when the dolls are delivered. Of course, he would like the dolls as soon as possible.

This should keep you busy.

With best wishes and affection,
Gabriel

Wei-chen was astounded at the order size. It was too large for him to fill within a short time, but he was prepared. He had spent the past several weeks observing people who lived in the neighborhood, most of them refugees like him. Two older women who were treated with deference by the younger ones had caught his attention. He decided to approach these de facto leaders with a business proposition.

"Nei hou. It is such a beautiful morning."

"Nei hou. It would be even more beautiful if we could find work," one of them said.

"Yes. It is a difficult time for many of us. Actually, I am hoping you could give me some advice. I have just received an order for some dolls I designed. I need people who can cut patterns and sew. Do you know anyone who could do this?"

Both women eyed him carefully, peering into his heart. They turned to each other and spoke softly. "It is possible we could help you, but we have some questions," this spoken by the woman who first replied to him. Her friend nodded in support.

"Shall we go to a teahouse? I will try to answer all your questions." After a candid conversation, Wei-chen said, "I cannot guarantee how long anyone will be employed, but I hope the first order will lead to many more. I plan to share any profits with the workers so the more orders we receive, the more money everyone makes."

Within days six seamstresses were sewing in Wei-chen's flat. Each day he burned incense before Uncle's Kuan-Yin statue, in remembrance of times past and in thanksgiving for the present. The first doll order led to a string of succeeding ones, which he enhanced by creating new designs.

Wei-chen celebrated the first anniversary of the business by quitting his night job. His flat swarmed like a beehive, with ten seamstresses sewing and four babies sleeping while their mothers worked. He found it impossible to turn away the young mothers and took delight in the little ones, walking around with them draped over his shoulder, patting them on the back to soothe them.

He didn't tell the women about being approached to sell the company. Watching his assistants cutting patterns, he replayed his conversation with the American.

"If you sell the business now, you could make a nice amount of money. You would still design dolls for us but, with our manufacturing operation, we could produce dolls more quickly and cheaply."

"And what about the women who work with me?"

"Well, I can't guarantee we would make the dolls in Hong Kong."

"I see. Do you know I paint the face on each doll? With your offer that would no longer be possible. Besides, this business supports everyone who works here. The more dolls we sell, the more each of us gets paid. We share the profits. How could I abandon my workers?"

That effectively ended the conversation. Without question, he had made the right decision. Contentment was seeping into his life but, concomitantly, an edginess shadowed him. A short time after the business offer, he was on his way to the Wan Chai wet market when he walked past an art shop. He lost track of time poring over the supplies. He left the shop empty handed but had defined the source of his anxiety. He needed to paint again. Smiling, he told himself, "Mr. Cheng was right. The singing bird has come to the tree in my heart."

Wei-chen decided to look for a larger flat with sufficient space for the sewing area and a small studio. The day after he moved, he purchased canvases, brushes and oil paints. A burgeoning creative energy consumed his evenings. Scenes of Shanghai littered his bedroom studio, some of them haunted by a beautiful, young woman. Vignettes of his new homeland - markets, temples, parks - competed for space with his paintings of China.

Sixteen

1968

In a cadence of distant friendship, Wei-chen and Knight corresponded regularly for twenty years. Knight's monthly letters sustained Wei-chen, confirming an old friend still cared about him and still took pride in his successes. Never in all those years had Wei-chen received a note from Olivia. He studied the letter before opening it. The delicate handwriting had to be hers. He made a cup of tea, sat at his work table and opened the envelope.

July 15, 1968

Dear Wei-chen,

I apologize for not writing immediately, but the past week has been a most difficult one. Gabriel passed away a week ago, and it is only now I have the presence of mind to write you.

His heart, which was never strong after his return from China, gave out while he was tending his flower garden. The flowers gave him great pleasure, and they have never been so lovely - a beautiful tribute to an exceptional man.

Your correspondence over the years brought him much happiness. Do you remember the small celadon vase you gave him when he left Shanghai? All these years he kept it on his desk, as if trying to keep part of you near him. I shall now keep it on my desk, a memento of your friendship and Gabriel's capacity to love those around him. He was a devoted husband and wonderful companion. I will miss him terribly.

Please keep me informed of your endeavors. Gabriel always read your letters to me. He was proud of you and the life you created after your flight from Shanghai. It would bring me joy to hear from you and know his dear friend continues to thrive.

With love,
Olivia

The teacup clinked onto the saucer. Wei-chen hunched over, sobbing. Tears of friendship lost slipped down his shirt. When the tears gave out, Wei-chen took the Star Ferry to Central District and climbed the hill to Man Mo Temple. Burning incense at the main altar, he watched the smoke drift upwards, bearing his wish of peace for Knight. Then he made the arduous ascent up Old Peak Road to Victoria Peak. After reaching the crest, he wandered off the path and sat on a grassy slope facing the South China Sea. A strong breeze raced up to greet him. Like a Chinese ink painting, outlying islands stretched across the hazy horizon. The timelessness of the scene held him captive.

When his consciousness re-engaged, he studied the kites spiraling on the ascending thermals. Identifying with the soaring flight of the big birds, he gave thanks Knight had encouraged him to flee to Hong Kong. Terrifying news was spilling out of China about a cultural revolution. The Red Guards were destroying churches and temples, imprisoning believers, arbitrarily sending intellectuals off to the countryside to be re-educated. He had no doubt his long association with foreigners would have identified him as someone to be watched, if not vilified.

In October Wei-chen and an assistant unpacked their inventory at a fall bazaar. While he was arranging the dolls, several nuns with a small group of

Chinese schoolgirls in tow stopped by the booth. He recalled having seen one of the sisters before - the small one. He couldn't place her nationality but she was definitely European. One of the girls and the nun were engaged in an animated discussion. Now that he thought about it, he had seen the student before too. He decided to approach them.

"Jo san, Sister." Wei-chen smiled and wished her good morning in Cantonese.

"Jo san, Mr. Chan." The nun smiled.

"Your students seem interested in the dolls."

"Yes, my student Anli especially likes these creatures. She also admires your paintings. Sometimes when we are out for a walk, she insists we stop at the gallery where your work is displayed. That girl is always drawing. Perhaps one day she will be an artist too."

"I am pleased that a budding artist appreciates my work."

"I also admire your work. By the way, my name is Sister Jayone and Anli... Now, where is she? Ah, there she is, talking to your assistant. Anli, please come here and meet Mr. Chan."

"Very good to meet you, Mr. Chan. I am Chan Anli." She bowed slightly.

"Well, we share the same family name. I am pleased to meet you too. I understand you have an interest in art." He smiled, trying to put the blushing girl at ease.

"Yes. I think your paintings are beautiful." She glanced at him, then quickly lowered her eyes.

"What do you like about them?"

"For many years I have listened to my grandfather and parents talk about China. When I look at your work, I see the world they have described to me and the life they left behind."

"Is your family from Shanghai?"

"No, they came from Guangzhou. But there is another reason I like your paintings. There is a beautiful woman in some of them. She is quite mysterious."

"Ah, yes, and she shall continue to remain mysterious." The smile slid from his face.

"Mr. Chan, customers are waiting to talk to you. Thank you for your time." Sister Jayone placed an arm around Anli to guide her away from the booth.

Wei-chen nodded to the nun. She nodded, looking deep inside him. His heart rate spiked. He sensed her strength of character, and it reminded him of Hui-lan.

———

Over the next year, Sister Jayone and Anli visited Wei-chen at most of his shows. He now anticipated their visits and felt disappointed if they didn't stop by. He was packing up after an October bazaar when Sister Jayone appeared at the booth.

"Good afternoon, Sister. Where is Anli today?

"I came by myself. I have been waiting to discuss something with you, and I think it is finally time. The first time Anli and I met you, she asked about the woman who appears in your paintings."

"Yes." Wei-chen raised his guard.

"On the way back to school that day, she said you smiled at her but your eyes looked sad. I noticed the same thing. Your face looks like the calm after the storm. Something very painful happened to you a long time ago. The war years were difficult for you. Am I correct?"

"Yes. They were life changing."

"I have a proposition I am sure will bring joy to you. I have known Anli since she was little. I taught in her village in the New Territories. Most of the families lost everything when they fled China, but they were still generous with the little they had. Anyway, Anli was an active little girl, very bright but a bit challenging. When I was transferred to the Franciscan Mission School in Kowloon, I encouraged her family to send her there."

"Perhaps you have some personal insight into this type of student." Wei-chen raised his eyebrows and smiled.

"That is true. I was also an active child, but this one has artistic talent. Every free moment she draws on any scrap of paper she can find. The school does not have an art program, so I was wondering if you might be willing to give Anli some instruction. Of course, there would be compensation. Our cook brews an excellent pot of tea."

Caught off guard by the suggestion, Wei-chen didn't respond immediately.

"It was just a thought. I know you are very busy."

"Actually, I think it would be interesting to work with Anli. In Shanghai I studied with an old Russian. He gave me an excellent foundation in art. There are some things I could teach her. And, as for your generous offer of compensation, I prefer jasmine tea."

"Thank you. I believe you two are meant to know one another. God works in mysterious ways."

He was about to ask what she meant but decided the smile creasing her face seemed sufficient explanation.

Twice a month Wei-chen stopped work early and went to the Franciscan Mission School for Girls. Anli's desire to study art surprised him. She memorized his comments, as if scribbling reference notes in her mind, and then presented him with new drawings each session. She touched his heart, bent over her work, looking so earnest. After several months, he surprised Anli with a set of watercolor paints and brushes. The warmth of her delight stayed with him for days.

Now that he was somewhat of a fixture at the school, students and nuns frequently joined him for tea after his classes with Anli. One afternoon everyone left early, leaving him alone with Sister Jayone, something he had wanted for months.

"Tell me, Sister, where did you grow up?"

" In the Basque region of Spain."

"I do not know much about the Basques."

"Not many people do. My name Jayone is a Basque name. It means to be born. I was born on December 24, the day before we celebrate the birth of Jesus Christ. When I grew up, we were not allowed to speak Basque at school. We were not allowed to sing our songs or dance our dances. We only spoke Basque at home. During the civil war, my region went through a difficult time. People were divided between supporting the Communists and the Loyalists. Hundreds were killed when Guernica was bombed. It was a dangerous time."

"I can imagine. China went through a similar struggle and continues to. When did you decide to become a missionary?"

"I was a teenager when I took that decision. It is a long story."

"I have time to listen."

"Very well then. After I finished secondary school, my parents expected me to attend university in Bilbao. However, my last year in school, I felt called by God to be a missionary. The Franciscan Missionaries of Mary operates schools and hospitals in Africa. I had always wanted to teach and, since I knew Portuguese, I expected to be sent there eventually.

"My family was upset with me. My mother cried for days. My brother begged me not to leave the family. My father insisted I attend university for a year. He even went to our priest and asked him to dissuade me from this decision. You see, in those years when sisters were sent to their missions, they were not allowed to ever return home."

"But that did not stop you."

She smiled. "No, it did not. Finally my family accepted that I was serious. It troubled me to cause them pain, but I knew God wanted me elsewhere."

"So, if you thought you were going to Africa, how did you arrive in Asia?"

"Well, that was a surprise for me, but I trusted it was also part of God's plan. Of the sixteen sisters who sailed to China, two Spanish sisters and I were the only ones assigned to Macau. The plan was that after we became fluent in Cantonese, we would be sent into China. The year was 1947."

"Did you ever make it into China?"

"No. By the time we arrived hundreds of missionaries were fleeing from China to Macao. It was a stopping point before proceeding to new assignments. The convent, designed to accommodate twenty-five sisters, was overflowing with twice that many. Cots and mattresses filled the halls and verandas. Although French is the common language of our order, a symphony in Polish, Spanish, Cantonese, Portuguese and English filled the cafeteria.

"Several months after I arrived, the Mother Superior called me to her office. She said my skills were needed at the colegia, the elementary school on the same campus as the convent. I was assigned to teach in the kindergarten. Because Macau is a Portuguese territory, we taught in Cantonese and Portuguese.

"Our convent, church and school were near the old colonial buildings and fortifications. I liked being there. You know, after Hong Kong became a dominant trading center, Macau lost its significance. It seemed sleepy, even with the unsettled political situation. What had once been a crown jewel was now an old family heirloom, shoved to the back of a dresser drawer."

"When did you come to Hong Kong?"

"In 1954 I was sent to work with refugees in the New Territories. After fleeing from China they had very little, but their spirits were strong. They were determined to survive. It was a blessing to work with them. After ten years, I was assigned to this school. I still have fond memories of the wonderful people in that village."

"It intrigues me you would leave your family and move far away from them. For as long as I can remember, I have wanted to be with family and that has always proven elusive for me."

"What do you mean by that?"

" When I was quite young my parents died, and I was adopted by a maternal uncle and his wife. My auntie died several years after that, and my uncle passed away before I finished secondary school. After his passing, I moved to Shanghai. During my university years I lived with a Russian couple who treated me like a son. At that same time I formed a friendship with an American who eventually became a combination older brother-father figure to me.

"When the Communists took over China, Gabriel Knight returned to America, and the Romanovskys joined their sons in Israel. The family I had created disappeared. My last strong link to China, an old scholar who was like an uncle to me, urged me to leave while I still could. He predicted only difficulty for me if I remained in China. So I fled here in 1948."

"What about the woman who appears in some of your paintings?"

The concern in her voice dissolved his reluctance to discuss Hui-lan. Wei-chen took a deep breath and stared into the teacup. "She was my wife, and she was killed in the rape of Nanking. She had many fine qualities - great intellect, emotional strength, familial loyalty. All I wanted was to share my life with her and create a family with her. It has been many years since her death. I still think of her everyday. Everyone who survived those years has a story. I am not the only one who cannot forget."

When he raised his head, Sister Jayone looked directly at him and said, "You are a refugee of the heart. You came to Hong Kong seeking political refuge, but there is much more to your story. I have seen this before - an abandoned child, a parent who loses a child, a survivor who loses a loved one."

Her stark words pierced his defenses. Tears pricked his eyes. She had named the burden he carried within him.

Seventeen

1970

After the Lunar New Year holiday in 1970, Wei-chen invited the sisters and students who usually joined him at school to visit his flat. Standing in his doorway, he heard the girls humming with excitement as they climbed the stairway, sounding like bees hovering over blossoms.

"Good afternoon. Welcome everyone."

Sister Jayone shepherded the girls into the flat. "Thank you, Mr. Chan. We are all quite excited to see the dolls and your artwork."

"My assistants left a few minutes ago." He led the girls over to piles of cut fabric. "Tomorrow they will sew the dolls together. We are working on an order for an American company. Here are some of the dolls we finished today. I just signed them." He pointed to his signature on a doll's foot.

Anli scanned the flat with eagle eyes. He assumed she was looking for his recent artwork. "I have several paintings underway. If you would like to see them, just come this way. My bedroom also serves as my studio, so I apologize for the clutter."

Now it was Sister Jayone who was looking with sharp eyes. He watched her assess the room, first taking in the pallet he slept on, the philosophy books crammed together on a bookshelf, the clothing line strung high above his mattress - which served as his closet - and finally his paintings.

"So you have an interest in philosophy?" She pointed to the bookshelf.

"Yes. Right now I am struggling through this. It is written by an Indian master."

She opened the book he handed her. "Sometime I would like to talk with you about these things."

"I look forward to that, Sister."

When the group was preparing to leave, Anli walked over to the workbench and examined a vest hanging above it. "Teacher Chan, this is a beautiful baby vest."

"My mother made it for me. The embroidery is beautiful. Look at the little butterflies."

"Ye Ye, my grandfather, has a vest very much like this. It also has a jade piece sewn on the right side with his name carved on it."

"Where was your grandfather born?"

"Near Suzhou. He was the first of two sons. When the boys were young, their father was killed by bandits and their mother died a short time later."

"And a paternal uncle adopted your grandfather." Wei-chen stared at Anli, heart pounding. "But that uncle, who was in financial difficulty and already had a large family of his own, sent the second son to live with a maternal uncle. This son grew up south of Shanghai, far away from his brother. Your grandfather is Chan Wei-da, my elder brother."

Anli gasped and grabbed the edge of the workbench to steady herself. "You are the missing brother of my grandfather. You are my great uncle. It never occurred to me the W.C. Chan in your business name could be Wei-chen." She mopped away tears. The hushed group circled her.

Wei-chen stepped over to her, folded his arms around her and patted her back. "It makes me immensely happy we are family." He tried to calm her, but he was also struggling for composure. His throat was tight. He glanced at Sister Jayone. Her eyes reflected the happiness surging through him.

"Is your grandfather in good health?"

"Yes, Er Da Ye, he is strong in mind and body."

Er Da Ye, she called him great uncle. Astonishment gave way to gratitude. "Please tell your grandfather I would like to see him."

"I am going home for the weekend. I will tell him my teacher is also my great uncle. It will be an amazing surprise for him. He will be very happy."

After the group left, he stood at the window and watched them cross the street. Just before they turned the corner, Sister Jayone turned back and waved. She frequently said he and Anli were meant to know each other. He wondered what she thought now, probably further validation that God works in mysterious ways.

The years of struggling to survive the war and then fleeing to Hong Kong had relegated the search for his brother to a distant dream. He never considered his family might have fled here also. Like a brilliant rainbow after a storm, it was an exquisite gift.

When the phone rang Monday afternoon, Wei-chen dashed to pick it up. He held his breath, hanging on Anli's every word.

"Grandfather was excited to know you are here and wants to see you. He would like you to join us for Ching Ming. I will meet you at the Kowloon train station Saturday morning."

"It will be an honor to spend Ching Ming with your family." The thought of sharing the ancient festival with his brother gave him an electric charge. Like a bud in springtime, energy burst open inside him. Feeling trapped in his flat, he rushed out and walked to the temple in Yau Ma Tei. The cloud of his offering swirled around him. For the first time since childhood, he would be with his brother to honor their ancestors and welcome the start of spring. Before returning home he bought paper money at the stationery shop.

Unable to sleep, Wei-chen arrived early at the Kowloon station and watched the harbor come to life while he waited for Anli.

After they boarded the train, she said, "Father will meet us in Sha Tin. Then we will take a bus to the village."

Years ago he had taken the train to Sha Tin to see the Temple of Ten Thousand Buddhas. It still looked the same, a sleepy fishing village nestled in the New Territories. When Anli introduced her father, he embraced Wei-chen warmly. Wei-chen scanned his nephew's face, sifting through distant memories, trying to discern the features of his long-lost brother.

They got off the bus at the village center and climbed a steep hill. Two-story stucco houses studded the path, separated by foliage that draped the hillsides. When the path doubled back to snake higher along the hill, Anli and her father stopped for Wei-chen to catch his breath. Wei-chen took in the view, a stark contrast to the density of Kowloon. Tiled roofs floated in a leafy green sea. Across the valley terraces of graves cascaded down the hill.

"My mother is buried there. We will make offerings at her grave tomorrow," Anli's father said.

Wei-chen took a long look at the man who had raised such a fine daughter. He took pride in his newfound family.

At the crest of the hill, Anli pointed towards a courtyard. "Brother and sister are playing in front of our home. That is mother standing in the doorway."

His nephew's wife waved to them. Her beautiful features and smile were those of her daughter. After introducing the family, his nephew said, "Grandfather is waiting for him. Let him pass." He bowed and let Wei-chen enter the home first.

A man about his height with silver hair stood up to greet him. Like most older men, his brother wore a mandarin jacket and loose trousers. Wei-chen blinked to see more clearly. He thought to say something, but his compressed lips wouldn't comply, too busy restraining tears. Regaining his composure, he walked towards his brother and bowed.

"Wei-chen, it is you." His brother extended his hands.

"Yes, Wei-da." Emotion strangled any further words. He didn't remember the face but the kindness was familiar. Distant impressions tugged at the edge of his consciousness.

"At last we are reunited, younger brother. Our parents' souls can rest in peace. Come sit near me." Wei-da pointed to a chair near him.

"It is a great pleasure to meet all of you." Wei-chen presented the family with a large package of preserved plums. The children gathered round him, eyes riveted on him and the plums.

After Anli's mother served tea, she and the children left to prepare the holiday feast.

"Let us sit in the courtyard and have another cup of tea," Wei-da said.

Wei-chen was about to leave the house when he noticed a photo and stopped short, causing his brother to bump into him.

"Excuse me, Wei-chen."

"No, it is my fault. I apologize for my clumsiness." Wei-chen couldn't take his eyes off the picture.

Wei-da walked to the desk and handed the framed photo to Wei-chen.

"I recognize this man. Years ago, shortly after I arrived in Hong Kong, I was at the Tin Hau Temple in Yau Ma Tei, desperate to find lodging. A man approached me and offered to help me. I am sure it was this man. I have never forgotten his face."

"That is our father. Come outside and bring the photo with you."

Wei-chen stumbled over the threshold. Catching himself, he took a deep breath and followed his brother.

"Please tell me what happened." Wei-da pulled two chairs into the shade.

Looking out over the hillside, Wei-chen relived that afternoon. "I went to the temple in Yau Ma Tei because there was nowhere else to go. I needed a room for the night, but the bed spaces I looked at were filthy and unsafe. I could not find work. I had barely enough money to return to Shanghai.

"I was sitting on a bench in utter desperation when this man approached me. He asked if I needed assistance. He had a gentle manner and spoke in the dialect of the Soochow region, so I decided to trust him. I told him I was a refugee and had no place to stay. Motioning for me to follow him, he said he knew a bed space that was safe. I stayed close to him on the crowded sidewalks. Eventually he turned down an alley and stopped in front of a door. He said the manager was trustworthy. After knocking on the door, I turned around to thank him but he was gone. I looked for him at the temple many times after that but never saw him again."

"I believe the ghost of our father guided you to safety. You were most fortunate to have seen his spirit. I have felt his presence over the years but I have never seen him. Do you make offerings for him?" Wei-da asked.

"Yes, of course, and also for Mother, Uncle, Auntie and my wife Hui-lan. I pray for their peace and ask their spirits to watch over me. I am still stunned at the thought of father leading me to safety." He looked at the photo again. "I have no memories of our family."

"You were so little when they died. I have a memory of you. Hold out your right arm? See this scar? Do you remember how you got it?"

"Many years ago I had a vivid dream. It seemed so real I was not sure whether it was a recollection or a dream. We were at home with mother. Then you and I went outside to play. When you were not looking, I climbed up the litchi tree. You warned me to stop and come down. Coming down was harder than going up. I could not seem to back down so I moved out along a limb. That is when I fell."

"And your arm was cut when you fell through the branches, causing this scar. It was no dream. When Father returned home from one of his trips, he and Mother talked about your little episode. They thought it indicated unusual independence for such a young child. That is why, after our parents' deaths, when our uncle was forced to make the terrible decision of which son must leave the family, they allowed Mother's brother to take you. Can you imagine how difficult it was for them, losing you from our family line?"

Wei-chen held his silence, hanging onto every word his brother said. All his life he was not sure his uncle's family really wanted him.

"When I grew older, Uncle explained his decision to me. As the first son of his brother, he could not let me leave the family. You were a delightful, independent little boy. Uncle did not want to lose you, but it was a desperate time. He knew Mother's brother and wife would be good parents to you. Having lost their daughters, he was sure they would treasure you."

"After all these years, it comforts me to know I was truly wanted."

"I believe Uncle always carried some sadness about your leaving the family. He did not forget about you and neither did I."

At that moment sunlight spilled across the courtyard and embraced the brothers. Wei-chen noticed it and felt renewed affection for his elder brother sitting across from him. Holding the photo of his father, his heart beat with steady assurance. Familial love penetrated every part of his being.

"My daughter-in-law is preparing special dishes to celebrate your return to the family. These traditional dishes were served in our parents' home."

Wei-chen slept on a cot in Wei-da's bedroom. Before they fell asleep, his brother said, "When we visit my wife's grave tomorrow, you will see a plaque I placed there in our parents' memory. It was the only way to show my family's continued respect. I wish we were able to cross the border and clean their graves."

The next morning they crossed the valley bottom and climbed the hill to the cemetery. During the ascent Wei-chen stopped and looked up. The smoke of offerings spiraled into the sky, while smudges from burned paper money and candles dappled the ground. On every level of the cemetery, families were cleaning grave sites and making offerings.

Wei-da stopped beside him. "Most of these villagers fled China decades ago. Ching Ming is doubly sad for them because, not only are they tending to the graves of loved ones who died here, it also reminds them of their untended ancestral graves in China."

After cleaning the grave, Anli's father spread a blanket nearby and the family shared their midday meal. The children chattered like little birds discovering strewn crumbs, and the adults summoned distant memories. Wei-chen savored each moment.

When they made their way down the hill, he said to Wei-da, "Being reunited with you and your family brings me much happiness."

"That is also true for me. We have memories to share and even more memories to create. You must visit us often." Wei-da bowed to his brother.

Wei-chen bowed to him, conjoining a fraternal arc.

Late Monday afternoon Wei-chen walked to the mission school. At the front desk, he asked for Sister Jayone and said he would wait outside for her.

A few minutes later she rushed to him. "Has something happened?"

"Yes, something has happened that I want to talk to you about, preferably not in the cafeteria."

"Of course, let's go to that bench." She pointed to one near the school wall.

A ginkgo's shifting leaves draped mottled shadows over them, and Wei-chen dropped his usual reserve. "As you know, I spent Ching Ming with Anli's family. It was wonderful to reunite with my brother. I have not seen him since I was three years old. I am still amazed at the coincidences that brought us all together.

"But what I want to discuss with you is yet another coincidence. My brother and I were going outside to have tea when I noticed a photograph. I was sure it was the man who led me to a bed space many years ago. Do you remember me telling you that story? How I looked for him and could never find him again?"

Sister Jayone nodded yes, intently studying his face.

"Wei-da said it was a photo of our father. He said I should bring it outside. I kept looking at it. It was definitely the face of the man who helped me. I have never forgotten his image. Wei-da thinks our father's spirit guided me to safety. What do you make of this?" Wei-chen examined Sister Jayone's face for signs of credulity or disbelief.

"I have seen God work in many ways, but I have not witnessed this kind of thing. What I have observed is this. When people extend their hands in prayer, many of them are hoping God will do something miraculous, but I think He often works through other people, sometimes complete strangers. I believe sometimes the veil between the material and spiritual worlds drops, and we have a glimpse of what lies beyond this physical dimension."

"So you think it is possible his spirit came to me?"

"Yes, but ask your heart what you believe. The heart knows things the mind can never fathom. This knowledge comes from the soul."

"I believe it happened. But what about your approaching me at the bazaar because you thought Anli should meet me? Do you think that was some kind of divine inspiration?"

"At the time I did not think so. I just thought you two should meet because Anli was fascinated with your work. I was not thinking beyond that. But look at all that has occurred since then, her being the granddaughter of your brother and you making that connection. When we look back at it, it seems different. It seems as if we were all guided to one another. Actually, I think many times this happens in our lives, but we never make the association that a larger force is guiding us. We just think we are lucky or that it was happenstance."

That evening Wei-chen reflected on Sister Jayone's comments. He took one of the books he had brought from Shanghai and opened it carefully. The ginkgo leaves he found after Hui-lan's death were still entwined, fibers still intact. From the back of the book he unfolded her final letter to him and reread it. "If something happens to me, my spirit will always carry my love for you. My love is strong, like the ginkgo. If I die, and if it is possible, I will always watch over you."

He wondered why her spirit had never appeared to him. Or, unrecognizable, had she had come to him in the guise of a stranger?

Like the full moon's faithful rise, Wei-chen returned to his brother's home each month. They talked in the dialect of their youth, laughed at each other's stories and shared the comfort of quiet moments. His visits reinforced the bond of brotherhood, forging an alloy of respect and affection. He was always pleased when Anli accompanied him on these visits. Life had given him a wonderful surprise, this delightful great-niece.

At his brother's request, Wei-chen brought photos of his paintings on one of the visits. After studying them for some time, Wei-da asked about the woman who appeared in some of them. When she heard her grandfather ask this, Anli sucked in her breath. Her grandfather looked at her with displeasure.

"Do not be upset with Anli," Wei-chen said. "She has wanted to know the answer to this question for a long time, and she understands it is something I have not talked about. I will tell you both about this fine woman who was my wife."

Wei-da and Anli hung on every word of Wei-chen's narration. He began with his friendships with Gabriel Knight, Mr. Cheng and the Romanovskys.

Then he divulged everything he had held back for years - his instant attraction to Hui-lan, her pursuit of him because of their class difference, the deep tenderness of their love, her devotion to family that took her back to Nanking, her pregnancy and her death. When he finished, Anli's eyes were red.

Wei-da took a deep breath. "I am most sorry, my brother. We Chinese have known much suffering. Leaving behind everything was difficult for us, but at least we fled as a family. You were brave to come here by yourself."

"I think it was not so much bravery as desperation. Mr. Cheng and Gabriel Knight convinced me that living under Communist rule was going to be very difficult. Can you imagine what it would be like for me if I were in China now? I would be vilified by the Red Guard, attacked for my association with westerners and sent to the countryside for re-education."

"What about Mr. Cheng. Has he remained safe?" Wei-da asked.

"Yes. He is quite old now but still has a great intellect. His long association with the Jade Buddha Temple affords him protection. The temple has a benefactor at a high level within the Communist government. As long as the monks keep a low profile, it seems the temple will be all right."

While lighting incense at the kitchen shrine that night, a mantle of tranquility enveloped him. Instead of pain, the disclosure of everything that happened with Hui-lan brought him a sense of peace. The pain in his heart no longer ran as deep. His heart was healing.

Just before Lantern Festival that fall, Wei-chen exhibited his latest paintings at a gallery on a side street off Hollywood Road. Most of them depicted vignettes of daily life in the New Territories, Kowloon and Hong Kong Island, but there were also a number of paintings of Shanghai, the city that still haunted his dreams.

On the opening night of the show, the full moon climbed an indigo sky, gilding the side street in shimmering silver leaf. The crowd thinned when closing time approached, and it was then Wei-chen noticed an attractive, older couple enter the gallery. Something about the man caught his eye. They looked American but were decidedly not tourists. This westerner wore his knowledge of Asia like a comfortable old jacket. He had to be an old China hand.

The man looked at Wei-chen, and Wei-chen threw his gaze elsewhere, feeling caught in his studied assessment of the gentleman. When he looked at the couple again, they were absorbed in his paintings of Shanghai, lingering over each one. Detecting something familiar about the man, Wei-chen struggled to place him. The moment they turned to him and began making their way across the room, he recognized Josh Ryan. Weaving through the remaining viewers, he rushed towards them.

"Josh, I had no idea you were in Hong Kong."

"Wei-chen, it's good to see you after all these years." Ryan extended his hand. "When I read about the exhibit, the article mentioned the artist's days in Shanghai. I had to see if it was the same Chan Wei-chen I knew so long ago."

"Thank you for coming to the opening. I never expected to see you again." Wei-chen dropped Ryan's hand and bowed slightly to the woman.

"This is my wife, Margaret." Ryan placed an arm around her shoulders.

"It is a pleasure to meet you, Mrs. Ryan. From my quick study of your husband, it appears you have domesticated that young man I knew so long ago."

She laughed, looked at Ryan and turned back to Wei-chen. "Thank you for the compliment, if indeed it is one. Your paintings are lovely. Josh said your scenes of Shanghai capture its essence, and the vignettes of Hong Kong are beautiful. You have quite a talent."

"Thank you." Wei-chen blushed and rushed to change the subject. It seemed ridiculous, but he still had difficulty accepting praise. "Josh, I have read your articles over the years but had no idea where you were living."

"We returned to Asia a decade ago. I've been traveling around the region, covering the Cultural Revolution among a multitude of other things. We leave for Singapore tomorrow."

"I would like very much to hear your observations about China."

"Are you free to meet us for dinner later tonight? There's a good Malaysian restaurant on Staunton Street, just a few blocks from here. The Mango Tree."

"I will be there as soon as the gallery closes." Meeting them later was an unexpected gift and delighted Wei-chen. Just before they left, he noticed the Ryans speaking to the gallery owner.

The moon threw Wei-chen's shadow ahead of him, guiding him down Staunton Street. The Mango Tree, wedged between two shuttered shops, was the only restaurant on that particular block. The windows were folded open, and light spilled from the candlelit restaurant across the cobblestone street. Ryan and his wife were seated near the front window, their hands interlocked. Feeling he was catching them in an intimate moment, Wei-chen stopped.

Seeing Ryan triggered memories of the war years in Shanghai. At that moment he felt as if a dancing butterfly grazed his cheek. He turned. There was no butterfly. He felt Hui-lan's presence.

Ryan waved to Wei-chen when he saw him crossing the street. The small restaurant felt inviting. Wei-chen quickly counted the tables - eight of them, an auspicious number, all of them full.

"We are so pleased you could join us," Margaret said.

"Thank you. It is a pleasure to meet the woman who captured my friend's heart."

She smiled and Ryan put his hand over hers.

The decades of time that had passed since their last meeting collapsed into the present moment. Ryan questioned Wei-chen at length about his leaving Shanghai and creating a new life in Hong Kong. "As difficult as it was for you to flee, you made the right decision to leave China."

"It took time to establish myself, but eventually it all worked out. What about you? Were you pleased to be reassigned to Asia?"

"Yes. I was immensely pleased to return. I couldn't get Asia out of my blood. It's still a maelstrom. What's happening in China is horrific. Good thing you left when you did. You would have been targeted because of your education and western ties. Speaking of which, what do you hear from Gabriel Knight?"

"He died five years ago. He returned to Massachusetts just before the Communists took over and eventually married Olivia, his longtime friend. They led a quiet life. I think he was very happy."

"And the scholar associated with Jade Buddha Temple?"

"Someone at a high level in the government is protecting the temple. The monks function inconspicuously. So far, the temple is safe. I communicate with Mr. Cheng through a temple in Yau Ma Tei. On quite a different note, before I left the gallery, the owner mentioned you bought the painting of the teahouse. Thank you. That was most generous."

"We didn't buy it for generosity's sake. It will give us great pleasure to have one of your paintings. Margaret noticed it as soon as we stepped into the gallery. I'm sure the longer we live with it, the more we will see in it."

"Yes, the reflection of the teahouse in the pond is exquisite. Perhaps the mathematical dimensions are the reason for its underlying beauty and balance - the five-sided teahouse, the bridge of nine turnings. The painting will always hold a special appeal for me," Margaret said.

Wei-chen was about to respond when Ryan spoke up. "The pensive woman in the teahouse window, it's Hui-lan, isn't it."

"Yes. I cannot separate her from my memories of Shanghai."

"I still vividly remember the night when you and Knight met me at The Papillon, when I told you..." Ryan stumbled.

"When you told me how she died." Wei-chen finished Ryan's sentence.

"Yes. Telling you about her death was one of the hardest things I have ever done. The brutalities of war that littered China were always difficult to cover, but somehow I managed to restrain my emotions and report the events taking place, letting the horrendous facts stand for themselves. Telling you firsthand of Hui-lan's death was quite another thing."

"Those were terrible years. Not just for me but for all of China and for all of Asia. Every person who survived the war has a story. Take Knight, for instance. Mr. Cheng and I were shocked at his appearance when he was released from Lungwha internment camp. He was extremely weak and malnourished and never completely regained his health."

"I can imagine how he looked. I saw survivors from some of the camps in Burma and Malaysia. God forbid we ever have another war like that one."

"When you arrived in Hong Kong, did you know anyone?" Margaret asked.

"Through Knight I had a contact at St. John's Cathedral, but his friend could only do so much. Hong Kong was flooded with refugees. I was in my early forties and had to start life all over again. Once the doll-making business took off, it consumed most of my time. Many of the women who sewed the dolls brought their babies to the flat with them. They became an extended family for me."

"So you never married again," Margaret said.

"No. After Hui-lan I never wanted to remarry. For a time one of my assistants and her young son lived in my flat. Her husband had been killed in a fishing accident. We lived as a family for several years until a flu epidemic took the life of her son. She was inconsolable and returned to her home village.

"However, several years ago something quite remarkable happened. I made the acquaintance of a nun, Sister Jayone, and some of her students. One thing led to another, and I ended up giving art lessons to one of the girls. Through an incredible twist of fate, we eventually realized my student Anli is my great niece, the granddaughter of my elder brother."

"What a remarkable coincidence. I wasn't aware you had a brother," Ryan said.

"Yes. When our mother passed away, a paternal uncle adopted him and a maternal uncle adopted me. After I moved to Shanghai, I tried to find him with Mr. Cheng's help. When he traced the family through temple registries, the last he learned was that the family had fled south. At that point I pretty much gave up the idea of ever finding them.

"But this is how the connection was finally made. One afternoon I invited Sister Jayone and several students to come to my flat. They wanted to see how the dolls were made and also look at some paintings. The previous evening I had set out my baby vest to study the embroidery work and left it on my work table. When Anli saw it, she said it looked like her grandfather's baby vest. I asked her where he was from originally, and it all came tumbling out. If I had not left the vest out on my work table or if the girls had visited on a different day, we would never have realized her grandfather is my brother."

"If, if, if. It was meant to happen. There is an Arab adage that says some things are written on the wind. You were meant to find her." Margaret's tone left no room for any questioning.

"I am beginning to trust that. Are you familiar with the concept of synchronicity? That seemingly unrelated occurrences are more than mere coincidences?" Wei-chen asked.

"I am aware of the term but haven't read about it. I like the idea of some kind of universal guidance."

"This talk of guidance reminds me of something else I wanted to ask you," Ryan broke in. "When I mentioned to a colleague we were going to your exhibit, he said, 'So you're going to see the old painter, the one who guides lost souls.' He said sometimes you help young people who have lost their way. He mentioned that you counsel them over a cup of tea and occasionally let them sleep on your floor when they have nowhere else to spend the night. That is quite kind of you."

"When I look back at my life, I see the extended hands of those who helped me along the way. How could I not do the same? Besides, there is much to learn from these unexpected guests who, from time to time, appear in my life. The older I become, the more I believe I belong to the world. Knowing that comforts me."

They left the restaurant late that evening, promising to meet again when the Ryans passed back through Hong Kong. Wei-chen caught the last ferry to Kowloon. Standing at the stern, he studied the strings of streetlights climbing their way to the island's skyline, now rimmed by moonlight. It would make a charming painting.

He mulled over Margaret's statement that some things are written on the wind. It reminded him of Knight's favorite passage from The Rubaiyat of Omar Khayyam. "The Moving Finger writes and having writ, moves on. Nor all they piety nor wit shall lure it back to cancel half a line, nor all thy tears wash out a word of it." For a long time he constantly wondered if he could have somehow prevented Hui-lan's death. Many years passed before he finally accepted he was not responsible for it, that there was nothing he could have done.

Just then he sensed a faint shimmer at his side. He felt Hui-lan's presence and turned sideways, half-expecting to see her. "I know you are beside me, Hui-lan." A sense of calm and composure enveloped him. For the remainder of the ferry ride, he shared the view with his invisible companion.

EIGHTEEN

1982

In 1982 Wei-chen sustained three losses. That spring Sister Jayone moved to the colegia in Macau to direct the care of elderly sisters and minister to the sick. Then in late summer Mr. Cheng and Wei-da passed on, leaving Wei-chen's tree of friendship almost bare. He felt as if he were the last leaf on the tree, twisting, clinging until a strong wind arrived to carry him away.

At age seventy-eight Wei-chen continued to make dolls, albeit for a smaller market. The art gallery still carried his paintings, but he painted fewer pieces. Each night he burned incense at his kitchen shrine, giving thanks for those who were still with him, wishing peace for those who were gone.

After Wei-da's passing, the family revered Wei-chen as the family elder. Anli, now a wife and mother, checked on Wei-chen frequently. When her daughter Anna begged for stories, he swooped her into his arms and held her captive with his imagination. Peace reigned in his heart.

On a beautiful fall afternoon, he set off to meet Anli and Anna in Kowloon Park. He was standing outside the park gate near Haiphong and Nathan Roads when Anli waved to him from the other side of the street. She was waiting to step into the intersection when Anna strained and broke free from Anli's grasp. At that same moment a taxi raced through the light, cutting ahead of pedestrians about to enter the crosswalk.

Before he could formulate a thought, Wei-chen knew Anna was going to be hit. Like an animal protecting its young, he charged into the street to shove her back towards Anli. Adrenalin surged through his body, forcing his legs to move faster than they had in decades. He was determined to reach her, knowing full well he would take the impact of the taxi instead of Anna. If this was how death intended to take him, he was ready.

Just as his extended hands pushed Anna into Anli's outstretched arms, he caught a glimpse of golden light shooting down his arms. An external force propelled him forward, keeping him narrowly out of the taxi's path. He came down hard on the street but turned his head to follow the light with his eyes. Hui-lan's image, swathed in a transparent golden hue, hovered behind Anli. The apparition of Hui-lan was beginning to fade when he heard her voice. "Long ago I told you I would protect you if I could. It is not your time, my love. You have more good deeds to accomplish." She vanished as quickly as she appeared.

Wei-chen wondered if he had passed to the other side. A cloud of knowing enveloped him. He comprehended many things at once. The golden light that shot through him released hidden inner feelings, the remorse that haunted him for years now completely stripped away. He thought he had freed himself from it years ago, but the incredible lightness he now felt told him otherwise. All remnants of his guilt at having survived Hui-lan were finally shattered. Peace and contentment swaddled him. The veil between the material and spiritual dimensions had dropped. Hui-lan had reached out to him and helped him save Anna.

"My Hui-lan, you never left me." He looked at his hands, surprised to find crushed ginkgo leaves in them.

At that instant pain radiated down his legs, bringing him back to the physical world. His trousers were torn where he absorbed the impact of the fall. People were yelling at the taxi driver speeding down the street. Anli was bent over him, calling to him. Anna stood beside her mother, crying.

"Don't leave us," Anli begged. Tears of familial love and devotion streaked her face.

Still feeling somewhat detached, as if suspended on the metaphysical continuum, Wei-chen considered it ironic that in his willingness to fling life away, new life had been given him. He needed to know what Sister Jayone would make of all this. As soon as he recovered from his fall, he would take a ferry to Macao. He wanted to have a long discussion with her.

72058321R00130

Made in the USA
Columbia, SC
14 June 2017